# Wings of Deceit

*One secret that changes everything.*

William Hoffman

ISBN 978-1-7339068-3-8

Second Edition.

*For my Mom*

*a passionate traveler*

*a fellow aviation nut*

*a ferocious reader*

Colleen M. Hoffman
November 21, 1963 – February 2, 2019

## Acknowledgements

My sincerest thanks to Allison Millea, whose editing master work made this project possible, and Elin Richey for her talented and artistic cover design. My wholehearted thanks to Kevin Golla, Kelli Pavlish, Shari Peterson, and Dan Schumann for the content review I relied on so closely. Thank you also to my selfless and patient wife Colleen, and to my sister Megan, who is my biggest advocate.

# Fact

The United States Federal Aviation Administration requires all airline pilots to undergo regular health screening by a certified aeromedical physician. If diagnosed with a medical condition, they risk the loss of their license, career, and often their life's passion.

*"Once you have tasted flight, you will forever walk the earth with your eyes turned skyward, for there you have been, and there you will always long to return."*

**Leonardo da Vinci**

# Chapter 1

February 2016 | Seattle-Tacoma International Airport
Seattle, Washington

Mac stood before the airliner's towering boarding door and let the hot air blow through his teeth. His burden pressed him further into the floor, but the world seemed to push back equally and indifferently. The rainy night weighed heavily on the airliners taxiing through Seattle-Tacoma's International Airport and damp air pulled the stale scent of time from every surface. Each muscle fiber in his neck ached in warm contraction and he didn't dare take his hands off his roller bag for fear they'd tremble. His muscular frame was draped over a reedy skeleton, shaped by years of intentioned exercise and a youth of doing without, but tonight, he felt weak. He was uneasy, knowing everything could change, but what it would mean was already clear to him. He garnered strength within himself, trying to forget all that had happened, and focused his mind. Just beyond the age of sixty, his experience was far more than suggested by his appearance, but tonight he hoped it would be enough.

The pilot's left foot came off the aged airport gate while his pulsing heart thumped in his chest.

He was risking everything, putting it all on the line, though his choice had already been made. He had everything to lose, and in stepping through the threshold of the door, he wagered it all. As he had thousands of times before, Captain Robert "Mac" Frank boarded the aircraft he would pilot around the world. *Home.*

The busy galley was freshly stocked with hundreds of meals and drinks to be served thirty-two thousand feet over the Pacific Ocean. His watch weighted in his pocket and he pulled it out to study its open face. 5:45. Though his mind was preoccupied, he would never permit tardiness. It fell back into his pocket.

"Fancy seeing you here, Captain Mac," smiled a stout woman closing an overhead galley door. She wore dark heels and a red scarf around her neck that danced off her shoulder. Her eyes were sharp and the years of flying in time zones around the world created furrowed lines beside her eyelids.

"Hi Shari," Mac was weary though her familiar face curbed some of his emotional dissonance. "I'm not sure I've seen you since our Amsterdam run last month." Her hair was wiry and pulled back tight out of her eyes. "How are things with the union?"

"Same complaints, different day." She opened the cooler and double checked the ice. "I like working for these cabin birds, but all of this office work is wearing me down." She walked with a slight limp and swung her leg to secure a galley door. "I jumped at the first chance I could to get back into the fleet and do a trip or two."

"I warned you when you agreed to this office job," said the pilot, but Shari leaned against the stainless-steel counter and rolled her eyes.

"I know, Mac. You don't need to remind me; I miss flying enough as it is." She took his cap and placed it on a shelf in the closet, "Although it has been nice to not live out of my suitcase for a few months," she said with a laugh and helped with his blazer.

"Living out of a suitcase is all I know," he mused as his left arm fell out of its sleeve. Their camaraderie brought life to those around them and their history made for quick jokes and easy laughter. Shari slid his blazer on a hanger while Mac reached into his briefcase and pulled out a mess of papers. He was paging through the passenger manifest in a routine that seemed to sooth.

"Think you can get us there in under six hours, Mac?" A second flight attendant came in from the cabin with a stack of dinners in hand. Her voice was gravelly, and her aged skin sagged under its own weight.

"I'll do my best Dawnis," Mac chuckled without looking up. These two flight attendants were among the most senior in the fleet and he'd flown them around the world dozens of times. "Looks like we're fully loaded tonight," he folded the paper back into his briefcase. "You guys will have your work cut out tonight."

"Well at least most of these problems can be fixed with an extra packet of pretzels and not a union complaint," Shari said with a folksy hint of a southern drawl. She took a seat on the rear facing crew seat near the boarding door. "You just get us there safe, Mac."

The captain's even facade shrouded the tension surging through his bones. *If only you knew.* His mind mercilessly recounted the past twenty-four hours on loop and uncertainty grew with each iteration.

"Of course," he looked away and his pulse quickened while he tried to level his breathing. Both single and living in Seattle, it was Mac and Shari's transient nature that kindled their friendship and their decade of working together that kept them connected. Mac and Shari's eyes met for a moment and he saw the warmth that had carried him through many difficult times. Tonight, he would disengage and focus entirely on getting these passengers and his crew to Hawaii safely under the burden of all he knew.

Pulling his bag behind him, he passed through the galley and made his way toward the cockpit. The bright lights of the first-class cabin were a treasured reprieve from the rainy Seattle night and the familiar setting eased his mind. Small bottles of water placed on each leather seat caught his eye and he saw them extend all the way into the coach cabin. "Looks like the airline is finally loosening up," he said over his shoulder. His eyes gestured towards the bottles.

"These passengers better enjoy it, because this crap is probably coming out of our end of the year bonus," Dawnis muttered from behind a galley cabinet and Shari laughed.

"We're happy to have you back, Shari," Mac tried to smile and forced himself onward.

■ ■ ■

Mac's ship was his home and he was reassured that the cabin was overseen by some of the airline's finest. Tonight was the first leg of eight where he and his crew would be trusted to bring a load of two hundred and sixty-seven people across the Pacific Ocean to vacations, funerals and everything in between. Though he had always been one to keep to himself, he knew his work brought people together and it was one of many parts of the job that brought him satisfaction. The end of the month would mark the thirty-eighth year of being an airline pilot and it was the only work he had known and loved. Even after all these years, the anticipation of a new trip energized him and commanding a 200-ton piece of roaring aluminum and steel down a runway left him wanting more. Being a pilot was all he knew.

At the first row of seats, he paused and considered the hundreds of miles of open ocean between Seattle and Honolulu. The route was routine, and he always approached it with a confident poise, but tonight the expanse was daunting and he ached for a shorter journey.

His steely eyes looked over the rows of empty seats and he ran his hand through his greying hair. Tonight, his responsibility felt more arduous than he had ever known and he hesitated before committing himself to the flight deck. Though he knew it was finally catching up with him, he would continue to fly. All he could do tonight was hope.

"The time has finally come," he said to the young woman sitting in the right pilot's seat. The green glow of the control panel cut through the rainy evening as he lowered his head to enter the cockpit. He slid his briefcase in a small closet behind the captain's chair before climbing into his seat, a routine he'd done a thousand times over.

"Can you believe it?" Mac could hear the anticipation in her voice. Her dark hair was pulled back neatly in a braid and her smile was full and bright.

"After all these years, did you think we would ever fly one of these together?" he settled into the left seat but felt uneasy.

"I wasn't sure if I would ever be able to fly one of these the last time I flew with you," she laughed. "Let alone fly one with my old instructor." If he had not known her, he would have said she was too young to be flying a Boeing 767, but the airline had been growing so rapidly in the past few years that faces seemed to be getting younger each day.

"Well, even though I was once your teacher, tonight, we are colleagues," Mac shuffled through the mess of paperwork from his briefcase. Fond memories from flight instructing years before elbowed some of the foreboding buzz in his chest. "How does the weather look?"

The copilot reached across the vast center counsel, with two large engine throttles and a crop of flight computers, to screen through a monitor.

"Once we get out over the ocean, we can get around the storms over the coast," she said. "Other than that, the weather in Hawaii looks great for a layover."

*If we make it to Hawaii.*

"Okay," Mac tried to keep his voice light. Through the windshield, hundreds of passengers were milling about the airport on the other side of the large terminal windows, waiting to board their flights. Seattle-Tacoma International Airport was busy at this time as airplanes departed on overnight flights around the world. "I also hear today is a big day not only because you're flying with your old instructor," he smiled but he already felt drained.

"I just graduated from type training just under a month ago," she said, her glee bounding and infectious. "I'm just starting my fourth week flying the 767."

Mac could feel the anticipation in her words and for a moment his troubles faded away, "Having an old student fly with me on the airplane I love is an exciting day for me too, Julie." He slid his headset on, "Congratulations," he adjusted his mic, "I am really proud of you."

As a senior pilot at the airline, Mac typically had a sense of the new pilots that came into the fleet and he quickly caught word when his most talented student was hired. Though they had not spoken since she left for college over a decade before, the company's check-ride pilot had good remarks and her reputation preceded her. Just under an hour before pushing back from the gate, he hoped tonight wouldn't put her skills to the test.

"Thank you, sir," she said while biting her right index finger absentmindedly.

"Are you still doing that?" he mocked. "I remember you chewing on your nails when you were a student in Virginia," the memory made him smile.

She let out a nervous laugh, dropped her hand, and cleared her throat, "It's a bad habit I guess."

Mac could always feel that Julie shared his insatiable love of aviation. From the technical skill of completing a difficult instrument approach, to the splendor of a jumbo jet leaping into the sky, the art and science of aerospace always had a way of rousing his imagination. He had sacrificed so much of his life for his career, but he would do it all again if he were asked, and he sensed his copilot felt the same. Aviators from different generations, they were connected by their reverence for flight.

A single knock at the flight deck door brought Mac from his thoughts. "When are we meeting, Mac?" asked Shari, stashing a few bottles of water in the small wall cubby. A pair of yellow reading glasses sat atop her head. Despite the lines worn into her face, she was striking.

Mac pulled the watch from his pocket again, "It's just after six and they're going to board in about twenty minutes. Why don't you round up the gang and we'll meet in ten at mid-ship." He made it a routine to meet with his crew before every flight and Shari knew the protocol. Only a few years from retirement, they had been flying together for decades and their work blended together seamlessly.

"I see you're still doing that too," Julie laughed, pointing at his watch. Mac slid it back into his pocket and smiled.

"I also had to call the ground crew," Shari spoke before leaving, "it was *quite* clear they neglected to service the rear lavatories and they needed some attention." Julie chuckled and she went back to her work.

Dawnis popped her head through the door and held herself against the side wall, "That's what you get when you find cheap help." Her leathery skin showed a love of getting roasted by the Phoenix sun and stood at odds with Julie's youthful glow.

"Today is a big day for our copilot," said Mac gesturing his thumb toward Julie. "This is her first month on the seven six," he said, letting himself fall into the energy.

Shari brought both of her hands to her mouth and beamed, "That's wonderful, dear," she placed a hand on Julie's forearm, "what an exciting time!"

"The company line-check airman just signed me off last week," she proudly muttered.

"Well it looks like we're going to have a fun trip," Shari smiled, "see you both in ten."

■ ■ ■

Fully loaded with two hundred and sixty-seven passengers and 23,900 gallons of fuel, the mighty 767 pushed back from the gate under the command of Captain Robert 'Mac' Frank. He brought the airliner to a halt at the head of the runway and looked off into the night. White lights outlined the asphalt paving forward into the horizon and lumbering airliners lined up on the taxiway beside.

"Jet Stream one forty-four heavy, cleared for take-off, runway 16 left," the controller crackled through the headset.

"Seattle Tower, Jet Stream one forty-four heavy, clear for take-off, runway 16 left," Julie responded in tempo. She looked over at the captain. "You ready, Mac?"

He put his right hand on the engine throttles, his left on the yoke, and thought of the years leading up to this moment. He tried to suppress the stress clawing into his mind and the lies churning like a swamp. He already made his decision.

"As ready as I'll ever be," he pushed the throttles forward and the engines began to groan.

335,000 pounds of steel, fuel, and flesh began to shudder down the runway in acceleration until, at one hundred and sixty miles an hour, Mac pulled back on the yoke. As the airliner soared into the night, the captain hoped he'd make it to Honolulu in the same seat.

# Chapter 2

February 2016 | Pacific Ocean

Two hours over the Pacific, Mac watched the long lines of the moon dancing off the ocean's surface. With no lights for hundreds of miles, the stars were expansive, and the water looked like glass to the end of the earth. He pondered the exact point where the sky ended and the sea began, and often wondered how something so majestic could be so deadly. He usually considered himself fortunate to have a front seat view of the world from this lens but tonight his mind wandered. The business of life and all its heartaches seemed to fade from the air, and he saw the world for its collective good instead of its individual parts. Now, he was preoccupied by each passing second. The engines hummed at just over 32,000 feet and Julie turned off the seat belt sign. *It could happen at any moment.* The autopilot was set, the weather was calm and Shari began dinner service in the cabin.

Julie's performance during their departure sequence was technical and precise. Countless emotions soaked his consciousness, but at this moment, he felt pride in his student from a lifetime ago. She had earned the privilege to land the airplane in Honolulu.

"Julie, why don't you go ahead and take your break in the crew hold," Mac said, tentatively.

Pilot breaks were routine for this route and company policy, but tonight Mac considered scratching it. "Maybe take an hour and we will switch out." If he canceled, he would have to field questions he didn't want to answer.

"I'll take a break, but there's no way I'll be able to get any rest," she joked. The glow of the instrument lights revealed her smile and underlying enthusiasm, a feeling Mac remembered fondly. The elation of a new pilot was parallel to nothing and her energy was infectious.

"We'll need you rested for your first landing," he rubbed his forehead and wanted to redact his words. *We need you to be ready.* He didn't want to raise any flags. "See you in a few hours."

Julie exited the cockpit by the books. A flight attendant stood guard at the door and a beverage cart blocked the aisle to prevent unwanted visitors at the front of the plane. Mac remembered the days of flying with the cockpit door open so stunning views from the windshield could be shared with curious passengers. All that changed in post-9/11 aviation. Security lines, locked doors and armed pilots were certainly among his least favorite parts of the job, but these days it came with the territory.

Julie crawled into the crew rest space after grabbing hummus and crackers from an extra first-class meal. The compartment sat just below the forward cabin and functioned as a space for the crew to recuperate during long trips. It was simple and economical, with a few sleeping bunks and two seats, but it did the trick when flying to another continent.

"You want a beer too?" yelled Dawnis standing at the top of the steps in the galley.

Julie jumped into one of the bunks with her uniform on and kicked off her shoes. "Sure, grab me one of those Miller Lites," the engines hummed and she giggled. The compartment door closed with a click at the top of the stairs.

• • •

*I'm alone.* The panel instruments dimly lit the cockpit and Mac sat with his hands resting in his lap. The walls of the cockpit felt suppressive and tight, and he shifted in his seat. The night sky was endless and seemed to merge with the ocean below. *Please, not tonight.* One thousand, two hundred feet of salty water sat above the ocean floor, stippled with vast crevasses and fissures full of invertebrates and predators below. Two hundred and sixty-seven souls were under his care, but his focus was elsewhere. When he first started flying, the responsibility weighed on him, but experience helped lighten the load. Tonight, the weight was more than he had ever known.

He tried to focus on his duties, but the chatter of the radio and the droning engines faded out of his awareness while his mind raced. With the autopilot engaged, his job was to take command of an automated system in failure, but he prayed he wouldn't be called to take action. Knowing dozens of other airliners were flying no more than fifty miles away offered some form of ease, but the sea below looked infinite and unforgiving. The miles could not pass fast enough, and he wished more than anything to see the dim hue of the Hawaiian Islands on the horizon.

Doom swirled within him with a tightening grip. Destiny seemed to be swallowing him like quicksand and he clasped the arm rests with each hand. He could feel it coming and his vision narrowed. He wanted to run but there was nowhere to go.

*Please, no.*

The beating of his heart became his central focus. Each contraction squeezed like a ticking watch as an internal lever slammed into a dreadful new gear. He tried to slow his breath, but chaos was unfolding in his chest like a crumbling dam. The final beat was fantastic, and nothing seemed to follow.

His chest was silent.

His eyes widened and the world was quiet.

*Please, no.*

Alone at the controls of a massive airliner, the captain's worst nightmare was unfolding. He slid his right index and middle finger into the space beside his windpipe, searching for a pulse. *It can't be now.* His face was tight, and each muscle contracted.

Finally, with sweet reprieve, he felt a single explosion in his chest. His heartbeat with such a tremendous force it nearly made him choke. *Breathe, Mac.* The glands on his forehead contracted in concert and the salty sweat of fear showered him. He looked down at his hands resting in his lap, searching for something familiar. The hair on his neck stood on end and the fear center of his brain whirled in panic.

*Boom, boom boom...*

*Pause...*

*Boom, Boom...*

Moments spooled together like beads on a string. His heart began to beat erratically. *It's not going to pass.* The sensation was one he was all too familiar with.

*Pause...*

*Pause...*

*Boom, boom, boom, boom, boom...*

He felt his heartbeat rapidly in succession, nearly out of control, followed by merciless pauses.

*Boom, boom…*

*Pause…*

*Pause…*

*Boom, boom, boom…*

There was the urge to slam his fist into his chest, but he knew he was helpless and small. *Terror.* Each heavy beat exploded behind his eyes and he was absolutely stunned. The sounds and views of his world faded, and time was held in suspension. *Why tonight?* He wished it was a surprise.

*I'm in atrial fibrillation.*

Alone in the cockpit, his mind raced desperately. *What do I do?* He considered reaching for the phone and calling Julie to return but didn't know what he could say to her. Certainly, it couldn't be the truth. *Think methodically.* His mind echoed the events of the previous night and his stomach sank, knowing the worst was yet to come. Like boiling hot oil pouring over an icy engine, pistons and rivets under his skin began to crack and ricochet. Without warning, a totally new sensation enveloped him like he had never experienced before in a commercial airliner. Amuck in confusion, time began to pass at a clipping new pace, and he could focus only on one thing.

The airplane began to spin.

Violently.

The force was so sudden and savage it thrashed him into the side of his seat. Panicked contraction of each muscle in his back couldn't keep his head vertical and it toppled to the side. The rotation would've thrown him from his seat had he not been fastened in. *What the hell is happening?* The airplane moved with a speed and might he didn't know was possible.

Adrenalin pumped through his veins and his breathing quickened. Knuckles turned white as he clasped the arm rests with all his strength, and he wondered if this was the end. He slumped in his chair under the force applied to his body.

*Boom, boom boom, boom…*

*Pause…*

*Pause…*

*Boom, Boom…*

*Pause…*

His jaw clenched and his abdomen fought to prevent his spine from snapping. It seemed the airplane was spiraling viciously toward the sea and he wondered how long the airframe could endure before it would break apart. *Why are we in a spin?* There was only a moment to act.

He mustered the strength to press his skull into the headrest as he squinted at the instruments. *Breathe, Mac.* He couldn't bring the panel into focus. The letters and numbers were indecipherable, and the clouds blocked his view of the horizon. *I have no reference.* His mind raced to explain the predicament, but the clues were murky and unclear. *Did we hit another airplane?* There didn't appear to be any red warning lights illuminated and the alarms were silent. *A collision is doubtful.*

It took blistering focus to ignore the thunder behind his eyes and dancing in his chest. Every cell in his body needed to be focused to the emergency at hand as he noticed the airplane's left wing dip below the horizon. *I wish I could see.* The tail seemed to be rotating just as swiftly as the nose. The wings couldn't withstand the force much longer before they'd break apart and the cabin would be in freefall.

*Did something fall off the plane?* He considered a United Airlines DC-10 that had an engine nearly fall off several decades ago, but the Boeing 767 had no similar reports. *Seems unlikely.* He pictured passengers being thrown around the cabin and his stomach squeezed. *The seatbelt sign was off.* He had flown through fracturing turbulence countless times in his career, but he'd never seen anything like this. Helpless and panicked, they were barreling towards the sea. *Where the hell is the first officer?* He could fill a room with all the things he didn't know. Only one thing was crystal clear: *I must do something.*

There was no more time for questions because he needed to act.

*The autopilot.* It remained on. The program held the airplane to specific altitudes and speeds, a valuable tool on an airplane flying ten hours over the ocean. It couldn't do the one thing he needed in this moment: *recover from a spin.*

*It must be turned off.* Mac believed it was complicating the picture. He needed to disarm it so he could fly the airplane. Spin recovery was not part of routine 767 training, but he had no other choice. *I'm not even sure it's ever happened before in this massive airplane.* The world beyond the windshield was grey with clouds and he couldn't bring the panel into focus. *I can feel for the autopilot switch.* He had to fly using his willpower and pure grit.

As he extended his arm to turn off the auto pilot, his arm struggled against the force. Waves of nausea crashed over him like a twenty-foot swell. His finger circled the target but finally managed it into the OFF position. *Ring, Ring.* A bell signaled its new state. The spinning was relentlessly torturous.

He held the yoke with both hands as he sat nearly slumped off the seat. *Focus, Mac.* He had recovered from hundreds of spins in small airplanes during his training, but never a wide body airliner. *I am alone in the cockpit.* He thought about the crew serving dinner in the cabin while every ounce of his training screamed at him to act.

```
Lower the nose.

Level the wings.

Full opposite rudder.
```

He put both of his hands on the yoke and pushed forward. *I need to get control.* The engines began to whine as they accelerated, and his weight pressed into the shoulder straps. `Level the wings.` Mac had no reference to build his judgement and had to solely rely on feeling. *The wings are in a deep left bank.* He pulled the yoke to the right and felt the aircraft respond. Accelerating air colliding with the fuselage bellowed as they soared towards the earth. The engine's shriek filled the cockpit as their speed grew. `Full opposite rudder.` *We're in a left spin.* His shoe pushed deeply into the right rudder pedal at his feet and swung the nose to the right.

*Boom, boom boom, boom…*

*Pause…*

*Boom, boom…*

*Pause…*

*Boom, boom, boom…*

The engine screamed and his brain was in chorus. Mac braced himself with every millimeter of his being. *Jesus, please be with us.*

The ship was hurtling nearly seven hundred miles an hour toward the sea.

# Chapter 3

September 1970 | Grafton, North Dakota

16-year-old Mac ran across the rolling fields of the North Dakota prairie. The vast blue sky paralleled the lush crops below without a single hill as far as the eye could see. The leafy tops of the sugar beet field neared the arc of Mac's knee as he ran, and a towering pile of white tubers sat a hundred yards away along the dirt road. Warm air blew through his hair and his bronze skin reflected off the midday sun. The only interruption of the endless field was the towering Frank family combine that pulled at the field's yield. A wide framed and bearded farmer sat at the wheel. In the midst of the harvest season, the tractor was operating nearly twenty-four hours a day to beat the season's first frost.

The teen hardly filled his baggy overalls held together by filth from the season's work. He approached the tractor as the roaring engines calmed and the side door opened.

"It's turkey," he passed a brown paper bag into his father's worn hands.

"Tell your mother thanks," he said evenly. The man took off his tattered baseball cap and wiped the sweat from his brow. "Any word about the rain?" He looked more tired this harvest season than Mac could remember.

"The radio said they're expecting it around seven tonight and to stick around for a few days," said Mac trying to catch his breath.

His father leaned left as he dug in his pocket for his watch and nodded. He was a man of few words, most of which were about farming.

"How is the field coming?" Mac looked across the remaining rows of crops. Far beyond the field, he could see the silhouette of grain bins and buildings in Grafton, where his mind was tonight. The high school homecoming dance was planned for later that evening and it was a longed-for excuse to get off the farm. Kids across the county were hastily finishing their chores to make it to the event that would be the talk of the town for the coming week.

"I'll bet we have a good six hours left in this field," said the farmer. He rolled up the top of the bag and placed it next to him. He worked the same fields as his parents and, though the crops had changed over the years, the fertile soil endured. "If the rain holds off, we're going to start on the south field. It's about time you put your books away and help me and your uncle out," Mac's jaw clenched. "You're up to drive the tractor first."

Mac swallowed hard. Though he was never one for crowds or these school functions, he needed to get off the farm for something other than class or church. Harvest season swallowed his life every year, leaving little time for anything else besides grueling field work and a few hours at school.

Even though they supported his entire family, he despised sugar beets. Their white conical exteriors were heavy and sheathed in clumps of soil, and the processing plant in town emoted a sour stench that made him nauseous. He thought the root vegetable looked like a paled, failure of a giant carrot but they seemed to thrive in the North Dakota soil and every farm in the county grew them. It wasn't hard for him to imagine a life beyond the fields.

"Alright, Pop," Mac said quietly. Mr. Frank powered up the old tractor and Mac made his way back towards the barn.

Mac's hometown was a part of the country where the hands of a family brought food to their table and a sense of duty held a family together. Not far from the Canadian border, the same family doctor cared for nearly everyone in town and had for generations. Grafton had a single grocery store and an equal number of churches and bars. Founded in 1881, the first postmaster named the village after his wife's hometown of Grafton, New Hampshire and was soon gifted the North Dakota State Institute for the Feeble-Minded. The first general store was resurrected only seventy years earlier and the community was still rebuilding after a ferocious flood that ransacked the town in the mid-1940's. The main street was quaint, with two bars and a women's clothing store beside a single screen movie theatre, but it was desolate during harvest. It was the type of place where humility was a virtue, and everyone stood for the VFW color guard at the July 4th parade.

Mac couldn't leave fast enough.

Known in town as a quiet kid often found in the rural small library, his world was suffocating. Moving hay before five each morning and working the fields far past dusk left him exhausted and yearning.

Many of his classmates prepared to marry, continuing the life of their parents, but the thought induced claustrophobia in Mac. Though dozens of Grafton boys over the age of 18 were being lost to the war in Vietnam, Mac hoped his lottery number wouldn't be his way out. Patriotism ran generously through the veins of most in Welsh County, but Mac found the war abstract and distant. Thousands of miles from Vietnam in America's heartland, the newspaper wasn't delivered to the Frank farm and the war was only evident during the shorthanded harvest seasons. Locked in the confines of his room, the only reprieve he could find from the oppressive walls of his small-town life was a good book.

"Mac, why don't you get in here and help your sister peel these potatoes for dinner," yelled his mother from the door as he made his way towards the house. The structure was two stories, with white wooden siding and a wooden fireplace for heat. Mac's grandparents built the house when they first got married and, now that the south side of the foundation was sinking, the house slanted slightly. He counted down the days until graduation in the spring when he would pack-up his room.

"Okay, Ma," he kept his eyes towards the ground.

A senior at the rural high school, Mac kept to himself. He had little to say to the forty-three classmates he'd known since kindergarten and he had a similar interest in their friendship. There was little purpose in being friends with people he'd never see again. Mac's mind eddied on a conversation he had the previous week at school.

*"So what is your plan next year, Mac?" asked his science teacher mid-bite of a peanut butter and jelly sandwich. Mr. Jackson was a sole outlet in this tiny school. A recent graduate from the University of Wisconsin-Madison, Mac identified with the young teacher who also kept to himself.*

*"I guess I'll be going to UND," he said, referring to the University of North Dakota about sixty miles south. He put his lunch tray on a desk and scooped into his potatoes. They had become some sort of friends during his junior year and Mac often ate his lunch in his classroom, thankful for the brief reprieve from the monotony of high school life.*

*"You're a smart kid," he said gauging his reaction, "have you thought about going somewhere else? Like out east?" Going to college was not expected nor always encouraged in this town. The fields always needed hands to work them.*

*"How would you suppose I'd pay for something like that?" said Mac looking up from his tray. "The only tuition money I will have is from my own pocket."*

*"UND is a fine place," said the teacher. He paused after swallowing, "you have what it takes to be a doctor, Mac."*

*Mac would've signed up for any degree if it meant he could leave Grafton. He had been a volunteer on the community ambulance since he took the course in his junior year and premedical courses at the university seemed like a natural step. Though he had never been on a true emergency, Mac found working on the ambulance interesting, but more so, it was a good excuse to be excused from his chores at home.*

*"I've been thinking about it," he said. "We'll have to see if I have what it takes."*

■ ■ ■

The sun set on the night of the school homecoming dance and Mac stood at the sink cleaning the last of the dinner dishes. He watched the spectacular blues and reds dance over the prairie horizon through the kitchen window over the sink. Though he dreamed of a world beyond North Dakota, he doubted there was another place with a more stunning sunset. His father and uncle headed out to the field to make use of the light that remained, and Mac would soon follow. As he dried his hands on the towel draped over his shoulder, the sweet sound of the community siren cut through the house. It was the signal of an ambulance call, which to Mac, meant the sound of freedom.

The siren next to the Grafton Town Hall was only two miles away, but its sound traveled for miles across the county. Its single metallic pitch cut through the air with the long pulse of its rotation and it was a lovely melody to Mac's ears.

The alarm beckoned community volunteers to the town ambulance and fire trucks to respond to an emergency call. It was Mac's chance, so he slapped the dishrag on the counter and bolted out the back door over the porch.

"Mom, I'm going to the ambulance call!" he yelled over his shoulder and ran towards the barn. His heart thumped proudly with excitement. Of the half dozen calls the ambulance responded to each year, there was usually only one true emergency. Tonight, it was simply a chance to avoid the field.

The family's barn was nicer than their house, with towering wooden walls and a new roof Mac and his father put on less than a year ago. A fresh red paint coated the exterior and Mac pulled the sliding barn door with his body weight to reveal the family truck. He jumped into the baby blue 1957 Chevy pickup, worn from years on the farm, and slammed it into drive before speeding east into town. The sun continued to set over the prairie and, as the headlights cut through the dusty farm roads, Mac smiled.

■ ■ ■

The pickup squeaked to a stop next to a single-stall barn, two blocks from Main Street. Any Grafton native would point the structure out as the ambulance garage but anyone else would have to assume it was an abandoned shed. It sat beside a two-story grain bin with wooden sides worn of white paint and a roof that sagged in the middle. Mac grunted as he lifted the sliding garage door to expose the ambulance that barely fit between the peeling walls. He pulled the yellow extension cord from beneath the hood used to keep the oil warm and jumped into the driver's seat while the siren still wailed. With a turn of the key, he brought the engine roaring to life. As he pulled the rig beyond the walls of the tired barn, another volunteer jumped into the passenger seat.

"Jesus, drive fast, Mac," said the middle-aged woman. She wrapped a yellow vest snug around her midsection.

Nearly out of breath, she grabbed the radio microphone, "Grafton Ambulance, en route to Grafton Municipal Airport," her voice was tense like she had something perched in her throat. Something else in Mac's stomach tightened.

"The airport?" he pushed his foot into the gas and looked over to his partner. His breathing quickened and eyes sharpened.

"Didn't you hear?" he could see the panic in her eyes, but her focus was back on the radio.

"Roger," a female radio dispatchers voice cracked through the speaker, "County Sheriff is also en route," she said, "you'll probably beat him."

"Do you have any..." she spoke into the handset and hesitated, "...report on the nature of the incident?" her gaze looked beyond the road. She had been a volunteer for over ten years and Mac was relieved they were partners tonight.

"There's been a report of an aircraft down on the field," they heard through the speaker. The dispatcher's voice was detached. "The call was made from a nearby farm house."

"Jesus," she slammed the handset into its holster. She looked at Mac whose blood drained from his fingers clasping the wheel. "I guess it's just going to be you and me on this."

■ ■ ■

Mac navigated the farm roads with the ambulance's siren howling and their red lights piercing the dusk. A mile ahead, a long grey line of smoke cut into the sky. Emotions were raw and growing, and the reality was difficult to comprehend. "We just need to get this guy in the ambulance," said his partner shuffling in her seat, "and get down to Grand Forks as fast as this thing will go." The larger hospital in the south was the destination for many of their patients but it meant they had to drive across country.

His hands were cold, his jaw tense and he wondered if she was talking to him or reassuring herself. She was a bank teller in her day job but probably had the most experience of all the volunteers. "Got it?" she looked over at her driver who was supposed to be at a high school dance. Mac tried to swallow but it felt like he had a mouth full of hay. He nodded. *What am I about to see?* Getting the patient into the ambulance wasn't what scared him, it was the sixty-mile drive to Grand Forks that made him sweat.

■ ■ ■

"My God," his partner whispered as he pulled onto the field. Mac drove the rig towards the smoke but from a distance he didn't know if it was a pile of farm rubbish or their nightmare.

"Jesus, Christ," she held her hand over her mouth and her eyes wide, "That's Terry's crop duster." Mac approached the pile slowly. There was a heap of displaced earth in front of the smoky mass and they passed a splintered yellow airplane wing on their left. Mac wanted to look away, but he kept his eyes forward because they wouldn't look anywhere else. The fuselage extended from the mound of dirt and the tail was elevated off the ground about shoulder height. The cockpit had buckled, and the back of the airplane angled to the right. It seemed to have flown straight into the earth.

"Don't park too close," she said gesturing her hand toward the driver. Mac slowed the rig to a stop. Glass, rubber, and aluminum peppered the scene and the sweet smell of aviation fuel stung his nares. It didn't look like an airplane but the only identifying clue was the yellow tail protruding from the mass with a crack along the top.

"You wait back here by the rig," she said stepping out. She studied the wreckage distantly as she spoke. "Get the gurney out and wait for me to call you over." With the blue medical bag in hand, she made her way toward the wreckage.

The scene was unlike anything Mac had faced before. The rig was in park, though his fingers remained tight around the wheel. He fought the urge to run, knowing there was no place to go. There was no evidence of a pilot and the wreckage was so complicated it was hard to know where to look. His partner set her bag down and put two hands on a section of fractured wing and began to pull. *The wing is covering the cockpit window.* She leaned back, using her weight to displace it. Some sort of grey smoke was billowing from the craft and he coughed as fumes burned at his throat. *I don't know if I want to see what's behind it.* Mac's heartbeat wildly, and his eyes widened. He should've been getting the gurney or the other medical bag, but instead he watched. A prisoner to his body, he could hardly move.

His partner widened her stance and she grunted through her teeth. A dark fluid leaked around the mess and his eyes burned. Standing next to the rig thirty yards away, Mac told his body to help her but it wouldn't respond.

"Get back from the airplane!" a voice cried from behind Mac and he looked over his shoulder. An old pick-up truck was racing across the field and a man yelled from its window. "Get away from that thing before it starts to burn!"

Mac was frozen. His eyes looked back at the volunteer climbing over the smoking wreckage. *Jesus, that thing is going to blow!* He wanted to yell out but his throat hardly permitted enough air to breathe.

"Move away, Goddammit!" the man pleaded. Mac recognized him as a farmer a mile down the road from the airport. He shifted the truck into park next to the ambulance and waved his baseball cap. "That thing is full of fuel!"

Just as the driver stepped out of the truck, Mac watched his partner use her entire body to pull back on the wing. She leaned her full weight and struggled against the mass. Her face was red, and eyes clamped shut with each attempt. He grunted with her. *It can't be.* She gave it one final wrench and the wing finally gave way. *My God.*

Mac's hips fell against the side of the ambulance and he tried to steady himself. *What am I doing here?* The hair on his neck stood at attention amidst the smoke and his feet were sealed in concrete.

"May God help us," said the farmer standing in front of his truck. He brought his fingers to his forehead and then to both shoulders, making a cross over his body. "Peace be to his soul."

The glass cockpit dome had collapsed. The muscles that controlled his eyes and neck were locked and Mac studied the mass carefully. His partner took a few steps back, looking into the cockpit heap, and was entranced for a moment. The glass that remained was red and dripping.

*May God help us.* The voice repeated in his head like a record.

The blood rushed so quickly to his feet that he had to take a knee. Mac tripoded with his right hand and he succumbed to the wave a nausea that crashed over him. *I don't have what it takes.* They waited an hour for the town's family doctor to pronounce the pilot dead. *I don't have what it takes.*

∙ ∙ ∙

Sleepless and alone that night in his room, he stared at the ceiling without blinking. *Why did this happen?* Life felt delicate and unjust. He knew the pilot and his family from church. He thought of the man waking up that morning, shaving and going about his day as if it wasn't his last. He pondered the undigested dinner in his stomach and pictured the children that would learn of their father's death when they woke.

*I don't have what it takes.*

He couldn't stop seeing the blood running through the pilot's veins that would later paint his tomb.

*I'm not strong enough.*

∙ ∙ ∙

Three days after the accident, there was a single knock at Mr. Jackson's door. The teacher looked up from his papers and didn't have time to disguise his surprise.

"Hi, Mac," he said and stood up from his desk. Like most in town, he had heard about the accident and assumed Mac was involved when he didn't return to school. "Please come in and have a seat," he gestured towards the desks.

"I can't do it," said Mac flatly. He came to the center of the room but did not sit. "I can't."

His teacher watched him closely and his mind raced, "You can't do what, Mac?" He took a seat in a desk one row from his student.

"I can't watch someone die again." His gaze was a million miles away.

The first-year teacher sat silently for a moment. "You don't have to do anything you don't want to do." Mac's eyes were glazed and absent. "I can't imagine what you've been through the past few days, Mac," he said.

"I don't have what it takes to be a doctor," there was a long pause. "I can't see someone die again." His right hand pulled at his left thumb.

"Give it time," the teacher sensed this was an important moment. "Just try not to think about it," he said. "Forget about it and move on."

Mac's eyes were tired and broken. A suppressive silence held the room while Mac looked across the prairie through the window. A flock of geese soared in the sky to the south, escaping the looming winter.

*Forget and move on.*

Their eyes met for a moment and Mr. Jackson slid his hands in his pockets. Mac wanted to say something, but nothing came. Outside, snow fell in place of the rain. It was the heavy kind. The kind that is beautiful, but impossible to move.

Mac did not return to the ambulance and followed the teacher's advice for much of his life.

*Forget and move on.*

# Chapter 4

August 1971 | Grand Forks, North Dakota

A brilliant blue sky painted across the prairie without a single imperfection. The lush fields of greens and browns carpeted deep into the horizon along the narrow, two-lane highway between Grafton and Grand Forks. The baby blue 1957 Chevy pick-up truck rumbled along the road and passed tractors pulling towering bushels of grain along on the shoulder. With both windows open, the cool fall air batted their hair as Mr. and Mrs. Frank and Mac sat silently on the bench seat. Shoulder to shoulder, they drove across the North Dakota prairie. Today was freshman move-in day at the University of North Dakota. *Finally, I am free.*

When winter still held its firm grip, Mac mentioned at dinner one evening he would be attending college. His father simply grunted during a bite of beef while the silverware clinked and nothing more was said. He didn't sense bitterness, but the loss of a farm hand during the fall harvest was met like a frigid gust of winter air.

When they pulled onto campus, his father helped him carry two suitcases up to an empty third floor dorm, where he shook his hand after he eyed the room. His mother embraced him for a moment but was silent.

"Come home if you need to," Mr. Frank said. Mac nodded and they left him alone. It was cold and simple, but Mac didn't care. He had left and would never return.

From a top floor window in Welsh Hall, an all-male dorm on the north side of campus, Mac was finally alone. He looked at the ornate academic buildings and the manicured courtyard between from his window and watched several students walk across the lawn chatting and laughing easily. The campus felt scholarly and he settled into a new sense of belonging. It was the fresh start he longed for and it was hard to believe it was finally here.

The University of North Dakota was built six years before North Dakota gained its statehood and only two years after Grafton became a city. It had a rich history Mac studied before he made his move, which cultivated an appreciation for the institution as more than a simple escape. The flu of 1918 ravaged North Dakota fifty years earlier, with UND serving as the single hardest hit institution in the country, but the university persisted and continued to grow. The campus closed a few years later in the midst of WWI to serve as an army base for training soldiers and was later dubbed "Camp Depression" during the financial hardship of the 1930s. The university provided free housing in empty box cars for students willing to do free labor during the Great Depression. New academic buildings were quickly built in the years of rapid growth after WWII and the tradition of the "Fighting Sioux" hockey mascot was soon to follow. When Mac enrolled, the university was in a phase of brisk growth and with it came swollen school pride and excitement as a new student.

In his empty dorm, he turned his back towards the window and studied the room. There were two of everything: a wooden bunk and mattress wrapped in plastic, a simple desk with a chair, and a lamp. The walls were white and the ceiling had a grey stain. The mattresses were thin, dimly lit by the small window, but it felt more like a home than any he had ever known.

There was a knock at the door, "Welcome to UND!" the perky voice followed. A man who looked a few years older than Mac waved from the door in a button-down shirt and tightly combed hair. Mac could hardly see his face through the width of his round, coke bottle glasses. "Can I give you a hand?"

"Uh no," it took Mac a moment to return from his thoughts. "I'll be okay, thank you."

"My name is Richard Sprout," he stepped into the room with an extended hand. "I am the floor leader." His corduroys were rolled up above his shoes and he happened to look like a sprout.

"Nice to meet you," the two awkwardly locked hands and Mac noted how his hair was perfectly immobile, "I'm Mac."

"Nice to meet you, bud," he brought his foot up onto the bedframe and rested his elbow on his knee. "Say, there is a freshman dance tonight at the Student Union on University Avenue if you're interested," he waited.

"Thank you," he paused, "Sounds like fun." *No way in hell.*

"There's a group of us from the floor walking down around seven," his teeth seemed too big for his mouth. "See you there?"

Mac hesitated, "I'll put some thought to it, thanks for asking." Richard left and Mac later lied he wasn't feeling well. By the end of the day, he learned where the cafeteria was and that he wasn't assigned a roommate. He was pleased with the first and didn't mind the latter. Always an introvert, he spent his first night at the University of North Dakota alone under a lamp paging through his new textbooks.

■ ■ ■

Sunday passed without attending church and Monday morning was welcomed. Mac crawled across the row of students sitting in a classroom larger than he had ever seen. The amphitheater seats were stacked over two floors centered around a daunting, green chalkboard dusty from a concluded lecture. His eyes tracked down the rows of students with their notebooks open and pens tapping. Mac couldn't even count the number of students crammed into the room that smelled like musk and old carpeting. He realized he'd better come to his chemistry lecture a few minutes early tomorrow if he wanted a seat.

"Good morning students," a short, bald man strolled to the front of the lecture hall from a side door, "I am Dr. T. R. Stemmer." His voice was sharp and nasally, and his belly protruded through his dress shirt. He arranged some notes on the podium then stood squarely in front of the crowd.

"Look around," Mac noticed late arrivals sitting on the steps. "There are over 200 students in this classroom and nearly all of you are pre-medical majors." Students shifted in their seats and Dr. Stemmer tapped a wooden pointer stick on the ground. He paused waiting for his words to sink in and someone coughed. Course registration was a few weeks ago and Mac panicked when it was time to register his major.

"Of the students in this room, 100 will make it through freshman chemistry." His eyes slowly scanned the room. "Fifty of you will make it through organic chemistry and twenty of you will make it through both histology and pathology." Mac was more nervous than he expected and felt like there were four hundred eyes on him. "Ten of you will go to medical school upon graduation." The plan had always been to go to medical school but the last year told him otherwise.

The freshman let his eyes wander around the room, but he kept his head still. Some students looked defeated while others looked on with resolve. He was somewhere in between.

Feeling small, Mac thought about the pilot and the seared memory of the crushed windshield. He had signed up for the pre-med courses for no other reason than he had no better plan. With a rather unceremonious commencement, Dr. Stemmer began Mac's first university lecture.

■ ■ ■

Weeks turned to months, the leaves turned bright, and no snow fell by the first of October. Mac struggled to keep his head above water in his courses. Despite late nights in the ornate Chester Fritz Library at the center of campus, Mac's early assignments were returned with C's and D's in the gradebook. Isolated in his studies, he knew few and was secluded in his cycle between the library, class, and his dorm. Though, he excelled in his high school classes with little effort, work at the university was beyond his expectations.

On a Friday afternoon nearing Halloween, Mac locked up his dorm and headed out to an evening in the library. His keys fell into his jacket pocket as he cut around the empty chairs and tables in the common area of his dorm floor. It was a large room, with white walls, fluorescent lights, and a dozen tables. The space was unoccupied beside for a single student seated at a corner table with his face down in a book. Mac recognized him but they had never spoken. He tightened his backpack as he made for the exit but slowed his pace as the student neared. Mac tried to make sense of the diagram he was so engrossed in. Scribbling into his notebook, the student had a crop of dark hair that bobbed as his head moved and Mac peered over his shoulder. *Is that a cockpit?*

"Um… Hey man," he looked up from his book and Mac blushed. "What's up?" The student was gangly, and his brown curls draped over his eyes.

"I'm sorry, I didn't mean to interrupt," Mac took a step back.

"Are you studying for the midterm too?" he asked laughing. His brown eyes were soft, and he leaned back and ran his fingers through his hair.

"No," Mac coughed and tightened his backpack straps again awkwardly. He thought of all the things he could say but instead, "I'm sorry, is that a cockpit?" came out and he pointed to the page.

"Sounds like you're all studied up," the student's white t-shirt was wrapped snug around his ribs. "I take it you're not an aviation student?" Mac noticed the thin stubble on his face next to the lush sideburns that fell below his ears.

"Pre-med," said Mac. He had the odd sense he wanted this guy to like him. "You're an aviation student?" he asked.

"You got it," he crossed his arms and raised his eyebrows like he was sizing something up. "Pre-med eh? You must be a pretty smart guy."

Mac thought about the C- on his last chemistry quiz and pretended to adjust his backpack for a third time. "I'm just trying to keep my head above water," he said. The student motioned to a seat at the table and Mac hesitated before sitting across from him. "So, what does a guy do with an aviation degree…?" his voice trailed. "I'm sorry, I didn't catch your name," he propped his backpack beside the table.

"No worries, brother," he brushed the hair out of his eyes again with both of his hands. "My name is Dennis Cullen and I'm going to be an airline pilot." His inflection was proud, but genuine.

Mac thought about the crop duster buried in the earth. *Who would voluntarily get in one of those?*

"Have you ever been on an airliner?" asked Dennis. He clapped the textbook closed and slid his notebook aside.

Mac shook his head. He'd never traveled far out of Grafton, let alone flown on an airplane.

"Yeah man, it's going to be great," he laughed and slid on a pair of aviator sunglasses. "My Dad flew in the war and has been shaping me to be a pilot since I was a baby." He spoke with a cool confidence but was so trim Mac wondered if he'd have the strength to fly an airplane.

"So, have you, like, flown by yourself?"

"Sure, I have man," Dennis pulled his sunglasses off. "I did my first solo when I was fourteen years old."

"Fourteen? My Dad didn't even let me drive the pick-up in town before I was that old." The two laughed and the tension eased. Mac felt himself smile with the first friend he'd met since August.

"I got my pilot's license when I was sixteen and have been flying since." Dennis interlaced his fingers behind his head and balanced on the back legs on his chair. "It's a family business, man, my Dad and Grandpa were both pilots too. You've never been up before?"

Mac didn't respond. *"May God help us," said the farmer. He made a cross over his body.* "No, I haven't," Mac thought of the red and wet cockpit glass. "To be honest I'm pretty afraid of those things." For much of the past year, he'd tried to purge flying from his mind.

"How's this, Mackie," Dennis leaned forward and slapped the table. "I'll bring you out to my parent's farm and I'll bring you flying. Heck I'll even let you fly if you want!"

Mac itched his nose, trying to buy time, "Sounds fun." He wondered if he should tell Dennis about the accident but decided against it. Words seemed to come easily when they spoke, and the somber memories of the ambulance call didn't seem to matter right now. Instead, the natural chatter of blossoming friends ensued. *I can study tomorrow.*

"I'll tell you what," Dennis paused and looked across the table thoughtfully, "Some buddies at Sigma Phi fraternity are having a little party tonight." Dennis opened his palms like he was making a deal. "Why don't you come along?"

Mac hesitated. He'd chosen to spend most of his time by himself since starting school a few months before, but something about Dennis put him at ease. He made him laugh and the world seemed lighter through Dennis's lens. With some encouraging, Mac finally agreed.

■ ■ ■

At a colonial style fraternity house east on University Avenue, Mac admired how Dennis spoke assuredly to many and he tried to follow suit. After the fifth beer, he too conversed effortlessly and, to his surprise, he actually enjoyed himself. There was something about being with Dennis that made an evening like this not so bad.

Though the night ended with a sudden exit and a bit of productive heaving, Mac considered the party a success. As Dennis put it with a slap on the back: "A little upchuck means you had a good time, my friend."

# Chapter 5

November 1971 | Grand Forks, North Dakota

Fall turned to winter and the first snow came in early November. The campus was peaceful with a fine white dusting and the temperature persisted well below zero.

As the semester wore on, Mac found himself spending more time with Dennis. Their friendship blossomed during their walks to class, meals together, and even some studying. It was comforting to have a companion to face the world with and in many ways, it was his first time in friendship. With the war in Vietnam in full offense, student demonstrations on campus were a common occurrence and their favorite hobby was to watch the disorder unfold between activists and the campus ROTC cadets. On calmer days, Dennis touted his pet rock with Mac at the Grand Forks' arcade where he spent too many of his coins in pursuit of his pinball champion dream. Mac found Dennis's energy surrounding aviation captivating, and he realized he spent more time thinking about it curiously.

As the third Monday in November loomed, Mac's mid-term exams approached, and the fun quickly dissipated.

Late nights in the library made his eyes bloodshot and the meat on his already thin frame leaned. The images of C's and D's circled on his chemistry assignments riled him and his mind homed in on his mediocrity. He wanted to drop the course weeks ago, but he'd have to disenroll from school and return in the spring because he didn't have enough credits to remain a full-time student. Going home was not an option so he simply had to press on.

*"Of the students in this room, 100 will make it through freshman chemistry... Ten of you will go to medical school...."* Dr. Stemmer's voice tormented him less about his medical school prospects and more about what his paltry achievement represented.

The library clerk approached Mac sitting at a long wooden table the midnight before his chemistry mid-term. "I'm going to turn off the lights in five minutes," he said. The lurking defeat would bring him to a new low. Coming to school was a dream but now he questioned if the path was his to take.

Staring at his notes diagramming chemical conversations and periodic trends, Mac felt helpless. *I don't understand any of this.* The library lights darkened, and the clerk locked the front door. *I'm screwed.* He wondered how he would explain academic expulsion to his father.

Mac lay in bed that night sleeplessly, aware of all he didn't know. A sense of inadequacy and dread sat in his throat. He thought of the crushed cockpit and Mr. Jackson. He wondered if he was destined to never get away from Grafton, but the thought was more than he could bear.

The metallic alarm pierced through his empty dorm room at seven the following morning and he arose from a sleepless night. Mac didn't bother showering and he didn't touch the eggs on his tray. He thought about a failing transcript and moving back into his room on the farm. The next year's harvest lurked in his mind and the dread he would carry with every day prodded him.

He walked across campus to the lecture hall with no open seats and several students sitting on the stairs. Dr. Stemmer had a gang of graduate student cronies policing the class as they passed out the exam without a single word.

"You have two hours, students," said Dr. Stemmer abruptly. The corner of his mouth curved up subtly. "You may now begin."

Mac felt the daunting white pages staring back at him.

General Chemistry Midterm Exam
Fall 1971

Name _____

He could hear his heart beating in his ears and both palms were damp and cold. He conjured the courage to finally turn the page and wondered if fewer nights at the arcade would've changed the outcome. It didn't matter now, and he held his breath:

If 5.0 moles of both hydrochloric acid and sodium sulfide are mixed and reacted according to the equation below, how many moles of hydrogen sulfide (H2S) are produced?

$$HCl + Na_2S \rightarrow H_2S + NaCl$$

The coils and wires in his head were knotted and rusty. He paged through the rest of the exam. *There are 100 questions?* Four hundred eyes around him were suffocating and somebody tapping a pen was the only thing his mind could focus on. The crushed airplane haunted him, and he could hear the billowing smoke. He thought of Dennis and the friendship that would certainly end if he moved back to Grafton.

He looked at the clock. *It's been twenty minutes. I need to answer some of these questions.* He read the first question again.

He felt the dread. The inadequacy. The cold sweat.

*"You have what it takes to be a doctor, Mac…"*

*"Move away, Goddammit!… That thing is full of fuel!"*

*"Only ten of you will go to medical school…"*

*Tap, tap, tap, tap, tap, tap….*

*"Peace be to his soul…"*

All eyes were on him. *Forty-Five minutes remaining.* He could hear everyone's breathing but he had to concentrate on his own air coursing through his lungs. He would return to his high school classmates and have to find someone to marry. They'd have kids, buy a house and he'd be working the fields next harvest. His pulse accelerated an it seemed the walls were closing in. His impending failure was approaching like molten lava.

How many moles of hydrogen sulfide (H2S) are produced?

*I don't have what it takes.* His body wasn't his own. College was his escape but now it was falling through his open hand. Floating and detached, he viewed his world through binoculars. *How many moles?*

In thoughtless panic, his eyes darted to the desk beside him. The student in the seat wore a yellow dress and Mac recognized her from earlier in the semester. He was conscious of the noise his breathing made and he tried not to move too much. She was active in class and appeared to be bright, but that didn't cross his mind at this point. Her answer sheet was nearly full, each multiple-choice question bubbled in, and sat openly on the desk. Mac felt like a marionette.

The whizzing of his eyes brought answers from the adjacent desk and his answer sheet quickly mirrored hers. *"Dad.... I'm sorry but I failed..."* The graduate student cronies didn't make a peep. *I don't have what it takes.* His cold and sweaty palms could hardly steady his pencil, but he made it to the bottom of the page before he realized what had happened. *I must get out of here.*

His backpack was closed, and he donned his jacket clumsily after hitting another student focused on their exam. He trotted down the stairs to the front of the lecture hall and smacked his exam on the table. He caught the surprised glance of a few students after being the first one to put an exam on the front table, but he maintained his pace. With his eyes on the floor, he shot up the steps, two at a time, and dashed out of the lecture hall. It felt like the room was devoid of oxygen and the ceiling was going to collapse. He knew Dr. Stemmer's eyes were burning into the back of his head as he retreated through the rear, but he didn't dare turn around. His fists crashed through the door and cold winter air slapped his face, finally permitting air to his lungs. *"Peace be to his soul..."*

■ ■ ■

"Jesus, Mackie. You look like shit," said Dennis as Mac passed his table on their dorm room floor. Dennis paged through his magazine and smiled but Mac fled into his dorm room without a word.

The freshman threw his backpack on his bed, closed the door, and sat heavily at his desk. Shame left him in a quiet daze and his mind churned like a boiling lake. *"You have what it takes to be a doctor, Mac..."* His future was fading and collapsing in the midst of a lie. He felt empty knowing what the pressure compelled him to do. *Is this who I am?* Every movement felt stolen and forged and his dorm was dark and closed.

A single knock at the door pulled him from his thoughts. He sat motionless and tried to hide in his skin.

"Don't come in, Dennis," his back was to the door but could hear it open.

"What's going on, man?" Dennis emerged slowly into the room and stood in the doorway for a moment. His tone was softer, but he was never one to go away when he was told to.

Mac's eyes were heavy and wet, and he didn't say anything for a moment. The plastic cracked as Dennis sat on the empty mattress and waited, "I screwed up." Mac didn't look up.

"Is everyone okay?" Dennis's voice was bouncy but concerned. "I mean if no one is hurt, things will be fine." He rubbed his hands on his knees. The two farm kids waded in the silence while Mac faced away from his friend, both irked and grateful for his presence in that moment.

"I cheated on my chemistry exam this morning, Dennis," he looked up but was conscious of his red, heavy eyes. He wondered what it would mean to his friend.

"Must've been a tough test," his brow raised, and he leaned back on his hands. He was airy and undeterred.

Mac nodded and widened his eyes, "I sat there for an hour and then copied the girl next to me." He wondered to whom he was explaining himself, "I had to get out of there," he brought his forehead to his hand. "I was even the first one done." He felt vulnerable and waited for the verdict.

"You idiot!" Dennis began to laugh, and Mac looked up scornfully. Mac's spine began to extend and his eyebrows creased, it didn't seem funny to him. "If you're going to cheat, the least you could do is wait until someone else finishes first!"

Mac could only hold his anger for so long before the strain began to dissipate. *You ass.* The amusement felt cruel, but the other freshman laughed easily and even slapped his knee a few times. "Dammit, Dennis!" and soon he too was laughing at the oddity of his reaction.

■ ■ ■

Mac walked across campus, battling the frigid air, to the Office of the Registrars the next morning. "Can I help you, young man?" asked Mr. Abram, a grotesquely slender councilor seated behind a desk. His brown locks were precisely combed and his long fingers rested interlaced on a dark, walnut desk.

"I would like to change my major, sir," he managed to get out. His mouth was dry and it was hard to swallow. *I cheated on my exam.*

"Might I ask the reason?" asked Mr. Abram, looking over the glasses perched at the end of his nose.

"I've just decided my current major no longer mirrors my interest." *I cheated on my exam.*

"I see, and what major might that be?"

"Pre-medical science, sir." *I'm a liar.*

"Oh yes," he pushed his glasses up his nose. "*Another* student leaving the pre-medical course work." If he were an animal, the counselor would be a snake. "And what field might better *mirror* your interest?" he said mockingly.

"Aviation."

The man's tiny eyes squinted across the desk and made some sort of snort. "And what do you plan to do for the remaining portion of the semester?"

Mac thought for a moment, "I suppose I will have to complete my classes unless I can transfer at this point in the semester." He tried to read the man's mind.

"That is simply out of the question," he snapped. "The drop date was nearly two weeks ago." Mr. Abram didn't try to conceal his disapproval. The UND School of Aerospace Science was only six years old but was quickly growing. John D. Odegard, a North Dakota crop-duster pilot and founder of the department donated two airplanes to the program that was drawing students from across the university. The new department was not always met warmly, *"Aviation is a trade that does not belong in an institution of higher learning," Mac once overheard a professor say.*

"You will complete your current courses and re-enroll in the spring," said Mr. Abram as a bead of saliva landed on the desk. Mac agreed and fled instantly.

■ ■ ■

"So Mackie, what ever happened with your test?" asked Dennis with a mouthful of lasagna. They spoke over the celebratory noise in the cafeteria at the end of final exams in January. Giant heaps of cafeteria food sat on trays across the dining room as students exchanged and howled in the cheerful, end-of-semester atmosphere.

Mac stopped chewing. They were speaking about Mac's aviation courses in the spring semester and the question blindsided him. He tried to pretend like he'd forgotten about it but the performance was lackluster. *Forget and move on.* His semester's marks were C's and D's and his first exam weighed on his mind daily

"Did you ever fess up?" Dennis prodded playfully with a bite of roll now joining the pasta.

"Well..." Mac swallowed heavily. "Of course," he could feel his words were clunky and loud. "I told him two weeks later." He set his fork down and blushed. It was the first deception of his professional life, but it wouldn't be the last.

"*Really?*" said Dennis, his brows elevated and sat back with his open hands. "You didn't say anything to me." Dennis had shaved his bushy sideburns but kept the underwhelming stubble on his chin for a reason even he couldn't seem to verbalize.

Mac laughed like a hammer hitting tin, "Yes, Dr. Stemmer gave me a few extra assignments and said don't do it again."

Dennis took another bite and slowly nodded his head, "Well I'm glad it worked out." His eyes sharpened across the table for a moment but decided not to press it.

Mac didn't finish his lunch. *This is who I am now.*

*Forget and move on.*

# Chapter 6

February 2016 | Pacific Ocean

Julie was lurched from sleep. Thrown against the wall in her bunk, she gasped into consciousness.

*What the hell is going on?* The noise was staggering.

She swung her legs from her bunk and grabbed the wall just before being thrown to the ground. Bottles and bags were sliding across the floor and the engines screamed. *The airplane is in a dive.* Her heart was beating wildly below her breastbone and her hands searched the walls for something to hold on to. She got to her feet but had to widen her stance to stay standing while the airplane's bank continued to deepen. Her breathing was sharp and staccato.

The co-pilot was alone in the crew hold; the two coach seats and handful of bunks were empty. The muffled cries of passengers above harpooned through her chest and she was acutely aware. Thunder echoed in her chamber from things falling heavily on the ground in the cabin above. The noise was overwhelming.

*I have to get to the cockpit.*

She struggled up the narrow staircase, pushing the walls with both of her hands to keep steady. The wind howled against the airplane hurtling towards the earth and she grit her teeth as she ascended. Her mind was darting from thought to thought as she used her shoulder to struggle against the door at the top of the stairs. She fought with it for several seconds until it finally opened. The scene before her eyes was out of a nightmare. *Chaos.*

The growing tumult of screaming passengers left Julie suspended in time and she watched Shari hunched over in the aisle pushing frenzied passengers into their seats. Cans and bottles were rolling about while bags were plunging from open overhead compartments in mushrooming disorder.

"Everyone into your seats," Shari wailed, "And fasten your seat belts!" She was desperately closing bins and shoving bags under seats. The sound from the wind and engines howled like the shriek of a thousand whistles blowing in unison. "Brace your heads forward!" the flight attendant begged.

Julie's brain could only take in what she was seeing but was otherwise frozen. Her lips were ajar and her eyes broad as she held the stairway door trying to fathom the scene. She studied the pained lines in a man's face while embracing the woman next to him before she turned her head and felt her blood go cold. With her eyes towards the galley, the gravity of the situation grew.

*Dawnis.*

The flight attendant lay face down across the galley floor with a growing stain draining from the side of her head. It took her a moment to realize that the entire pool was blood.

"Dawnis, are you okay?" Julie knelt and tried to shake her awake amidst the howl.

The flight attendant was limp and laid oddly across the floor. The airplane's dive was so deep that the first officer struggled to stay vertical. *Is my foot wet?* She tried to focus her mind but so much stimulus begged her regard. She looked down and realized she wasn't wearing any shoes and her socks were sopping with blood.

"Watch out!" the panicked cry from a passenger called from the cabin. Julie looked up and she held her breath. A beverage cart was accelerating down the aisle directly in their path. One man pointed at the cart growing in speed while others looked on helplessly.

Shari leaped out of its course in the aisle and Julie felt her body plunge into action. She jumped back to her feet and pulled the flight attendant's entire weight by the shoulders of her uniform. The back of Dawnis's white blouse waded through the maroon pool as Julie schlepped her across the galley floor. The cart's acceleration roared through the galley, inching closer with each passing millisecond.

"Get out of the way!" the passenger wailed again while another screamed. A man in the front row of seats held his hand on his balding head and simply let his mouth hang open.

The cart collided with the cockpit door just as her feet were pulled out of its path. The clamor was deafening but the copilot didn't flinch. Her mind was sharp, and the world looked vivid. Julie propped the flight attendant against the exit, blood still pouring from the side of her head. She pulled the cart away from the door and locked it into its slot before eyeing the cabin sweltering in emotion. The cries of a screaming baby echoed over the rows of seats and she watched a greying woman press her head into the seat, clasping her eyes shut. *We're all going to die if I don't do something.* She unlocked the cockpit door and embarked, sensing everything was about to change.

■ ■ ■

"Captain Frank!" yelled Julie over the whine of the engines, her urgency palpable. "What is happening?"

She closed the flight deck door behind her and struggled to the empty copilot seat. The only thing she could see through the windshield was the drab greyness of nighttime clouds, punctuated by glimpses of the Pacific Ocean. *We're crashing towards the sea.* The howling wind sung with the engine's whine.

The captain was askew off his seat, leaning forward into his shoulder straps. He said something unintelligible.

"Captain Frank," she twisted into the seat and buckled the straps over her shoulders. "What is happening?" There was no reference through the cockpit window and she skimmed the controls, trying to orient herself.

Artificial Horizon: *Steep bank, a deep dive.*

Airspeed Indicator: *Too fast, 520 knots... nearly six hundred miles per hour.*

Altitude: *Passing through 25,000 feet... dropping quick.*

Turn Coordinator: *Uncoordinated... like a car skidding on the ice.*

Autopilot: *Off... why is the autopilot off?*

The Boeing 767 airliner was diving towards the ocean.

"Mac!" She yelled into her headset over the wind inundating every nanometer of the plane. "Why are we in this dive?" The airplane was trembling and the muscles in Julie's neck and side burned to keep her upright. She looked over at the captain, who was leaning over onto the yoke and turning the wheel in the direction of the bank. Her fear seared like hot oil.

"I'm not sure what happened," the captain's words were slurred and odd, "Everything was fine until we entered this left spin!"

*Tick, tick, tick, tick, tick, tick, tick.*

The airspeed warning alarm began to ring. *Left spin?* She looked at the controls again. *We're not in a spin.* Julie fought the urge to freeze.

*Passing through twenty-two thousand feet.*

"There must be a structural failure, that's all I can think of," it was a wounded voice. A red warning light flashed on the dash and the clouds rushed over the windscreen. The green glow from the instruments in the dark cockpit was punctuated by the ominous beacon of the airspeed warning light.

*Both engines seem to be working, no other warning lights are on.*

*"WARNING... AIRSPEED!"*

*Tick, tick, tick, tick, tick, tick, tick*

Mac was leaning heavily into the yoke, pressing it forward. *Could the captain be causing this?*

"My airplane!" she yelled, her mind was racing. She was initiating a standard procedure called 'Positive Exchange of Controls'. She waited for the captain to respond, *"Your airplane!"* indicating he no longer had hands on the yoke. *Come on, Mac.* She waited for one hair-raising second, but the captain said nothing.

"Captain Frank!" her voice cracked. "My airplane!" *Passing through twenty-one thousand feet.* The airspeed warning horn filled the cockpit and another warning light began to flash. She was running out of options. *Is the captain trying to crash this airplane?*

"I've got to pull the plane out of this spin!" he yelled. He looked disoriented and pale and she could see the glisten of sweat on his forehead. The airliner was barreling towards the dark ocean below.

Julie grasped the yoke and pulled back with the entire strength of her arms. Usually, she could move the airliner's controls with little effort but now they felt heavy and muddy. It became clear she was fighting his weight on the controls. "Sir, please let go of the yoke! We have to pull up!"

"What the hell is happening with this plane?" Mac yelled through his teeth. He was sweaty and would've piled onto the floor if it weren't for the straps over his shoulders.

"*SINK RATE…. PULL UP!*" The automated voice continued aloof and heartless. The airplane's dive was unlike anything Julie had seen in training and its bank was growing.

"*WARNING… AIRSPEED!*" The computer voice filled the cockpit in loop and the engine blared. Every bolt, wire, and sheet of steal stirred in fierce vibration.

The copilot pulled back harder on the yoke and began to overcome his strength. *Come on!* She could feel the airplane trying to respond. *The captain put us in this dive.* "Sir," she pleaded to the captain. The noise was deafening, and her muscles were tight. "Please let go!"

The co-pilot was in an impossible position: *I must take command from the captain.*

"Sir, my airplane!" she tried one last time. *Is there another option?* She raked her mind but nothing else came.

"Step down, Julie and let me correct this spin!" he yelled, his eyes were wild.

"We are *not* in a spin, sir! *You* are causing this," she pulled back on the yoke with all of her strength. "Now *please let me take the controls!*"

First Officer Julie Sampers pulled back again, this time with all the force she could garner, and the controls yearned to respond. *Gain control.* "Sir, please!" She pulled again but this time the yoke broke free. *Yes!* She could feel the airplane begging to end the madness.

She pulled the wheel towards her as the sole pilot in control of the 767. *Thank God.* The copilot pulled the engine throttles back, adjusted the rudder pedals, and cautiously brought the wings back to horizontal flight.

Her pulse was still bounding and her breathing wild. *It was almost all over.* Julie held the airplane level for several moments while she tried to gain her baring. *Nine thousand feet.* The reality was strange and disturbing. She opened and closed her jaw, stretching the muscles that ached with tension. Her eyes turned over the counsel towards the captain, his arm hanging off the chair and contracting every muscle in his face. Gleaming and pale, he quickly turned his head away and began retching violently. The contents of his stomach spewed below his feet.

"Full opposite rudder, Julie!" he yelled between waves. "You have to recover from this spin!"

"Sir…" she was at a loss. The airliner was slowing and no longer descending. "We're level now." She was confused and almost hurt. *There is something terribly wrong.*

*First, fly the airplane.* Her training was ripe at her fingers and she brought her focus back to the controls. *I can do this.* She exhaled, rolled her shoulders and brought the engines to full power to bring the massive airliner into a climb.

A ring from the cabin phone.

She simply watched it for a moment, not sure if she had the strength to answer the voice on the other side. Eventually, the receiver pressed into her ear. "Yes," her voice was quiet but even.

"Julie, this is Shari. We have an emergency in the cabin," her voice was sharp and concise. "Put the captain on."

She eyed Mac from her seat. He heaved again and more contents fell onto the floor before he leaned back into his seat. "The captain is incapacitated," her voice masked her lurking fear. Something in the bottom of her belly swirled like she was in a transient moment of free fall. "I am in command now." Both ends of the line fell silent, considering the implication.

"Direct the crew how you'd like to proceed," said the senior flight attendant. Her voice was calm and detached.

Julie had trained for this: thousands of hours at the controls, head in the books, mind in the sky. *I took command from a pilot who has been flying longer than I've been alive.* The twenty-nine-year-old had more responsibility in that moment than most do in their lifetime. "What is the emergency?"

"Several passengers are seriously injured. At least one crew member is unconscious and severely bleeding," she said. It reminded Julie why her feet were wet.

"Secure the cabin," Julie thought methodically and thoroughly but she permitted her thumb nail to come to her mouth and began to gnaw. "Get everyone seated and get me a head count of the injured," she reached up and turned on the seat belt sign with her other hand. "Find a doctor and send them to Dawnis immediately."

Shari's words were crisp and placid, but nothing could fill the hundreds of miles of open ocean that lay before them.

"And Shari," Julie continued just before the call ended, her nail clicking between her teeth, "Send someone up to remove the captain from the flight deck." She hung up the phone and looked at her colleague who heaved again. *I'm sorry, Mac.*

"The aircraft suddenly began to spin to the right," he groaned but managed to get out. "I turned off the autopilot to correct it manually."

"Sir, I was in the crew hold and felt the airplane bank left and dive," she hesitated, "I do not think we were ever in a spin," she began to absently pick at her cuticle with the other hand.

"The hell we weren't!" he grit his teeth through a wave of nausea. "I felt it." He pushed himself up in the chair by the armrests and wiped his mouth, "To be honest, it still feels like we're spinning now..." his voice trailed off. He paused but seemed to already know. "Julie, something is wrong."

"Try to relax, Mac," her voice tendered as she looked at the man who taught her how to fly over ten years before. *I have my life's calling because of him.* "They're sending up a doctor." He was the reason she was a pilot but now she felt penitent and afraid. It was clear she was the sole pilot responsible for their wide-body airliner.

Another call from the cabin phone. It was Shari.

"Seven with moderate injuries plus Dawnis," she said quickly. "Many more with bumps and bruises." She hesitated, "Dawnis is not doing very well, Julie. The doctor is worried."

"Bring the doctor to the cockpit," Julie ended the call.

# Chapter 7

April 1972 | University of North Dakota
Grand Forks, North Dakota

Fall semester turned to spring in the North Dakota Prairie and Mac began his aerospace courses just after the first of the year. Over the holiday break, Mac dove into his new textbooks and the content didn't disappoint. He began his first day of lecture having read most chapters in the book and each page seemed to inspire the next. The science of barometric pressure moving weather fronts and Bernoulli's laws left him captivated and curious. He found airplanes to be a work of art and understanding how something so complicated can function was gratifying. He eagerly awaited his aerospace lectures as one week passed to the next and, though he had yet to actually fly in an airplane, something felt right. *This is what I'm supposed to do.*

Dennis was one full semester ahead of him in the program and appointed himself Mac's tutor. *"I'll teach you all you need to know, Mackie,"* he said, though Mac had already earned straight A's on his early assignments. *"Aviation is tough stuff and you need someone who knows what they're talking about,"* but Mac rolled his eyes.

Though Mac learned the technicalities from his books, Dennis inspired him to dream about the future. *"You'll fly people around the world, Mackie,"* he said. *"You'll see places most people never see in their lifetime."* Mac's eyes were wide. *"You'll command the most sophisticated machine humans have ever created,"* Dennis tended to get a little ahead of himself. *"And the best part?"* he looked back at him. *"You'll get paid to do it!"*

Though he grew to love life in the university, Mac found his required liberal arts courses to be burdensome and distracting from his new interest. Usually the humanities stimulated him, but he now grew to loath the obligation and let them occupy only a modest corner of his mind. Something about flying invigorated him and competing priorities seemed unimportant and bothersome. The course "Introduction to Sociology" was required for his degree in aerospace and he approached it with dread. *Why do I need to learn about this to fly an airplane?* Perhaps it was Mr. Abrams, sadistically smiling from the Registrar's Office. Mac endured the lectures, dry and monotonous, but anything he learned came from the textbook because it was impossible to learn from the droning lecturer.

On a sunny Friday in late January, blustering wind whipped Mac's face as he trekked across campus. As part of his course, Mac was scheduled to participate in a small discussion group led by one of the graduate students and decided to attend without enduring the required reading. *I'll blend into the walls.* He'd spent most of the night studying for a weather quiz anyway.

Tables were set in a semicircle around the blackboard occupied by fifteen students who looked tired and indifferent. It was a course required by many majors so students from departments across the university occupied the seats. At exactly three in the afternoon, a portly and unfortunate looking graduate student collapsed into the podium at the front of the room and drank something out of a bottle. Mac wondered if the grad student at the podium or the people in the seats wanted to be there less, but decided it was probably equivalent.

"Now we will discuss this week's chapters," his words were without inflection as he opened his book. He looked down at his roster, "Mr. Merrell, please start us off." He sounded like a vacuum cleaner.

Michael Merrell's eyes went wide and began to fumble his way through a question. Each passing second was full and merciless and the second hand of the clock clicked apathetically. Before the grad student decided the question was sufficiently answered, Mac counted three people had coughed and one who'd presumably gone to the bathroom. The graduate student went down the line of students, each question becoming more difficult, until he neared Mac. He was daydreaming out of the window about his first flight lesson scheduled in a few weeks when Mac found himself in the hot seat.

"Mr. Frank," the graduate student looked hot. "Please describe how Auguste Comte worked to unify humankind through the scientific understanding of the social realm."

Mac sat silently and someone coughed again. He was racking his brain but could produce nothing and suddenly wished he would've read. *Who is Auguste Comte?* He could feel his cheeks begin to warm but didn't feel particularly worried.

"Mr. Frank, have you done the reading?" the graduate student looked bored.

"Of course," Mac stumbled, "I guess I didn't read this section close enough." There was shifting and giggles.

"Perhaps you did not," he scratched his nose. "Does anybody else know the answer to Mr. Frank's *important* question?"

There was silent disinterest in the classroom. The fleshy grad student inspected the room and exhaled through puffed cheeks until a crystal voice pierced the lull like a song.

"I think I can answer that question," she said. Mac immediately recognized a face that he wouldn't soon forget. "Comte believed that human life passed through historical stages and one could prescribe the remedies for social ills if they could grasp the progress." Her voice was calm but assured. Her soft features brought out her warm smile and buttermilk skin veneered around her eyes and lips.

"Indeed he did," said the graduate student. He looked lighter and seemed to come back to life. "Miss…," he looked down at his clipboard.

"Thomas," she said. "Susan Thomas." *She is beautiful.* "To Comte, all basic physical sciences had to arrive first, leading to the most difficult science of human society itself." She spoke melodically and each word flowed into the next. Mac watched her in a daze.

"Yes, Ms. Thomas, I find your assessment quite fine. It seems you have an interest in the subject," said the graduate student.

"How can one not be interested in understanding the human experience?" she said. *Is she a freshman?* It was a face he knew without a source.

"I couldn't agree more," the eyes of the other students watched her reverently. "Might I ask what your major is?"

"I am a premedical major," she smiled, "with an interest in the classics."

She was the most interesting person he had ever encountered. Susan sat poised in her chair, and her blouse pulled at her breasts. *She has an interest in the classics.* Mac admired her every movement and the fodder left him craving more. He flushed when he realized he was staring but instantly darted his glance when a new awareness came to him.

*How is this possible?*

He knew why her face was familiar and worried he would be sick. The room began to spin, and he sank in his chair. *Why have I done this?* He grasped the desk, pulling himself forward, and tried to regain composure.

*I cheated off her chemistry exam.*

His mind roiled and his pupils were full. *I'm a liar.* In his moment of weakness, he defiled her perfection. He glanced at her again but this time she looked back and grinned. A small dimple imprinted her cheek when her soft and pulpy lips smiled, and his stomach dropped into his feet.

*I'm in love.*

■ ■ ■

At the end of the hour, the graduate student broke the class up into groups of three and assigned topics to present at the end of the course. *Please don't be in her group.* The graduate student droned out the names one by one for the group assignments.

"Steven Golla...

...Mardi Herald...

... and Felix Joseph. Next,"

He breathed self-consciously and kept his eyes low.

"Susan Thomas..."

Her name made the room vibrate. *Please, no.*

"...Kevin Gleason..."

His pulse bounded in his neck

"…and Robert Frank."

*Shit.* Mac tried not to react, but it looked more like a sneeze. Nervousness and excitement simultaneously circulated through him like he'd never experienced before, and he had to concentrate to appear unruffled.

"Let's meet on Wednesday afternoon at three," said Susan as the classroom cleared at the end of the hour. "How does the library sound?"

Kevin, their hunched over third partner with a wide space between his front teeth, agreed. Mac simply nodded. *I'll do whatever you say.*

"Alright boys," Susan winked, "See you then!"

■ ■ ■

Mac couldn't contain himself. *I'm in love.* His head was brimming with Susan the entire walk back to his dorm. *She is beautiful, smart, and confident.* He cheated off her. *She can never know.* He detested himself for it and wondered how he could have tarnish such a flawless being. The universe had cursed him by putting her next to him that fateful day.

"And what are you smiling about?" Mac walked onto their dorm floor and Dennis sat at his usual table in the corner flipping through the pages. He was midway through a cafeteria cookie and his sideburns were growing back with a force.

"Nothing," Mac was pulled from his thoughts. "I guess I'm just glad my discussion group is over." Crumbs were falling onto Dennis's copy of *Flying* magazine on the table.

"It's unusual for you to come home from that class so perky," Dennis eyed him suspiciously and twisted towards him.

Mac felt intoxicated and warm, "I guess you could say I'm just inspired by Comte."

■ ■ ■

Mac's weekend was exaggerated and long, and his nights were sleepless and protracted. With his first flight lesson nearing, there was so much to study but the effort was useless. *I just can't focus.* Wednesday afternoon throbbed in his brain until, with sweet compassion, the morning finally arrived. His eggs sat on his tray untouched among the noisy chaos of the cafeteria.

"Are you not going to eat?" Dennis was chewing his way through a pile of pancakes.

"I guess I'm not really hungry this morning," said Mac. Nerves had always squashed his appetite. They feasted on pancakes, eggs, and sausage every morning together since the beginning of the year. *Habits from growing up on a farm.*

"What the hell is going on, Mackie," Dennis slammed his fork on the table playfully. "You haven't even *wanted* to talk about airplanes the past few days. Are you sick?"

Mac felt his face blush and he began to tap his foot. "I'm fine Dennis, I'm just nervous for my group today."

"Why the hell are you nervous about that?" he reached for the syrup. "You hate that class."

Mac was up all night reading his sociology book for the second time. He wasn't going to be unprepared for today and he decided maybe he liked the classics after all. He had never felt this way about someone before, and he let himself be pulled into the warm current that it brought.

"You sonofabitch!" Dennis's eyes shot up and he dropped the syrup on the table. "It's a girl, isn't it," he clapped in delight. "Isn't it!"

"Will you shut up!" Mac's eyes darted around for eavesdroppers.

"I knew it Mackie!" It annoyed Mac how giddy he was and his growing scene only cultivated it, "I knew there would be a girl eventually!"

"I *never* said it was a girl." Mac threw his napkin on his tray and got up to leave.

"Who is the lucky lady, you stud?" Dennis stood too. To be honest, Mac thought about asking him for some advice earlier in the week but he decided against it for this exact reason. Dennis had a way with the ladies and it was a skill he embraced. Mac had to eat dinner alone more often than he preferred while Dennis brought a date into Grand Forks over the past few months.

"Jesus, Dennis. Can you keep it down?" Mac looked over his shoulder for any drawn attention. "There is a girl in my class and I'm supposed to do a project with her," he whispered.

"A project, eh?" he winked. "She's pretty foxy?"

Mac had to fight the urge to punch him. Susan wasn't just any foxy girl on campus, and he responded to words on the contrary like an allergy.

"What?" he said. They stood and walked their trays to the dish belt, "I can't be happy for you, buddy?"

"There's nothing to be happy about, I'm just going to my small group."

"Invite her out with us this weekend," Dennis held Mac by the shoulders in front of him.

"What are you talking about, there is nothing to invite her to," they stepped out into the crisp winter air.

"Alright, alright," his voice leveled. Mac was thankful he seemed to let it go. "Where is your class? I'm walking to Leonard Hall."

"I'm heading to the library, I'll catch you later," Dennis jabbed him in his shoulder with a smile and they parted ways.

■ ■ ■

Usually, Mac savored the oaky scent of old books at the Chester Fritz Library but today it made him queasy. The building was a cherished sanctuary for his dive into aerospace but today he felt vulnerable and uneasy. He ambled through the book stacks like they were new and unfamiliar until he wandered into the soaring walls of the central study hall. He took a seat at the end of a long, wooden table away from other students paging through notes. His book echoed against the table under the towering ceilings and the grandiose university crest on the wall.

With palms wet, his heartbeat at the bottom of his throat. *Maybe I should take a lap around the building.* He wished he wasn't the first one there. Windows were fixed from floor to ceiling and Mac looked out across University Avenue over the snowy prairie and waited. *Don't do anything stupid.*

He pulled his watch out of his pocket and realized that the three minutes he had been waiting were the longest in his life. His foot began to tap, and his eyes darted around the room nervously. Four other students sat some distance away scribbling into notebooks while another snoozed with his head down on the table.

Mac's mind dwelled on the chemistry exam and taunted his lies. His body urged him to leave but he fought the impulse that instead manifested as quickened breathing and a pale face. He pulled out his watch again. *Nine minutes.* He could hardly tolerate it any longer. Her smile made him melt and he ached to smell her perfume again. He was a liar and was now about to face her.

*She's here.*

He was frozen like a mummy and only his head could swivel. She surveyed the room and smiled after seeing Mac in the chair, who sat fully erect and several inches off the back. The gesture was large and fast as he tried to wave Susan over and he blushed when she laughed. Stomach acid churned in his belly, but he managed to curb an impending heave. Even in winter boots, she was graceful. Her bell bottom jeans covered down to her shoelaces and her scarf spilled over her coat. Her blue eyes sparkled from below her winter hat and her teeth completely filled her smile.

"Hi there, Mac," her voice was like a song. She took her hat off and a pile of wavy brown hair fell on her shoulders.

Mac tried to smile but instead he gritted his teeth, "Hi, Susan."

"It looks like we're still waiting on Kevin," she took a seat across from him.

"Yes, Kevin," honestly, he'd forgotten about their other partner, "I'm sure he's on his way." Her skin was smooth and he wanted his fingers to explore its nuanced curves.

She pulled a foiled plate out of her bag and exposed the pile of treats, "I made us some cookies," she smiled, and he melted.

Mac grabbed one and shoved it into his mouth reflexively. He chewed in short, clipped contractions and swallowed before he should've.

"Hungry?" she laughed and Mac reddened. "I was at my parents over the weekend and made them for today."

"Thanks," he swallowed again but didn't taste the cookie. *Easy does it, Mac.* Her laugh made his tension fade. She was beautiful and he felt a warming calmness when she spoke. *I could listen to her forever.* They talked about the winter and the cafeteria chicken and every moment was a treat.

"You just look so familiar," she said, her chin lightly resting on her fist. "What classes were you in last semester?"

His breathing ceased and his stomach dropped. How many moles of hydrogen sulfide (H2S) are produced? His mind was turning and began to jeer. "Well…" *I cheated off your chemistry exam, Susan.* "I took biology and freshman English," her eyes squinted thoughtfully. "College algebra," he paused, and his eyebrows spiked. "…chemistry?"

She snapped her fingers, "That's where I know you!" she pointed and beamed. "We were in chemistry together last semester!"

"Hey guys," Kevin set his backpack on the table. "I'm sorry I'm late." Like a gift, their third partner interrupted before either noticed he had arrived.

"You haven't missed anything," Susan said and Mac exhaled.

In an attempt to recollect his thoughts, Mac peered across the study hall. The wooden study tables were long and expanded across the entire room and shelves stacked with books boarded each wall. The winter air cut through the towering windows so the air was crisp, but his blood went cold when he saw who else passed through the doors. *No.* Mac's jaw dropped and prayed he was mistaken. *Dennis?* He was marching right towards them with his stupid grin. Mac couldn't imagine what the hell he was doing there.

"Well hi there guys!" his peppy words filled the entire room. He helped himself to a chair and slid right up. "You guys seem to be working *so* diligently." Kevin shot Mac a look and Susan laughed nervously.

"We're just getting started," Susan said and Dennis unzipped his winter coat half way down.

"Well, I was walking to my history class when I saw my dear friend, Mac, over here," Dennis slapped his arm over his shoulder and pulled him in, "*left* his textbook on his desk." Dennis dropped a book on the table. "Can you believe it?" his voice elevated like a question and Mac recognized the cover. *Wait that's not my textbook.... that's your book.* Mac's blood went from cold to hot.

"I *just* couldn't bear the thought of him going to class without it," he winked at his friend and Mac fumed.

"Wow," Susan said, shifting in her seat, "That's very nice of you." Mac couldn't get a word out.

"Anyway, I don't want to take up too much of your time," he stood up and pushed his chair back in. All three students watched the performance in silent surprise. Just as he took a step towards the door, he dramatically popped his finger into the air and slowly turned back to his audience. *Jesus, you're a bad actor, Dennis.*

"Say," Dennis's head was cocked to the left. "This is certainly a fine-looking group." Mac was screaming through his eyes. "Mac, why don't we bring them to our little party on Saturday?"

"Our party on Saturday?" *There's no party on Saturday.* Mac couldn't take it.

"Yes, our party this weekend," Dennis's voice was political and smooth. "We always welcome fine people like yourselves!" Susan worked to conceal a smile and Kevin's mouth hung open.

"I'm sure these guys already have plans," Mac stumbled over his words and looked around the table. *Please just go, Dennis.* His voice came from the back of his throat and was a little loud. "There's no need to…."

"…you're planning a party, Mac?" said Susan, leaning forward in her chair. She seemed to be enjoying the scene. "To be honest, I'm a little surprised."

"Well I wouldn't say I'm *planning* a party…," blushed Mac.

"What a humble guy!" Dennis slapped him on the back again. "So, it's a done deal. Mac will give you the details on Friday." He waved as he walked towards the door, "Good luck with the project and see you this weekend!"

The room fell silent for several moments. Kevin eyed Mac, who looked at his feet. *See you this weekend?* Mac was stunned and Susan was giggling. *Dennis did it.* He couldn't believe it. *Was that a dream?* Now looking across the table, he tried to conceal his smile. He was going to see Susan this weekend.

■ ■ ■

A few favors were called in to the fraternity down the street and Dennis managed a lively party that looked months in the making. *"I told you I could throw together a good party, Mackie!"* Mac got a haircut, put on a tie and stood guard at the door until Susan finally arrived. *She's here alone.* He didn't leave her side for a single moment and they laughed almost as much as they drank. By the end of the night, a budding romance began that would shape the rest of their lives.

# Chapter 8

March 1972 | Grand Forks, North Dakota

Swaths of oranges and blues painted the eastern sky as the day's sun peeked over the horizon. The rolling prairie ventured into distant lands and snow dust danced in the wind. Northern cardinals and blue jays sang, their color kissing the snow. The flawless North Dakota sunrise was genuine and each passing second was novel and unique.

The control tower watched over the taxi and runways with a red beacon pulsing atop. Five single engine airplanes were tied down on the tarmac, undisrupted and orderly. The airport was perfectly calm. *A beautiful morning for flying.*

Mac recoiled reflexively as the wind whipped his face, the only skin exposed to the winter air. He lowered his head under the wing and opened the cockpit door. The propeller sat motionless at the nose of the craft and the tail rested on a single wheel. On the panel, the rows of dials and selectors looked foreign, but a moment of focus made them familiar.

Today would be more than just his first flying lesson. *Today is my first day in the air.*

Hours of study would see their application and the inspiration that stemmed from books would come to life. Nervousness turned into a concoction of eagerness and curiosity but most of all he was excited. The culmination of Mac's aviation experience came out of a lecture or Dennis's mouth but today, *I am a pilot.*

The aluminum airplane sparkled in the sun and a single green stripe marked from nose to tail. Mac and his instructor fought the cold as they checked the fuel and the flaps, wheels and oil. They crawled into the cockpit when their external pre-flight checks passed the inspection. *She is beautiful.* They pulled the harnesses over their shoulders and turned on the master power switch, which brought the cockpit panel to life. Most importantly, they flipped on the cabin heater.

"Clear prop!" Mac yelled out of the window and the engine jolted to life. The instructor walked him through each step methodically just as he'd practiced countless times in his dorm room. The engine hummed, Mac's heart bound, and daydreams were coming to life.

Clumsily steering the airplane down the taxiway, Mac struggled with the foot pedals. He had never steered anything with his feet before, but he was getting the hang of it and relished every second of it. Not only was Mac the first student of the morning, their aircraft was the only one operating on the field. *This is my blank slate.*

The Cessna idled at the head of the runway and they ran the checklist. The runway extended wider than the wings and the lights outlined the field like a holiday tree. *A work of art.* Mac's heart bound as the engine began to roar, and they unlocked the breaks. With one hand on the yoke and the other on the throttle, they began to accelerate down the field and towards the horizon.

The wheels shuttered under his seat and the wings became lighter. Mac held his breath. He fiddled with the rudder to keep the nose on the center line and their airspeed grew.

"Okay, Mac," said his instructor. "You can lightly pull back now."

The yoke felt warm and natural in his hand. He pulled it toward him and felt the airplane respond like a dance. Disconnecting from the earth required less strength than he thought, and it felt like a captured fish being released back to the sea. He was pressed back lightly into his seat and they climbed higher over the prairie. The direction combines combed the fields came into focus and the snow highlighted the nadir between each row. Farm roads cut the land into vast squares, a full mile on each side, and Grand Forks looked like a period at the end of a sentence. Mac was captivated. It was an entirely new way to view his world and it was spectacular.

The instructor guided the student through turns, climbs, and dives while a smile painted his face every moment. The movements felt natural and intuitive and he wished it would never end. Flying conjured something that guided him into a state of peace and inspiration. Like an artist in his work, he was absorbed and these first moments in the sky were a revelation of his life's calling. There was no question what he would do for the rest of this life.

*"Now, many of you have likely been bitten by the 'flying bug' early on,"* his mind replayed his aerospace professor the first day of class. Mac was at a loss. *Bitten by a bug?* Dennis later clarified, *"It's the moment a person falls in love with flying, Mackie!"*

Soaring three thousand feet above his home state, Mac knew he was not only bitten by the bug but was fully septic with the disease. The condition was anything but a malady.

■ ■ ■

As winter became spring, Mac studied and flew with a new energy. He treasured seeing his textbooks come to life and, when he wasn't flying or studying, he was talking, thinking, or dreaming about it. For a field he stumbled upon, his place in the world seemed to reveal itself and the sweltering seas of life finally seemed to calm. He would give anything to do it for the rest of his life.

Freshman year ended and sophomore year came and went as American history was being written. Hundreds of students vanished from classrooms across campus to required military service in the persisting war in Vietnam and student peace protests were frequently on display. A demonstration of 300 traditional people from the Pine Ridge Indian Reservation in South Dakota conjured discussion about reservation poverty and violence in classrooms across campus. Several UND students made the ten-hour trip to participate in the 71-day ordeal, symbolically held at the 1890 site of the Massacre of Wounded Knee. The finale unfolded on TV sets across the country where FBI agents, US Marshals and the National Guard opposed protesters.

Despite the precarious state of world affairs, Mac was insulated by his studies. Courses ranging from engines to navigation were in the books and he thrived with the rigor. The news seemed to fade into the background and both Mac and Dennis continued to be top performers in the school. Mac found the courses intuitive and Dennis even took a few courses in the business school to kindle his airline business ambitions. When President Nixon ended the draft during the spring of their sophomore year, the two friends breathed a sigh of relief knowing their numbers were never called.

■ ■ ■

The years at the University of North Dakota - an exciting degree, a dear friendship, and a blooming romance - would be the happiest of his life. The trio spent most of their time together and their camaraderie was clear. The pilots would talk endlessly about their time in the air while Susan would patiently wait, often reading a book. They laughed over breakfast in the cafeteria and played cards together on Saturday nights. During their junior year, Mac and Dennis rented an airplane and flew Susan down to the buzzing city of St. Paul, Minnesota for a burger and fries. On their way home, they nearly ran out of fuel and had to land at a single grass strip in Park Rapids, Minnesota to siphon enough fuel out of a crop duster to make it home. It was a trip they would remember for the rest of their lives.

Though flying was his first love, he relished every moment with Susan. They took long walks together through University Park and shared their most treasured dreams and memories. Also a bookie introvert from a farm town, she was the only person in the world that he felt truly understood by and their companionship gave him confidence to press on. Freshman chemistry was a faded memory, and though aspects of their relationship seemed to dwell in the shadowy silence, a youthful love seemed to flourish.

Susan was an impressive student, and everyone seemed to know it. A notorious academic all-star, she had her hands across campus. She was elected president of the pre-medical club and was a teaching assistant in the Anthropology Department. She studied fruit flies in a genetics lab two days a week and managed to volunteer on the weekends. At 20 years-old, her name was on an article published in the esteemed journal *Nature* on a topic Mac was never able to quite fully understand. Her life bound with success, her personality charismatic and spirited, but she kept most of her thoughts to herself. Mac struggled to understand her inner monologue and, when a divergence seemed to arise, it was often faced with scornful silence and avoidance. Their young love seemed to work during their two and a half years together and, though Mac often longed for a deeper emotional connection, he emulated her behavior.

Medical school applications were submitted the summer before their senior year and interviews were soon to follow. Susan intended to stay in the Midwest for Mac, but her parents insisted she apply to Georgetown University School of Medicine because of a distant aunt in Washington, DC. She made the trip east in the fall and immediately fell in love with the stone streets of Georgetown and the scholarly buildings of the historic campus. Her decision was made before she stepped foot back on the grounds of UND.

Susan Thomas returned to her dorm to find a hand-written note from the president of the university on December 1, 1974:

*Congratulations, Susan. The faculty and I could not be more proud.*

*Yours,*

*Thomas J. Clifford, President*

She accepted a seat in Georgetown University's School of Medicine Class of 1979 without mentioning a word about it for over a week.

# Chapter 9

January 1975 | University of North Dakota
Grand Forks, North Dakota

"I don't know anyone out there," Mac said late one night. "What would I do?"

"I'm going to medical school, Mac. You'll have to figure it out."

The years looming beyond graduation were uncertain. Susan made her plans to move out east and Mac finished up his last flying course. *"We're fully qualified pilots, Dennis, can you believe that shit?"* Mac tried to push Susan on the thought of a move across the country, but she was cold and had little to say.

In late February, Mac was 21-years old and the time had finally come to apply for his first professional job. The petroleum crisis left many in the department unsure of commercial aviation's future, but growing airlines and cheaper seats made air travel a household normality. The winter issue of *Flying* read passenger numbers more than quadrupled since 1955 and half of all Americans had flown. Dennis and the other seniors did not lose sleep over finding a job.

The face of commercial air travel changed during Mac's time at UND for the better. In 1975, ticket prices were closely regulated by the federal government, leaving cabin service the only means for airlines to set themselves apart. Dennis learned about innovative advertising platforms in his aviation business courses like Braniff Airways' *"End of the Plain Planes"* campaign that dropped conservative airplane paint jobs for colorful and artistic designs. The airline industry embraced changes in social attitudes with the introduction of thigh high, curve hugging stewardess uniforms and continued requirements for flight attendant weight and waist size. *"Some uniforms even have a clear helmet to protect hairdos on windy tarmacs, if you can believe it," Dennis explained.*

The iconic double decker 747 made its maiden voyage from New York to London under the colors of Pan Am Airlines just before Mac went to college and every student in the department dreamt of flying the double-decker airliner that was the largest in the world. Professors often noted it was an exciting time to be an airline pilot and Mac shared the sentiment.

■ ■ ■

Mac and Dennis, along with nearly two dozen other seniors, donned their black suits and made their way to the Student Union on a blustery winter evening in March. Airline executives from around the country gathered into one ballroom in hopes of recruiting North Dakota's best pilots to fly for their company. *"Don't forget, Mac," said Dennis the day before, "It's a buyer's market so play hard to get!"*

The aerospace department had been bustling with anticipation for weeks as the job fair neared, and students contemplated moves and careers around the country.

"I think I want to work for American Airlines," said Dennis as they walked across campus. "I'd love to see the west coast." His hands hid from the wind deep in his pockets trying to avoid the frigid whip of the wintery air.

The west-coast based airline originated as an airmail route first flown by Charles Lindbergh and recently made news by hiring the first African American airline pilot in history. "Plus, I hear California beaches are crawling with surfer babes."

"I think I'll probably stick with Northwest," said Mac, "Maybe I can stay in Minneapolis." Many graduates signed on with the Minnesota based carrier over the past few years. Northwest Airlines was rapidly growing in the orient and their Minneapolis base allowed many pilots to remain close to their families in the prairie.

"Northwest won't get you very close to Washington," prodded Dennis. His shoulders nearly touched his ears and his nose was pink and eyes watered.

Mac didn't look over, "Perhaps it won't." *You don't think I've thought of that?* He had been privately looking into jobs based in Washington, but his future remained uncertain. He found the idea of living in the nation's capital rather intimidating and Susan didn't seem interested in weighing in on the move. He had only seen the Nation's Capital on the front page of the newspaper but living in the center of the free world was met with growing intrigue. The newly built "Metro" subway conjured a cosmopolitan air and access to a grocery store open past six would be a welcome reprieve. It was a world away from North Dakota.

The two rehearsed sample interview questions back and forth until they made it to the Student Union. They shook the frigid winter air off when they entered the ballroom and double checked the math in their logbooks to ensure every tenth of an hour was accounted for. Larger sums of flight hours meant better bargaining power and, with airplane rental going for $22 an hour, every second had to count.

The atmosphere was festive, and Mac gauged the room in a daze. Men in brown and corduroy suites jabbered behind tables around the room and banners draped off the wall exhibiting the various recruiters. Some tapped their foot to *Abbey Road* by The Beatles playing in the background and everyone seemed to have a cup of punch. *This is where I find my first job.* Recruiters from all the big shot firms were there with pressed suits and greased back hair:

**Delta Airlines** from Atlanta

Continental Airlines from Houston

*Pan Am Airlines* from Miami

United Airlines from New York City

***Northwest Airlines*** from Minneapolis

The booths were painted with enormous, engaging signs and intricate model aircraft pulled prospective employees in. Men with clipboards in hand stood ready for on-site interviews while others passed out airline postcards. There were a few companies Mac had never heard of who worked the crowd even harder:

**Evergreen International Airlines** from McMinnville, Oregon

***Air Pacific*** from Eureka, California

Aloha Airlines from Honolulu, Hawaii

America West Airlines from Tempe, Arizona

Aspen Airways from Denver, Colorado

*These people are here for me?* Mac stood by the table of crackers and cheese while Dennis was pouring himself some punch. The only female in his graduating class stood at the Continental Airlines table from across the room and he watched her from the corner of his eye. She was poised and tilted her head back as she laughed with the interviewer. All other girls in the Aerospace Department were in the Airline Stewardess Program, training to work air cabins around the country, and surprisingly had little interaction with the pilots. The Texas based interviewer put out his hand and she shook it assuredly. *If she can do it, I can too.*

Mac exhaled through pursed lips and tried to prop his shoulders back. *Be strong, Mac. You can do this.* He started to walk the line of booths, gauging which carrier he'd attempt first. A heavy recruiter of UND students, fourteen students stood in aggregate in front of the Northwest Airlines recruiting booth. The airline started in 1926, flying mail between Minneapolis and Chicago, but quickly expanded westward into Seattle and Portland. With the company growing into Asia and Central America, they were in desperate need of young pilots to fly passengers around the world. Mac considered waiting in the line but decided he would come back after doing a loop.

The room was bustling with conversation and energy as he continued down the line, regarding the action distantly. Recruiters reeled prospective pilots in with promises of travel and adventure while students recited sweaty, rehearsed answers. The energy sizzled like bacon in a skillet.

Beside the exit door, a short man with a thin flock of hair pulled across the top of his head stood alone. This booth was modest with a single table, a handful of pamphlets, and lapel buttons. They locked eyes and he smiled as his first student approached.

"Come on over, son!" the recruiter was waving. "Tom Jonas," he extended his hand. His woolen coat was too short for his extended arm, but his smile was genuine.

"Mac Frank," he had rehearsed. He reached out his hand but stopped a little too far away. *'Eastern Airlines'* read the sign in capital blue letters. The canvas behind the booth was strewn with pink cherry blossom trees along a winding river and a white obelisk pierced the sky at its center. *The Washington Monument.*

"Have you ever thought of working in our nation's capital, son?" He bounced emphatically on his toes when he spoke, and Mac reminded himself to play hard to get.

"Not really, sir," Mac lied. He was trying to suppress his nerves. *Don't put all your cards on the table.*

"Have you ever been?" he asked, but Mac shook his head. He had never been out of North Dakota, let alone to the east coast.

"Eastern Airlines is looking for young men just like you to live and work in one of the most advanced cities in the country," the recruiter arched his hand.

Mac studied Eastern Airlines diligently for this very day, though he never mentioned it to Dennis or Susan. Eddie Rickenbacker, a race car driver, WWI ace, and commercial aviation tycoon, bought the company from General Motors in 1938 and made it the most profitable airline in the country into the proceeding decades. Dominating the air between New York City and Florida since before WWII, the company was the launch customer of the Boeing 727 and had a reputation for being employee friendly. Despite its success, the news media had been rather harsh on the company in recent years. A report came out showing the 1972 crash of one of its L-1011 Tri-Stars was due to a distracted crew. The airplane continued to descend while pilots fixed a faulty cockpit landing gear light until it barreled into the everglades killing 101 aboard. It was second deadliest aircraft disaster in the United States to date and the topic of Mac's senior aviation safety course. Despite all the noise about the airline recently, it had a hub in Washington, DC and seemed to be the natural choice if he were to follow Susan.

Mac didn't know what to say and simply stood there and sweat.

"Mac Frank, eh?" the recruiter put his hands on his hips. "You have yourself a pilot name if I've ever heard one." Mac coughed. "Where are you from, son?" He spoke fast and tight.

"Grafton, sir," Mac shifted his weight. It was his first job interview and he felt it showing.

"Grafton? I don't even know where the hell that is," he laughed. Mac finally placed his accent. *New York*. "Is your Dad a crop duster pilot?"

"My parents are farmers, but I never flew before coming to UND," Mac wished the words weren't so bulky and taxing.

"Well, they grow good pilots up here," he said, "we like to recruit you guys to fly for us." Mr. Jonas passed him a pamphlet. "We have a new fleet of DC-9s that we're flying up and down the east coast," he tapped his finger on the color photo. The polished aluminum aircraft had a crisp blue paint job along the cabin windows and two engines below the high wing, 'T-tail.'

"These new state of the art jets seat 100 passengers and the airline hopes to begin flying them between Washington to New York every hour!" he was jumping on his toes again. As a North Dakota boy, Mac wondered how there was enough passenger demand to support the business but instead smiled and nodded.

"How many flying hours do you have, son?"

"Just over four hundred," he said pulling out his logbook.

"That's respectable, kid," he waved off Mac's logbook. "Have you ever been in any trouble?" Mac shook his head. The early months of freshman chemistry prowled in his mind, but he didn't react. "Good because trouble seems to be the only thing keeping people out of the cockpit these days." Mac shifted his weight and kept his hands at his side. "Are you a good pilot?"

"My instructor seems to think so," Mac blurted and Mr. Jonas laughed. The extent of his flying experience was in the single engine Cessna and the twin-engine Piper Navajo. It was hard to believe he was ready to fly the ultra-modern DC-9.

"Well, son, if you are interested in moving out to DC when you get your degree, Eastern Airlines Shuttle is interested in you," they shook hands again. "You could start as early as August."

With that, they exchanged contact information and Mac conducted no more interviews. He felt light and bounced on his toes as he walked out of the job fair after his decision was settled. Whether or not Eastern Airlines was the right company for him didn't seem to matter. His priorities in the world were Susan, second only to flying. Though the first was doused in growing uncertainty, he would give anything for the latter.

Dennis held his ground for several hours at the fair, interviewing five airlines. *"I played them off each other, Mackie,"* he said. *"They were bargaining and it was hilarious!"* Dennis accepted an offer flying Boeing 727s for Northwest Airlines out of Minneapolis starting in the fall. *"You know why you're flying a 100-seater and I'm flying a 180-seater?"* Dennis asked. Mac knew what was coming. *"Because of my extraordinary flying skills!"* he winked. With their careers in focus, their future looked bright.

■ ■ ■

From the Memorial Union Ballroom, recruiters and students migrated to *'Whitey's Wonderbar'* in East Grand Forks to continue schmoozing. The airlines foot the bill for an open bar at the posh restaurant and all parties were generous with their pour. Opened in 1933 by a New Yorker who named the restaurant after himself, *Whitey's* was the most expensive restaurant in town and Mac and Dennis weren't about to miss out. They drove across the Red River in Mac's pickup truck and strolled in the door with their shoulders back and chin up. *We're employed, boys.*

The energy was electrifying.

The buttery light filled behind a film noir, cigarette haze and a chattering orchestra of knee slapping and dish clanking rang in chorus. Dennis floated around the room and Mac followed behind with the warmth of alcohol flowing through his veins. Bow tied waiters with baked brie and pork dumplings drifted through the crowd and the wine seemed to flow out of the walls. The roar grew and high shelf liquor was pulled for congratulatory rounds.

Smiling figures blurred and rings of light formed around the sconces as minutes turned to hours. Brassy conversation muddled and the floor began to rock like a ship. Mac wished he ate something more than cheese and crackers to support the liquid sloshing in his belly. *Where is Dennis?* He hiccupped and ran into a shoulder. *It's only a few miles.* He felt the truck keys in his pocket and needed to go home. He tried to grapple the keys out of his slacks, but they fell onto the floor and the room spun as his arms swung around to pick them up.

He found a coat that looked like his and nearly tipped over a tray of beef samosas before he felt the winter air. He found the truck and searched around for a key hole until he finally got the door open. *Dennis can find a ride home.* He fell into the driver seat and decided against a nap. The oil fought the cold until the engine came to life and Mac fought with his eyes to focus on the road. *Nice and easy now.* The truck popped into reverse and he pushed the accelerator.

Mac's body fell forward against the wheel and his foot pressed deeper into the pedal. His mind spun and the world felt lax. *Nice and easy, buddy.*

*Shit.* The truck roared back but came to an explosive and sudden stop. His head fell back against the headrest amidst the commotion. He muttered something to himself and steadied his feet on the ground once he got the door open. *Didn't make it very far.* He left it open and stumbled to investigate. The tailgate was embedded into the driver door of a red 1975 Chevy Malibu. *Sonofabitch.* The driver window lay shattered across the seat and the windshield was cracked.

Mac's breath steamed and he looked around the parking lot. Muffled music from the restaurant drifted into the winter air and he thought about retreating into the party. He was alone and snow fell into the Malibu's open window.

*"...trouble seems to be the only thing keeping people out of the cockpit these days."* Nausea began to swell and his eyelids drooped. *We're employed, boys.*

His vision was foggy and doubled but he eventually managed to focus his eyes on the Malibu. Snow began to blanket the fractured glass and his truck, already worn from years on the farm. *Shouldn't have parked here.* The decision came to him easily and he climbed back into the truck. With his clumsy foot on the accelerator, he dislodged the truck from the Malibu's side panel and managed it across town to his dorm building. Embarrassment and dread preoccupied him as he stumbled up the stairs and fought with the lock. He fell into bed without undressing and drifted into a sleep that persisted until noon the following day.

■ ■ ■

"Did you hear about the hit and run on Saturday night?" It was the talk of the department for the next week. *I'm moving to Washington, DC.* Mac grit his teeth. "The car belonged to one of the recruiters and he was furious when he came outside!"

"You left about that time, did you see anything, Mac?" Dennis asked at breakfast on Tuesday morning. They were in the final bites before heading off to their senior capstone course.

Mac swallowed, "I didn't see a thing."

# Chapter 10

February 2016 | Pacific Ocean

Mac pressed into the headrest and held his seat, praying the motion would relent. Stunned by the velocity of his spinning world, he worried about the fate of the Boeing 767. He gritted his teeth through crashing waves of nausea, determined not to add to the mess sprayed across the cockpit floor. Only minutes before, he was commanding the airliner flying 32,000 feet above the Pacific Ocean until his world lurched into a violent spin.

*The airplane was going to fall into the sea.* The situation was bizarre, he never experienced anything like it before.

*Nose down...*

*...level the wings...*

*...full opposite rudder.*

His training played in his head like a refrain. He had to dissipate the circular momentum over the wing and generate enough lift to bring the aircraft to level flight. *Nose down, level the wings, full opposite rudder.* He practiced recovering from spins in smaller airplanes, but never on this massive airliner. *I had to act.* He turned the autopilot off and trusted his instincts.

*"Mac, what is happening?!" the copilot exploded into the cockpit in panic.* She took command and disobeyed an order. *"We are not in a spin, sir! You are putting this airplane into a dive!"* He was confused and humiliated. The first officer reassured him the aircraft was level, but his brain screamed an alternate reality. *"Sir... we're in level flight."* His stomach turned. *Something is wrong.* Another wave of nausea crashed over him like a ship running aground.

The dreadful rhythm of his chaotic heart boomed in his ears.

*Boom, boom, boom...*

*Pause...*

*Boom, boom...*

It was distressing but not unfamiliar. Endured countless times, he had never told a soul. Weeks would pass and his heart would beat in regular cadence until an episode would present its ugly head. *When it happens, my world comes to a stop.* The chambers would beat wildly, like in a sprint, only to be followed by a merciless pause. The cycle repeated until pity brought resolution. *This will end my career.* He worked to purge the thought from his mind, though it was pervasive and lurked. It weighed heavily on his mind each moment of his world but he continued to fly.

*Tonight, something is different.* The moment he felt his pulse change, the airplane seemed to fall out of the sky. A murky fog of regret was swallowing his consciousness and there was no means to battle it.

A single knock at the cockpit door. Two women appeared in the doorway. Shari first, followed by a trim woman with caramel hair pulled back out of her eyes.

"Julie," said Shari, "this is Dr. Delaney. She is the only physician on board." The physician had a bright complexion and striking blue eyes. Shari paused for her to say something.

"Um, hello Julie," stumbled the doctor. Skin was pulled tight beneath her jaw and her eyes wandered around the intricate illumination of the cockpit instruments, "I'm Megan Delaney." Julie looked over her shoulder and forced a momentary smile.

"Thank you for coming forward, Dr. Delaney." Julie wondered how she was old enough to be a physician. "I'm worried about the captain." Megan looked over at the greying man, grimacing and sweaty. "Perhaps it would be best if you brought him back into the galley."

Julie looked back to the senior flight attendant, "What's the situation in the back?"

Shari rubbed her hands down the front of her uniform, "It's not good Julie, some people are really hurt. What happened up here?"

Julie looked at her superior, a man from another chapter in her life, now feeble and destitute. "Honestly, I'm not sure what happened but I think there is something wrong."

Megan jumped in, "There is a nurse on board who helped me triage the injured." The young doctor was self-assured, but her pitch elevated after each phrase. "The flight attendant has a significant head injury and is the most critical. From my count, we have two more with moderate injuries and five others with mild injuries." Each of her sentences inflected like a question.

"We haven't been able to wake her up," said Shari. Her calm was wearing. "Dawnis is really hurt, Julie." The lines in her forehead radiated in the cockpit lights.

"I asked one of the passengers to stabilize her neck in case she has a spinal injury," said the doctor. She pulled a strand of hair behind her ear and shifted her weight. "There is not much we can do for her at this point other than get her to a hospital." Her dark jeans and baggy, mustard sweater played on her youth. "How long until we can land?"

"We are at least two hours away from any airports," Julie looked at the GPS. Her lips were tight and her shoulders tense. "At this point, we have to make it to Hawaii." The twenty-nine-year-old was racking her brain. "Have you pulled the EMK?" The first officer needed to exhaust all options.

"Yes, I asked the nurse to start an IV and give some pain medicine. We'll need to monitor her breathing closely," said the physician. The airliner's emergency medical kit was stocked with supplies only a licensed physician could access like IV medicines, obstetrical supplies, and a simple intubation kit. "Sir, can you tell me what happened?" The two began helping the captain out of his seat.

Mac fought to get every word out over his powerful gag reflex. "Everything was fine but," he made some sort of noise, "then the plane suddenly began to spin." He managed to get untucked from his seat but fell heavily onto the cockpit floor. Megan looked over at the copilot who grimaced and subtly shook her head.

"Do you feel like you are still spinning?" They helped him lean against the center console with his feet splayed out. Shari loosened his tie and unbuttoned the shirt at the collar, damp with salt weeping from his pores.

"Yes..." he paused. His eyes were compressed shut and the moisture caught the light. "To be honest, I still feel the spinning."

With one arm around the senior flight attendant and the other around the doctor, Mac was hoisted off the floor and escorted off his own flight deck. Julie wanted to comfort him, tell him it was all going to be alright, but the future loomed with uncertainty. Her duty tonight was only beginning, and she wondered if she was ready for the task. She felt small, compressed by her charge, but knew it would be her alone who could shepherd this situation to resolution. Before the cockpit door clicked shut, Julie called out, "what kind of doctor are you anyway?"

Dr. Megan Delaney looked over her shoulder, "I'm a family doc."

■ ■ ■

Julie concentrated back on the controls. *First, fly the airplane.* She called air traffic control in Hawaii and declared an emergency. *We need help up here.* This permitted landing priority once they made it to Oahu and would ensure fire trucks and ambulances would be on the runway waiting for them when their wheels were on the ground.

*"Please describe the nature of the event that precipitated the injuries,"* asked the controller.

She kept her answer vague. *Honestly, I have no idea.* The night was unfolding like a movie before her eyes but to rewind or fast-forward seemed equally petrifying. The stakes were high for hundreds of reasons and she knew her every step would be meticulously scrutinized in the coming months.

At this moment, she had two priorities: *I have to fly the airplane and manage the situation in the cabin.* Her years of training prepared her for the former, but the latter left her hands trembling.

■ ■ ■

The forward galley held the two most-injured passengers aboard while both Dr. Delaney and Shari stretched the limits of their equipment. The flight attendant guided Mac onto the crew seat folded against the wall and found an airsick bag. She closed the galley curtain and digested the scene before her.

Dawnis was lying face-up across the galley floor beside an open medical bag. A passenger knelt at her head with one hand behind each ear. There was blood pooled on the floor sourcing from her swollen and blue temple. Her right eye was engrossed with fluid below the skin, making the tissue surrounding the eye lid protrude, and dried blood flaked down to her chin.

"It's very important her head does not move," the doctor coached. An IV bag hung from the wall and open medication packages were thrown about. A black uniform blazer was pitched over her thorax, covering her from neck to waist, and her shallow breathing could only be witnessed by close inspection. Shari knew this moment would cut into her memory like a gutted deer but now she felt calm and detached.

The doctor brought her ear down to Dawnis's mouth and listened prudently for several seconds. Some excess cloth from her draping sweater waded through a tarn of the satin liqueur. Her fingers were tucked along the windpipe, probing for a pulsing carotid artery. The engines hummed and no one said a word. Passengers in the forward rows seemed to remain still while the galley was frozen in a moment of time.

"She is breathing, but very slowly," Dr. Dulaney cut through the silence. She motioned for another passenger to come into the galley and grabbed a breathing assistance device from the bag. It had a clear mask on one end and a collapsible bulb on the other. Air pushed through the device with each pump.

"Can you help breathe for this person?" Megan asked. Her voice was mild, but the passenger could only stare at the scene before her. "She needs your help." The passenger snapped from a daze and came to her knees. "Have you ever learned how to do CPR?" She pushed a strand of hair behind her ear.

"I mean," she hesitated, and the other passenger watched mutely. "I took a class in college but I've never done it in *real life.*" It sounded like she was going to be sick, like something was going to crawl out of her mouth.

"It's easy," Megan's voice was gentle. "Place the mask on her face and make a good seal with your fingers," she demonstrated. "It is important air goes into her lungs and not through the sides of the mask." Her face was focused but not intense and Shari watched on. "Now take the bulb in your hand and squeeze it only until you see her chest start to rise." She watched to see if her words registered, "Do you think you can do that?"

The passenger nodded and they switched spots.

"Now squeeze the bag every six seconds and no more. Count aloud if you need to." She watched and made sure it was done exactly right. During residency, she learned to pull in bystanders during an emergency to free herself up for complex problems. She wasn't the only one depending on her training today.

"I'm worried she has swelling in her brain," she rummaged through the medical bag and tested an LED pen light against the palm of her hand. "It is possible she hit her head and now blood is collecting around her brain." Dr. Delaney pulled the flight attendant's eyelids towards her and flashed the light in her patient's eyes. "Do you see how her pupils are the same size on both sides?" she looked at the man holding Dawnis's neck and he nodded. "I need you to check them every few minutes. Tell me immediately if this changes. Can you do that?" He nodded and the doctor moved on. She was methodical and worked with precision.

"Captain Frank, tell me exactly what happened." With her most critical patient assessed, she came to the stowaway crew seat and studied the pilot. She pulled the redundant cloth from her sweater past her elbows and adjusted another strand of hair. He was buckled in and the color was returning to his face.

"I keep throwing up," he looked at her through on eye. His top button was undone, and his black necktie was pulled down below his name tag. Both his feet were planted on the ground and his white dress shirt was lined and muddled. "I don't know how to describe it," he was searching for the words, "It feels like we're spinning."

"When did it start?"

"When I was flying," he replayed the situation in his head. *What do I tell her?* "It just came out of nowhere."

"Has something like this ever happened before?"

"What do you mean?" The words were sudden and defensive and the doctor recoiled. *Easy, Mac.* There was so much he couldn't say.

"Have you ever experienced the sensation of spinning before?" the doctor eased back. She knelt beside him so they were at eye level. The galley felt small amidst the five other breathing bodies.

"No, this has never happened before, if that is what you are asking," Mac felt vulnerable and wished he could focus. The thumping and spinning made it impossible to monitor his expression.

The doctor slid a blood pressure cuff around his upper arm and mulled the oddly sensitive question. "Did you notice anything unusual before this happened?"

*If I could only focus.* Mac's mind raced to think of the right thing to say. *You mean the medical condition that was supposed to end my career?* The moment his heart flipped flooded his mind, closely followed by the past 24 hours and then the preceding years of lies. It was all too much.

*Boom, boom, boom, boom...*

*Pause...*

*Boom, Boom...*

*Pause, pause...*

*Boom, boom, boom...*

"No, nothing happened."

"Your blood pressure looks okay," she pressed the stethoscope to his chest, "let me listen to your heart." She focused intently for several moments. He closed his eyes again wishing for a miracle and wondering how he got here. He sensed the looming march of a thousand-man army advancing towards him and he was without defenses. She looked up, "do you feel any palpitations?" Her tone changed.

"Do you hear something?"

"Your heart is beating unusually," she wrapped the stethoscope around her neck. "It sounds like an arrhythmia called atrial fibrillation. Have you heard of this before?"

*It didn't take you long to put that together, doctor.* The army's cadence drew closer. Atrial fibrillation was the name Google gave his symptoms years before. Hooves of mounted horses rumbled in his chest and every cell in his body buzzed in anticipation. He thought of all the doctors he lied to over the years but knew he was becoming the victim of his own actions. Flying was the only thing he had in the world and he wasn't going to let this end it.

"No, I haven't heard of it before," Mac was backing himself into a corner and was surprised by what he was willing to do. He pulled his head off the seat and tried to steady it to meet the doctor's candid gaze.

Dr. Delaney checked the strength in his arms and legs and Mac denied any numbness. She worked with quick accuracy, neither adding nor neglecting an extra step. Shari knelt beside the flight attendant in quiet reverie while she looked on.

"Follow your eyes on my finger," she said as it passed from right to left. Megan closely studied the movement of his eyes as she held his chin in place. Shari cautiously came over to watch over the doctor's shoulder. Megan stopped her finger as far left as the pilot's eyes could go with his head forward, "do you see how his eyes drift slowly to the right and then snap back?" Shari inhaled in surprise. "That's called horizontal nystagmus." She elicited the same response on the right side.

"It looks like you have bilateral horizontal nystagmus, Mr. Frank," said the doctor.

"Bilateral *what?*" Mac held on to his seat again and sweated through his undershirt. The maneuvers disturbed the symptoms precisely balanced in a state of mild reprieve and he gritted his teeth. His head fell back onto the seat and sweat continued to seep from his brow.

"I think there may be a problem in your brain, and I can see it in your eye movements, "she said. "Now, take your finger and touch your nose."

Mac yearned to stay still but brought his index finger towards his face as he was told. As it neared, it circled in a growing radius and nearly barbed into his eye. Mac shifted uncomfortably and his breathing quickened. He looked to the doctor for answers, but she continued unfazed.

"Now touch my finger," she held her pointer finger an arm's length away and waited for his digit to meet hers. Mac extended his same finger but found he could not make them connect. It jutted around wildly and missed the target entirely. Shari knelt and held her hand over her mouth. His finger was lost in space and he discovered it was mirrored on his opposite hand.

"What the hell is happening?" Captain Frank's voice was sharp. Shari rubbed his shoulder absently, trying to comfort him in a scrubbing motion. A new panic was boiling within him and he wanted answers.

"Captain, obviously I have no tests beyond my exam to confirm my suspicion," she explained concisely. She sat back and studied her patient.

"Please doctor, just tell me what is happening to me." The leer from the two passengers was palpable. He'd read the list of complications from atrial fibrillation countless times and knew them to be a chilling concoction.

"I think you've had a stroke, captain," her voice was composed but not indifferent.

There was lingering stillness until Shari broke the spell. "I don't understand," she continued to scrub while she thought back to her cabin-crew first aid course, "he doesn't have weakness or droopiness in his face." Her brow crinkled in the center and her cheeks flushed.

"Most of the time a stroke can cause arm weakness or changes in speech but not always." Mac was trying to process the news, but the load hit repeated barricades. "A stroke in the back of the brain can cause a spinning sensation and difficulty with coordination. It's an uncommon type of stroke that happens most often in patients with atrial fibrillation." She came to her feet and let her eyes connect with the crew in the small space. "It would also account for the sudden onset of your symptoms."

Mac could feel his eyes dilate. *A stroke.* Scorching panic flooded to his toenails and the chaos in his chest was relentless. His arms tingled as if crawling with spiders and his foot began to tap in brisk tempo. "Okay, well let's do something about it." They had talked about it enough and he needed relief.

The young doctor racked her brain for options. "Obviously, there's no clot busting drugs in the airplane because we don't have a CT scanner," she was back over the medical bag shuffling and thinking aloud.

"What about aspirin?" asked Shari. "Like for a heart attack."

The doctor's fingers ran through her hair like a fork and she continued to hunt.

"We can't give him aspirin because we don't know if he is bleeding in the brain," Megan said while pulling the cloth past her elbows again. They took her at her word. "But we can try some of this," she pulled a bottle out of the bag and studied its label. "This should help with your nausea."

The doctor palmed two pills out of the vial and placed them in his trembling hand. Shari promptly shuffled to the cabinet and made a bottle of water appear. Mac swallowed the pills as the doctor put her hand on his shoulder. "We just need to get you to a hospital, Mac," the pilot looked up at her, longing for more, "that's the best we can do."

"Doctor, you need to come see this!" the man with the flashlight was trembling and the energy in the cramped galley shifted. The beam from the flashlight he held was striking the flight attendant's retina while the passenger held her head with one hand. Growing fear besieged her like an odor and Megan sprang into action. She pushed the passenger aside and peered deep into the flight attendant's eyes.

"Her right pupil suddenly became huge!" the passenger stood and paced.

"Squeeze the bag faster," Megan said evenly, "if she hyperventilates and increases the oxygen in her blood, the pressure in her brain may go down." The doctor knew this was only a temporizing measure.

Shari crawled back to her original post and held her old friend's hand, "What's happening, Megan?" She began to softly cry.

"The pressure in her brain is too high," Megan pushed the mask aside and listened to her breathing, "She's likely bleeding into her brain."

"Oh my god," Shari covered her mouth. She brushed the grey hair off Dawnis's forehead and tilted her head as she watched helplessly. "It's going to be okay, dear," she fought heavier tears, "Just relax."

The silence was crushing.

*What have I done?*

Mac's eyes darted from person to person, begging for someone to do something, but it became apparent that there was nothing left to do. Still hundreds of miles from land, they simply watched destitute and powerless against the terminus of life. Megan pulled the mask off Dawnis's face, smeared blood on the plastic, and felt for her pulse. The onus pressed him further, knowing this was the culmination of his work, but he couldn't look away. The doctor leaned back and met Shari's eyes with the scourge of new grief.

"I do not feel a pulse," she looked down at her patient one final time. There was dolefulness, and sorrow, but mostly there was shock.

The hum of the engines played in accompaniment and two hundred and sixty-three voices seemed to quiet. "She has passed."

Over the moonless Pacific Ocean, there was one fewer soul aboard.

# Chapter 11

May 1975 | University of North Dakota
Grand Forks, North Dakota

In their black graduation regalia, Mac, Dennis, and Susan proudly displayed their diplomas at the 1975 University of North Dakota's graduation ceremony. Susan and Mac's parents met for the first time at the commencement and the couple revealed their intention to move to Washington together at dinner later that evening.

"Certainly, there will be a wedding," said Susan's mother in a surprisingly blasé way. She placed her napkin over her untouched dinner.

Susan had little to say on the matter and they found themselves passive subjects of the proceeding series of events. They met with the priest weekly during their spring semester and held a quiet ceremony at St. John's Catholic Church in Grafton the last Saturday in June. Only their parents, siblings and Dennis occupied the pews and the couple made for Washington the following Monday.

■ ■ ■

"Cheer up guys," Dennis tried to hide his red eyes. Everything the newlyweds owned was heaped into the pick-up truck running in the driveway outside of the Frank farm. The prairie sky was cloudless and a combine was already tilling the field for the season's seed. "We work for the airlines now so we'll fly and visit each other." Dennis was preparing for his own move to Minneapolis in a few days and had stayed on the farm over the wedding weekend. "Now make sure Mac doesn't hold himself up in his room with a book, Susan," he laughed, and they embraced.

Mac climbed into the left door of the pick-up truck and throbbed in the sting of farewell. There was nothing left to say so he didn't say a thing. He felt bound to Dennis, almost indebted, and felt his life's normal agitate into something new. Spun in uncertainty, he waved goodbye to his friend and all he knew life to be. He thought about his uncertain promises, the marriage that came so quickly and his new life across the country. Susan remained silent as emotion sparked uneasy contraction in his belly and he put the truck into drive. Pulling down the gravel driveway, he looked over at Susan, whose gaze searched over the distant cusp of the prairie horizon.

■ ■ ■

Mac drove across Minnesota and through Chicago while his bride mostly read. Past Ohio, he navigated Pittsburg and drove south through Maryland. They slept in a tent at rest areas off the highway and ate sandwiches out of a cooler. They listen to the newly formed National Public Radio and sometimes Susan slept. On the third day, they arrived at their new home: a small, one-bedroom apartment a twenty-minute walk from Georgetown's campus. The neighborhood, called Glover Park, was quaint with row houses and sat adjacent to the historic Wisconsin Avenue that ran toward the Potomac River.

The verve of the city was unlike anything Mac had experienced before and it didn't take him long to feel the buzz all around him. Their building was built during World War II and the rent was higher than a semester's tuition at UND. Emptying the truck into their third-floor apartment without air conditioning was a harsh introduction to Washington in July but, Mac felt cheerful and Susan seemed to hearten in the energy of their new adventure.

Their honeymoon would be in the city, a metropolitan playground that was exotic and alluring. They explored the infinite rows of books at the Library of Congress and milled the Greco-Roman pillars at Union Station. Mesmerized by the painting *Apotheosis of Christ,* they spent hours in the National Capitol rotunda and ate turkey sandwiches on the lawn of the National Gallery of Art. It was the happiest Mac had ever been and their solidarity in a new city seemed to nurture their relationship that remained new but precarious.

The night before Susan was to begin school, they stood hand-in-hand on the top step of the Lincoln Memorial. The Washington Monument sparkled in the Reflecting Pool and the sun was setting behind them. A full moon rose above the dome of the Capitol and a warm breeze danced on their skin. Mac peered into Susan's eyes and brought his lips to hers. *I love you, Susan.* They admired the majestic splendor of the National Mall while her hands were holstered in her pockets and his wrapped around her shoulder.

■ ■ ■

Her first day of medical school was on a sweaty Monday in the first week of August. Susan's body was still adjusting to the crushing humidity, so she walked to campus just after six in the morning to avoid sweating through her long sleeve blouse and dress pants. It was a practice she kept until it finally cooled in October. *"Why are you wearing long sleeves, Susan?" asked Mac. "It's a hundred percent humidity out there."* She was one of only a few females in her two-hundred-person class and, *"it's important I'm viewed as a professional."*

Within a few days, she was submerged in the complicated world of biochemistry and physiology. Spending countless hours memorizing facts and concepts, she settled into her modest new home: the basement of the university library. The academic rigor was far beyond anticipated, coming from a degree she excelled in rather effortlessly, but she was determined to make her mark in the class.

As weeks grew to months, the couple occupied less of each other's time. Late nights in the library left only weekends together, and even that time was punctuated and distracted. It didn't take long for the already delicate light between them to dim. A young person in a new city, Mac filled the time by touring the Nation's Capital alone while his wife was away. He was accustomed to spending time by himself, but he couldn't help but feel displaced. With penetrating anticipation, reprieve finally came when Mac began his first day at Eastern Airlines.

■ ■ ■

On the tenth of September, an Eastern Airlines 707 bound for Miami-Dade County Airport was parked at terminal one of Washington's National Airport. The sweltering Washington humidity conjured sweat from every pore and the sun's heat ricocheted off the concrete tarmac. Mac climbed through the boarding door in the suit he wore to the North Dakota job fair and sat eager to head to flight training. In the auditorium of Eastern Airlines pilot training center, Mac sat among thirty other new pilots who conversed pleasantries with nervous energy. His chest was expanded at the thought of being an employed airline pilot, a sentiment that seemed to be mirrored by all other rookies in the room. The energy was electric and swollen with pride. Frank Boreman, the new president of the company, welcomed the pilots and training began that afternoon.

"You'll be with us for three months learning how to fly the Douglas Company 9," the instructor pointed to a diagram and chewed on a cigar. "You will be challenged, it won't be easy," no one moved. "But if you work hard, you will be out on the fleet in no time."

The culmination of his work was finally manifesting as his dream and nothing else mattered. The company's headquarters were recently moved from Rockefeller Center in New York City to Miami amidst a shift in the company's target market and Mac didn't mind the move. With books under his arm, he'd make his way right to the beach after his first day of class.

The group was recruited to support the airline's revolutionary concept of hourly shuttle service between cities on the east coast. The idea was debuted in 1961 when Eastern Airlines Shuttle used ten Constellation aircraft to connect Boston, New York's La Guardia, and Washington National airport every two hours. The program was so successful, they expanded to charter flights every hour, seven days a week from seven in the morning until ten at night. They dropped the initial turboprop fleet for a fresh crop of fast and modern DC-9 jet aircraft. *"We're transforming the industry, gentlemen," the instructor said. "Emphasizing convenience and simplicity when most people consider flying a luxury."*

By 1975, the DC-9 had proven itself to be a valuable ship and Mac was eager to get out in the fleet. He hit the books day one. The airplane had two rear mounted Pratt and Whitney engines and a T-tail so the wing flaps, uninhibited by engines, could extend deeper. This permitted the 100-seat jet to land at slower speeds and smaller runways. It was built with rapid ground turn around in mind: stairs built into the front and rear passenger doors enabled boarding without a ramp and a fuselage low to the ground made for easy bag loading. Mac learned the details of the electrical system and the cockpit workflow. He studied the hydraulic pumps and emergency procedures while growing to respect the engineering marvel as a work of art.

When he finally left the classroom for the cockpit, Mac found flying the airplane to be a physical experience. The cockpit yoke was directly connected to a series of mechanical pulleys and wires that ran to the control surfaces on the wings and tail. The pilot had to rely on his own strength to physically move the surfaces in flight. At the end of a grueling check ride, Mac would sweat through his undershirt from both the mental strain and physical exhaustion but every second was a rush.

Though the rigor required his attention most hours of the day, he found himself becoming friendly with his classmates. Eastern Airlines put the new pilots in a luxurious hotel near the beach with a generous per diem, apt for regular trips to five-star restaurants and extravagant clubs around Miami.

Nearly all the pilots were unwed, and they courted more women than Mac cared to count. A favorite pick-up line usually had something to do with Eastern Airlines' sponsorship of the *If You Had Wings* ride at Disney World or a pilot's *"powerful engine,"* but the creativity bar was pretty low. Their prestigious career made picking up women in the Miami clubs successful with only minimal effort.

Mac went along on some of their uninhibited evenings but often returned to his hotel early or spent the evening alone altogether. The physical distance from his wife strained their relationship and Mac missed her dearly. They exchanged brief stories over the phone on Sunday and Wednesday nights, but Mac sensed Susan was undergoing a period in her life that he could not fully understand. She was detached and Mac longed to return to Washington to be with her.

"I love you, Susan," he sat at a payphone in the hotel lobby one evening in his fourth week of training. He was longing and lonely and twirled the phone cord in his hand. It was just after eight in the evening and six other students were anxiously waiting for him in the hotel lobby.

"Me too," she sounded distracted and he could hear papers shuffling on the other end of the line.

"Me too?" the bruise couldn't be masked by their distance. Outside of the glass phone booth, hotel guests shuffled about the lobby, some formal while others in beach attire, and one of the pilots was gesturing to him.

"That's what I said," Susan's words were crisp and quiet, "me too." The gesturing student pilot approached from the lobby and raised his open palms after knocking on the glass. Mac waved him off and posed a single finger.

"I'm excited to see you dear," his eyes searched for her warmth, "I miss you."

Some muffled sounds came through the receiver and Susan worded something inaudible. "Listen Mac, I need to go," she said something again off the line that Mac couldn't hear. "I'll call you on Sunday."

Before Mac could say anything, coins fell into the tray and the line went quiet.

■ ■ ■

Graduation for DC-9 pilot training came in mid-December and Mac began his first official trip in the fleet after the first of the year. Susan walked Mac to a Wisconsin Avenue bus stop in the early morning hours and offered a partial smile as he climbed aboard the bus bound for Foggy Bottom Metro Station. He buzzed with excitement amidst the flock of morning commuters on his way across town. He climbed off the train at the National Airport Metro Station and fielded polite nods from businessmen and two children that pointed and smiled. He began to walk a little taller when he felt the unabated glances from passersby and found himself smiling back. It was unearned respect he was quick to embrace. Though his love for flying flourished, it wouldn't take him long to become accustomed to the status and his first four-day trip was everything he'd hoped it to be and more.

■ ■ ■

Susan's new position as class social committee chair kept her busy on the weekends and Mac frequented clubs with other single pilots on his trips. He remained faithful in action, but he soon was quick to return a wink to an admiring lady. He started flying trips into the airline's headquarters in Miami during Susan's junior year and it soon was his favorite overnight spot.

The disco movement was gathering momentum and, with clubs popping up all over South Florida, Miami was a leader in the charge. In the summer of 1978, Mac was 24 and his single, 27-year-old captain brought him to one of Miami's most talked about spots called *Casanovas*. The towering ceiling echoed beats from bands across the city and people from around the world boogied on the dance floor in time. The elaborate lights show drew huge crowds and Mac roamed the party into the early hours of the morning.

"I didn't know you could dance like that, Mac," said the captain as they waited for passengers to board the next morning. Mac's head throbbed.

"Me neither," he was looking for his sunglasses. Just before they pushed back from the gate, Air Traffic Control announced an Eastern Airlines Lockheed L-188 Electra was blown up by a ground bomb at Boston's Logan Airport and their flight would be cancelled. Shocked by the news, Mac returned to his hotel subdued. The thought was sobering and he decided he'd best not drink before flying any longer.

■ ■ ■

As the years went on, his love for flying expanded and matured. The roaring engines on a takeoff roll or breathtaking sunsets from the air were certainly gratifying parts of the job, but there was something intrinsic about being in transit that Mac found soothing. The calm between trips was quickly replaced with restlessness that was relieved only in the front of a DC-9. There was little at home for him to return to, so every waking hour was devoted to his work. He treasured the respect of his uniform and his audience of passengers, but the journey was where Mac sourced peace.

Susan graduated in the spring of 1979 and began a residency in general surgery at Georgetown University Hospital in the fall.

The detached couple bought a house across the Potomac River in Virginia, but with Mac's travel and Susan's hospital schedule, only obligation, silence, and a cast of their marriage remained. They became accustomed to autonomy and cold indifference permeated when their paths crossed. His voice was harsher than he intended, and she didn't always return his calls. He spent more time alone, often in hotel rooms or quiet restaurants, and his chronic absence from Washington left him with only a few acquaintances in the city. With Susan's odd hours, they began to sleep separately. He only saw her after a backbreaking, 15 hours a day in the operating room and even then, they usually exchanged only a few words. He couldn't always ignore the ache of what their marriage should've been, but his accelerating career seemed to distract him from the void. Not knowing how to combat her growing indifference, he simply mirrored it because he didn't know what else to do.

■ ■ ■

Resident physician, Dr. Susan Frank became an attending physician after she passed her boards in the spring of 1984. Mac was 31-years-old and hoped the conclusion of her training implied more time to mend their fractured marriage.

Nearly 10 years into their lives together, they made more money than their parents could have ever dreamed of but their home in suburban Washington was hostile and empty. Susan's personality won a rich and separate social life and she remained close with several surgeons at the hospital. Mac never found the strength to explain the crushing loss when she didn't come home at night and any attempt was met with detached silence.

In desperation, Mac made a reservation for two at the lavish Old Ebbitt Grill on Pennsylvania Avenue next to the White House in mid-1985. He hoped the Victorian rooms and buttery light of one of Washington's esteemed historic restaurants would be an appropriate backdrop to discover something to fight for.

"Susan, I know it's been hard the past few years," Mac had pulled out his old suit and got a haircut for the occasion, but his hands were sweating under the table. "I think those days are behind us now." Susan put her fork on the table and swallowed. Nearby diners spoke easily among laughter and a soft waltz played. "I love you, Susan," his mind was racing. He coughed out the words, "I think we should have a child."

She didn't breathe and reflexively looked over her shoulder. His pupils dilated to watch every muscle in her face.

"Mac, I'm not sure what to say," she spun her wine glass in her fingers. "Work is just so busy right now and…" her voice trailed. "I'm just not sure I'm ready."

"I miss you, Susan," he pleaded.

"A kid's not going to fix that, Mac," she took a sip of wine and let her face say everything.

He wanted to hold her and piece together what remained but knew it would be like embracing a pile of chalk. He wanted to see her laugh and remember their first year together in North Dakota. He longed to be her partner, build a life and kiss again under the moonrise of the Lincoln Memorial. He craved an emotional connection, the intimacy of knowing everything about someone, to miss and be missed. Instead, Mac knew it was the beginning of the end. He was swimming against an unbeatable current and could feel the tide of loneliness gurgling down his throat as the water submerged his face. Life was thinning, and he was grasping for anything that would give him justification to go on.

Instead, Susan paid the bill and they drove home to sleep.

# Chapter 12

May 1984 | Washington, District of Columbia

Mac Frank was promoted to co-pilot on the L-1011 TriStar not long after Susan graduated from residency. The iconic, three-engine, wide body aircraft was affectionately known as 'El Grandote' - *the huge one* - and was the flagship Eastern Airlines airplane used to ferry passengers into Central America. The promotion was a timely means to occupy his mind.

Mac began a four day trip the morning after his dinner with Susan feeling adrift and hollow. He fell through the motions of getting to the airport, filing paperwork and checking the weather for the first leg of his trip, wondering how life could proceed. Calculating fuel payload, the Tristar's captain walked into the flight deck.

"Well shit, if it isn't Mac Frank," the greying man was round and short. He had a cheerful face and a belly that protruded. "How the hell are you?" Mac strained to clear the clouds in his brain.

"Hello," Mac was tired and spoke slowly. The captain's face looked vaguely familiar and Mac shook his hand. "It's Tom, right?"

"You damn right it is, Tom Fesinki" Mac could only describe him as jolly and he wanted to evade. "So, I guess it's you and me in this pile, eh?" Mac suddenly placed his fleshy jowls. Tom was a captain on the DC-9 when Mac first started flying with Eastern and he had a personality known as anything but reserved.

"I guess so," Mac tried to laugh but was listless and distracted.

"When did you start flying the Tristar?" he stowed his bag and climbed into the left seat. "I started about three years ago and had enough seniority to make the jump as a captain." Like many companies, Eastern Airlines had a seniority system that determined the type of plane, position, and schedule a pilot would fly. *More senior the pilot, the better the job.*

"I've flown this pig around for a few months," Mac said, his mind throbbing.

"You damn right, you sonofabitch," he shot back and Mac gave a surprised laugh. "I love this pig!"

The Federal Aviation Administration required airplanes greater than 80,000 pounds to have a third crew member, but the rule was set to change in the coming years. In the meantime, their flight engineer, skinny and fresh out of training, came aboard. "Morning, gents!"

"You damn right it's a good morning," the captain twisted his shoulders towards the engineer, his belly precluding full rotation. "Let's fly, boys." Something about the cowboy captain and the boyish flight engineer seemed to click and the distraction seemed to slowly dissipate the lingering grief.

224 passengers boarded their wide-body airliner and they navigated the grounds of National Airport, congested with Eastern Airlines aircraft.

The fleet was split between airplanes painted white and others bare and silver. Those manufactured in the United States had an exposed aluminum exterior, which decreased its weight by 100 pounds, while the European airplanes were coated in paint to cover their composite skin panels. The California manufactured L-1011 Tristar glistened in the sun as the crew pulled the beast into the sky and towards Juan Santamaria International Airport in San Jose, Costa Rica.

■ ■ ■

"Where'd you learn to fly, Mac?" asked Tom running through the post-takeoff checklist and flipping the landing lights off. He was in the midst of a jelly donut that crumbled on his dress shirt, pulling snug over his belly.

"Flying school up in North Dakota," Mac fiddled the radios and took off his sunglasses.

"So you're a Sioux guy," he said. "Did you freeze your nuts off up there?"

"I went to UND too," the flight engineer leaned between the two forward seats. He was sporting stubble on his chin and a lush comb of black hair. "I love that place, but it's damn cold."

The captain leafed through some papers and Mac laughed. Air traffic controllers instructed them to climb to thirty-one thousand feet and they turned south. "Eastern actually sent me up there a few years ago to recruit when we were growing so much in the early seventies," the captain looked over the Gulf.

"Did you make it to Red Pepper?" asked the flight engineer. Mac plugged in the new flight information into the autopilot on the top of the panel. Memories of the notorious Mexican sandwich shop frequented with Dennis during their stint on campus eased some tension pulling at his shoulders.

"Everyone kept telling me to go so I finally went," said the captain. He brushed a crop of crumbs onto the floor and used a piece of paper to wipe jelly off his chin. "That decision kept me no more than a few steps from the shitter for the rest of the night."

■ ■ ■

They unloaded in San Jose and prepped for their next leg to Miami, where they would stay for the night. The cadence of Mac's work had preoccupied his mind and it was difficult not to enjoy the approach over the island's tropical beaches. Mac was breathing easier now that he was away from Washington. The Tristar took on over twenty-four thousand gallons of Jet-A fuel and twenty-three carts of meals and drinks for the trip. The L-1011 Tristar was unique in that it had a lower level galley for meal preparation and a lounge facility for the crew. As he did on many quick turnarounds, Mac stretched his legs below the cabin while the plane was cleaned and equipped for the trip.

"Can I get you anything?" a satin voice came behind him. He stood amidst the windowless chamber of wall-to-ceiling galley cabinets, rolling his ankles and squatting slightly. He turned and couldn't get a word out. "You guys must get so cramped up there." Her glistening red hair was pulled behind her ears and freckles peppered her nose. The cut of her uniform dress avowed the nuanced curves around her hips and her skin pulled snug as she smiled.

"Hi," Mac struggled and made some noises, "I'm fine." He wanted to say something else, but nothing came so she giggled lightly. She opened a cabinet door and found a bottle of water, which she passed to him. "At least take this," her fingers grazed his she pressed the bottle into his hand. Her head tipped to the side somewhat as their gaze met. Her eyes were vast and dark, and her uniform skirt didn't hide her toned, velvet legs. There was a visceral yearning to feel each curve at the tip of his fingers.

"Let me know if there's anything else I can do for you," she winked and not discretely. Just before she disappeared into the cabin, she turned back on the stairs and smiled at him, "First Officer Frank." An enchanting warmth tickled in Mac's stomach and he stood with the bottle of water just as she'd passed it to him. The sensation was so sudden and intense it left him entranced in a stirring wind of curiosity and lust. The moment sparked within him a new energy.

"She's single, Mac," said the captain. The first officer walked up the steps, looking for the red headed flight attendant again. Tom stood in the upper galley trying to hide his smile in a cup of coffee. "You can't argue with the way she was eyeing you up," another jelly donut had appeared in his hand.

Mac blushed and reflexively slid the bottle of water in his back pocket. He would've said anything to fill the silence and he coughed before speaking, "So, are we all fueled up?" Both pilots pressed their heels against the wall as a cart of meals was pushed through the boarding door.

"You sure are," the captain winked.

■ ■ ■

*Her red hair.* Mac tried to focus on his responsibilities, but his mind wandered endlessly. *Her lips.* It had been years since he felt seen by a woman and desire stirred within him. *Her soft neck.* The Tristar climbed over the southern border of Nicaragua and the clear, blue waters of the Caribbean Sea north towards the United States.

"So boys, have you heard what Bakers is going to try to get this company out of its financial shit storm?" The captain pulled Mac from his thoughts and looked over the center panel. He was slinging handfuls of peanuts in his mouth from packets piling up next to his seat. Phil Bakers became president of the nearly bankrupt Eastern Airlines a few years before and promised he'd bring the company back to financial straits.

"They're going to start loading people up on overnight cargo flights for cheap fares," he raised his open hand in surrender. "Can you believe that shit?"

"You mean they're going to put seats on our cargo planes?" the flight engineer leaned forward. When he pressed his lips together, the baby fat in his cheeks bulged.

"They think cheap fares are going to prevent the airline from going flop?" he laughed and waved off the idea. "I'll eat a green vegetable if those tickets do a damn thing."

Eastern Airlines did begin selling *Moonlight Specials* between 18 domestic cities in the US through the mid-1980s. Passengers flew on cargo flights between midnight and seven in the morning for discount fares. The bulk of the cargo airplanes held mail, textiles, and machine parts so passengers had to pay $10 to bring a bag that only made it onboard if there was extra room. Years after the program ended, an Eastern Airlines flight attendant told the *New York Times* passengers were "a cross section of college students, illegal aliens, and weirdos from L.A."

■ ■ ■

"Come on guys, let's go have a little fun," Captain Tom Fesinki said as they pulled their bags off the crew shuttle to their hotel. "We've worked hard today," he clapped, "so now let's play hard!" Tom insisted the crew go out for dinner together in Miami.

The flight engineer was young and eager to see the town and one of the stewardesses said something about being ready for a drink. Mac looked over to the red headed flight attendant, whose perfume danced in his nose. He regarded the hair dancing on her shoulder while she gathered her bags under the hotel awning. *I didn't even get her name.* The Miami air was heavy and humid, but Mac walked with the lightness of steam.

Within the hour, all three pilots and five of the cabin crew members piled into taxis and made their way to a steakhouse just off the beach. The captain wore a collared Hawaiian shirt and Mac was happy he brought along a pair of slacks and a polo. First the drinks came, then the food and the cheery conversation was not long to follow. Mac decided to forgo his drinking rule and tried to keep up with whatever the captain ordered. *What's wrong with a little fun?*

The red headed flight attendant sat across the table from him and his eyes kept catching hers. He returned her smile and she looked to her shoulder. With the help of Tom's drinks, they began to talk and discover how their worlds came together. *"I moved from Wisconsin to see what else is out there,"* she said. He could make her laugh effortlessly and he never wanted the moment to end. They talked about places they've been and airplane food. Tom was telling a loud story at the other end of the table and the restaurant rumbled in music and conversation. The pours were generous and didn't seem to end, though Mac was only drunk on one thing. Her name was Mel and at twenty-two, she was a woman.

Outside of the restaurant, Mel stumbled on the curb as the group walked into the Miami night warm and engorged. Taxis honked on the bustling street and tourists shuffled on the sidewalks beside. Waves of the Atlantic Ocean crashed onto the beaches beyond the road and muffled beats played from clubs nested in both directions. Mel reached for Mac's arm and caught her balance but didn't let go. Her touch was electrifying, her skin delicate and tender, and Mac swelled. He guided her into the cab, and they rode shoulder-to-shoulder on the congested streets of Miami. He felt like a man and relished every moment.

■ ■ ■

"Let's plan to meet down here at eight tomorrow morning to shuttle to the airport," said the captain in the lobby. Someone mumbled something and the group split to their rooms.

Mel took a step towards the hall but looked back at Mac intimately before completing her stride. He peered into her eyes and the discs between each bone in his spine extended. Her dress nestled along the small of her back and each strand of her hair seemed to glisten in the light. Mac's eyes were sharp, and his heart bound. A craving cascaded within him, but he didn't dare move. Alone in the lobby, she swallowed and her breasts moved with each breath. "I suppose we should get some rest before tomorrow," she said. He felt strong and faced her completely.

"I suppose you're right," he stepped towards her and could feel her hips close. They were like magnets and he wanted to yield to their attraction. Mac was breathing through his mouth and she bit her lower lip.

Mel took a step towards him and pitched her chin slightly into the air. The world seemed to lean in, and a primal urge was gaining. Her rib cage expanded when Mac took her hand. She exhaled, her lips separated and wet. He finally surrendered. His lips fell to hers.

*With her, I am a man.*

An electric buzz coursed through his veins and he longed to freeze time itself. His hand fell on the small of her back and, before he opened his eyes, her hand was guiding him down the hall. She unlocked the hotel room door, never moving her eyes off his, and stepped into the darkness. Mac stood frozen in the threshold of the door and looked into the void. *Susan.*

The sweet fragrance of her perfume twirled in his nostrils. *Is this who I am?*

He heard her shirt fall to the floor.

Mac stepped forward and closed the door behind him.

# Chapter 13

## June 1987 | Miami, Florida

Mac climbed into the co-pilot seat of the Tristar L-1011 with his skin tingling. *It was a touch I haven't known in years.* The captain shot him a smile, pulling the harnesses over his shoulders, but didn't say a word. The evening was an utter catharsis that brought new strength and Mac questioned if something that made him feel this way could be wrong. In the cockpit, his mind eddied on his lonely years with Susan and their bleak future before he finally conceded. The realization came briskly but without angst. He was another pilot with an affair.

The Tristar leaped into the air over the swampy Everglades on its way towards Mexico City. *The way she looked at me made nothing else matter.* The captain leveled at thirty-one thousand feet as they traveled west over the Gulf of Mexico. *Her skin melted into mine.* Mac couldn't identify the feeling but knew he liked it. The crew began breakfast in the cabin and the pilots sat back as they flew over the stunning ocean waters.

"Alright boys," said Tom. Beyond the gravelly voice bent by a night of tequila, Mac could sense an uneasiness in his voice. "It's that time of year again for me to get checked out by the doc." They sipped on some coffee brought up by one of the girls and he adjusted the visors to shield the Pacific sun. "I had the same guy doing my exam for the past 25 years, but that sonofabitch retired," he shifted in his seat.

The Federal Aviation Administration published an extensive list of symptoms and diseases deemed medically disqualifying to maintain a pilot's license and each year pilots had to be checked out by an FAA doc to ensure they were fit to fly. "You guys know of anyone?"

"I'm sorry to hear that, Tom," said the flight engineer. If health was questioned, even the best were vulnerable to losing their wings. "Losing the right flight doc is a bad deal."

"You damn right it is," said the captain. One misstep could bring a quick and unceremonious end to a career. "He was a good guy, didn't ask too many questions, you know?" He tapped his fingers on the dash as Mac was rebounding from a moment of musing.

"I know what you mean," said the flight engineer seated behind. The program's goal was to ensure America's pilots were fit to fly but pilots ran the risk of losing their medical clearance every time they attended an appointment. To many, it seemed the program left frustrated pilots who avoided doctors like the plague. "I knew a guy who went to a new flight doc a few years back for some heartburn," the engines roared in the background. "That trigger-happy S. O. B. put something about chest pain in his medical record and he got grounded for like *six months*."

"Jesus Christ," the captain combed his hand through his hair and shook his head. "What the hell happened?"

"It was heartburn!" The youthful flight engineer laughed but the senior captain wasn't amused. Mac knew these situations were not uncommon and wouldn't forget how his aerospace professor summed up the sentiment years before: *"avoid by all means necessary."* He knew plenty of pilots who struggled with headaches or sinus problems because they worried about what a trip to the doctor might mean for their livelihood.

"I understand they need to be cautious and what not, but it just feels like nothing good comes out of seeing the doc," said the flight engineer.

"Have you heard about Jack Sternson?" asked the captain shaking his head. The cockpit was silent and tense. "This guy was about 10 years older than me and we used to fly the Tristar together." The tone of his voice implied where the story was going. "He was at home one day and started to have some chest pain," the captain looked over at Mac. "He was too damn stubborn to go to the hospital because he didn't want to tell the FAA about it."

"Well, fuck man I get it," said the flight engineer leaning forward between the seats, "I wouldn't want to either."

"Right there at the kitchen table," the captain clapped his hands together and the skin below his chin rippled, "that son of a bitch had a heart attack." Mac grinned his teeth and shook his head, "His wife said he sat there for three hours and when she came back from the store, he was dead at the kitchen table." Mac turned his head over the Gulf and the crew was silent.

"I'm really sorry to hear that Tom," Mac shook his head again and studied the lines in the captain's face. Tom looked older for a moment and the energy in his voice dimmed. A pilot complaining about doctors was far from novel but something about this seemed different. Mac had the fortune of good health but knew the thought of a yearly medical evaluation plagued many of his colleagues. Only the roaring of their three engines echoed in the cockpit for several seconds.

"The system is just fucked up, man," said the flight engineer. "I know a flight doc out in Virginia known for being the kind of flight doc a guy looks for." Mac adjusted the sun visor again and the captain looked back.

"What's the guy's name?" the captain tried not to sound too eager. "I need to get a medical eval in the next month to keep my currency."

"Edward Klemson," he said. "He as a small office out in Arlington and I hear he is also a private pilot."

"Finally, a guy who understands," said the captain, scribbling notes into a small notebook.

Mac discretely wrote down the doctor's name on the corner of his notepad, knowing he too, would need an evaluation. The flight engineer said something about the premiere of the cartoon *The Simpsons* and the captain mentioned President Reagan's upcoming speech at the Berlin Wall, and the cockpit lit up again.

■ ■ ■

Mac remained thrust into Mel's passionate amour two years after their first encounter. Crossing paths in Miami made their affair convenient and filled a pervasive longing for companionship, given his marriage was built on unspoken anger and growing indifference. Mel's energy made him feel alive and a night together left him revived. Certainly he wasn't the first pilot with a struggling marriage and affair, but it seemed his was unique and it didn't feel wrong. Most wives remained at home, caring for kids and available for the capricious life of a pilot, but Susan's career was thriving. At 35-years old, Susan was a rising star in the department and was recently awarded teaching responsibilities in the medical school. Sure, he was happy for her, but he was many other things too.

*"We'll only see each other in Miami," Mel said.* Her apartment was three miles from Mac's suburban Washington home, but they kept their pact and lived in two separate worlds.

He didn't know if he had the strength to leave Susan and sensed Mel knew it too, but their time together wasn't spent dwelling on the future. They were lost people, searching for something they couldn't find, and sweltered in the distraction of visceral emotion and lustful thirst. Mel was young and had a child, paying support to an ex-husband who left her with scars. Mac would buy her posh jewelry from the Caribbean and spent sleepless nights craving her. Their romance cultivated in time and brought some direction to his life. There was someone in the world who thought of him too and, though their lives were complicated, their time together in Miami was simple.

■ ■ ■

In 1989, they dined on crabmeat cocktails and double rib lamb chops at Mel's favorite spot. *Arthur's Eating House* was not far from the Miami ocean and always had a trio playing a somber tune. With bare skin against the sheets later that night, Mac propped himself up on his arm and gazed into Mel's eyes. He pressed his lips to hers and he could feel her soft smile. In that moment, Mac realized he was happy.

"So, have you been updating your resume?" asked Mel pulling the comforter over her bare chest.

Mac rolled on top of her playfully, "Updating my resume?" He kissed her again.

"I'm not sure what all of you boys are chatting about up in your cockpit, but I've been hearing that the airline is going to belly up soon." Mac rolled off her and propped his head up on his hand. The sliding door was open to the night and salty air whirled around them. "I'm not going down with this ship," she said.

"Now, where did you hear that?" asked Mac, playing along.

"All of the ladies are talking about it," she said. The blanket was at Mac's waist. "I guess someone in the corporate office spilled the beans and it's spreading like wildfire." Mac admired the contours of her lips and arms above her head.

"Is that so," he said lightly. There had been chatter in the cockpit about the airline's financial situation and many seemed to be on edge. He knew the airline had been through it before, so he didn't dwell much on it.

"I don't think it's good, Mac," she pushed the hair out of her face. "Some of the girls are looking for other jobs." Her tone changed.

"Are you telling me you're looking for a new job?" Mac was smiling and distracted by her eyes and creamy skin.

"I can't say it hasn't crossed my mind," she climbed out of bed and wrapped her bra around her chest. "What am I going to do if I lose my job, Mac?" She rummaged for her shirt. "Being a flight attendant is the only thing I know how to do."

"The airline will be fine, Mel," he got out of bed and pulled on his pants. The motion in the room changed and he wanted to crawl back into bed where life was clear and carefree. There had been recurrent turnover in the leadership and the airline recently cancelled an order of new Boeing airplanes. *Things may be different this time.*

"I hope you're right Mac," she walked around the bed and placed her hands on his hips. "I guess all we can do is update our resumes," she kissed his cheek.

■ ■ ■

Congress passed the Airline Deregulation Act of 1978, heralding brutal new competition in the commercial aviation market. The federal government once controlled the number of passenger seats and ticket prices between cities in the U.S., but the new legislation freed the industry of regulation and left a Darwinian marketplace. Established airlines struggled to remain profitable amidst skyrocketing fuel prices and dozens of new budget carriers offering abundant seats at low fares.

Cockpits across the country were filled with anxious pilots chattering about jobs at other airlines or even careers outside aviation. Eastern Airlines was a historic institution, with a rich history dating back to the 1920s, but the fierce war for revenue left the clumsy giant unable to keep pace. Frank Lorenzo acquired the airline and began moving assets into his other companies like Texas Air and Continental Airlines, foreshadowing the fate of the once powerful carrier.

"I've applied for a job with American Airlines out in LA," said Mel. She draped the napkin over her plate. "I think I'm going to get it." It had been over two months since they'd last been together and he sensed a looming change.

"Congratulations, Mel," he spun his wine glass and tried to mask what he couldn't deny. "When would you start?" Back at *Arthur's Eating House*, the jazz trio crooned the final melodies of *Lush Lullaby* in the key of D flat.

"I'll start as soon as they will let me," she said. He regarded her beauty across the table. *I was lucky to be with her.*

"So, you're moving to LA?"

"So, I'm moving to LA," her voice graveled. She answered fewer of his phone calls and made an excuse the last time they were in Miami. "It's time to get out of this rut," she said longingly.

Mac played with his napkin on his lap, avoiding her gaze, and she put her fork on the table.

*You were more than an affair, Mel.*

"It's time to move on, Mac," her eyes sparkled. He didn't say anything.

*You're my friend.*

"We don't have a life together."

*I don't have a life with anyone.*

He thought about his empty house in Washington and the hollow days on the road. He thought of Susan and their fractured marriage. Soon, the empty promises to Dennis and the children that never came followed. Mac was accustomed to feeling alone in the world but now it was morphing into something new.

"So, I can't see you again?" It was loneliness and it cauterized his esprit.

"I'm sorry, Mac, but I need to try and start over. I can't be another pilot's affair." She wiped a tear falling down her cheek. A reason to endure vanished, leaving only daunting despair.

Outside the restaurant in the oppressive Miami air, they stood apart. The bustle of tourists laughing around them and someone on a bike chimed a bell. Cars honked and swerved while seagulls circled a nearby trash can. They blended into the busyness of the city and Mac wondered what was left in this world. He kissed her lightly on the cheek and watched her turn away into the night.

"And, Mac," her coat draped over her shoulders, and she looked back. Her lipstick was red and perfectly outlined her lips. "You need to find what's missing in your life," Mel's eyes glistened in the moonlight, "because it's not me."

■ ■ ■

The airline told 4,000 employees that Friday not to return to work the following Monday. Within a few weeks, ground crews suffered a staggering pay cut, triggering a historic strike across the country. Concerned theirs would be the same fate, flight attendant and pilot unions called for a sympathy strike, which completely halted domestic operations across the fleet. The episode brought staggering financial loss to a company already in economic trouble and the airline filed for bankruptcy in just three days. 5,000 people immediately lost their jobs followed by 18,000 more. Eastern Airlines Shuttle, the successful entity Mac flew for out of college, was sold to Donald Trump and renamed *"Trump Shuttle"* while the rest of the company was liquidated to pay its debts. Unaware of the closure, reservationists mistakenly continued to sell fares until midnight the night before the final Eastern Airlines flight landed.

# Chapter 14

February 2016 | Pacific Ocean

Julie methodically evaluated the instruments aboard the empty 767 flight deck and found the ship to be functioning by the book. With plenty of fuel aboard, she pressed the throttles forward and accelerated the airliner towards Oahu.

With an emergency declared, Pacific Air Traffic Controllers vectored her directly to Honolulu International Airport. *"We'll have emergency medical personnel immediately available when you're on the ground,"* said the *controller.* Her mind etched from one concern to another, but she had to remain sharp if she would get those aboard on the ground safely. With the throttle forward, the two turbo-fan Pratt & Whitney engines roared through the misty ocean night.

There was a knock at the door before it clicked unlocked.

"We have a situation in the galley, Julie," Shari said, exhausted. Her eyes were puffy and she looked shaken.

*What else could have possibly happened?* The pilot waited for the senior flight attendant to continue. The copilot noticed the bothered, swollen skin around her eyes and the lines stacked on her forehead.

"Dawnis is dead."

Microscopic muscles under Julie's skin pulled the hair on her neck erect. She reflexed to say something, but her mouth was arid. Instinctively, her index finger began picking at her thumb and she wished she'd better concealed her reaction.

"Dawnis is dead," Shari was trying to hold back tears. "I watched her die, Julie." She braced herself on the cockpit wall and her hand trembled. The pilot wanted to comfort her but her body wouldn't move. The delicate stack of ceramic cups would collapse at any moment and the cockpit seemed tight.

"The doctor was there," she tried to swallow back the emotion skulking below. "Something about bleeding and pressure in the brain…" the words were too much.

"Do you know what happened?" the answer didn't seem to matter because the damage was already done. Her mind whirled in all the possibilities.

"It looks like she fell backwards on the corner of the galley counter when the airplane started to dive," her eyes were opaque as it replayed in her head. "Her blood is all over the galley."

The pilot wanted to grieve but couldn't. *First, fly the airplane.* Her mind replayed the words but she knew she had to focus. She longed to be back in the basement of the Jet Stream Air training facility running a scenario in the simulator, but cold reality condescended.

"Where is her body?" Her thumb nail made it to her teeth.

"She's lying on the floor," Shari was salvaging her composure. She dabbed below her left eye with the arched back of a finger. *She watched her friend die tonight.* Some muffled radio chatter came through the speaker while the two women, generations apart, suffered in the cockpit light.

"We'll have to move the body away from the passengers," she was running through the options. It was imperative that everyone remained calm. "Quietly move her to one of the berths in the crew quarters," Julie's voice was even but felt vanquished. "Who else knows?"

"Two of the first-class passengers helping the doctor," said Shari. Her dark uniform looked worn, and the red scarf around her neck lay limp on her shoulder. "I'll talk to them." Everyone aboard would know soon enough.

"What about the captain?"

Another knock at the door and Shari let Dr. Megan Delaney forward into the flight deck. "I guess you can ask her yourself," Shari looked at the doctor in the slack yellow sweater. "What's going on with Mac?"

"I can't say for certain," she pushed a strand of hair behind her ear after the door clicked, "but I'm highly suspicious he's suffered a stroke." She had eyes of concern but not of worry. Julie was so accustomed to white coats and suits that seeing this person in vacation clothes as her medical expert was a little odd. "Based on some of my findings," her head tilted and nodded as she spoke, "the stroke is the likely cause of his vertigo."

"Vertigo?" the pilot remained strapped into her seat and looked back over her shoulder. She was familiar in the context of flight but not as a form of stroke.

"His physical exam suggests he's had a stroke in a part of the brain called the cerebellum. It would account for the spinning and discoordination." Julie nodded like she followed along but the details didn't seem important. "If we can get him to the hospital soon enough, he may still be eligible for a clot busting medication."

Dr. Delaney and Shari stood in the cramped space behind the cockpit seats while Julie stewed over their options. The flight attendant rubbed her hands down the front of her uniform, and the pilot chewed her nail distantly. It seemed all that mattered was the airliner got on the ground as quickly as possible.

"The medicine can be used within six hours of a stroke," said the doctor. She was factual and concise. "But no longer. Every second he is on this plane, more of his brain is dying," *Every moment counts.* Tissue plasminogen activator had been used over the past twenty-five years for ischemic stroke and worked by breaking up the culprit thrombus. In contrast to hemorrhagic stroke where blood leaked into the brain, blood obstruction in an ischemic stroke caused brain cells to die within seconds. *We have to get him to a hospital.* "There are other possibilities, but this seems to be my most likely," the doctor paused, "and the most urgent."

Julie studied the control panel, *six hundred and fifty miles to go.* They were hurtling through the sky as fast as the airframe could tolerate and she wished she could push harder. "Just under two hours," she stirred in her seat and looked at her thumb, now bleeding. "They'll have an ambulance on the ground when we land."

"We will have to move Dawnis into the crew hold," said Shari. The lines in her forehead seemed to smooth and her neck lengthened. "It's under the first-class cabin."

"Discreetly," said the pilot. Her thumb ached as the exposed nail bed touched the air. "What about the other injured?"

"One person is in a temporary sling for what looks like a broken arm but everything else is relatively mild."

"Thank God more people didn't get hurt," said Julie. Words were curt and she stared back at the eyes waiting for her leadership. The fate of the hundreds of people aboard were in her hands and those of this young physician. The years spent preparing for this moment suddenly felt insufficient but there was no other choice.

■ ■ ■

The looming blackness of the open ocean painted deep into the distance and touched the horizon at infinity. Alone again in the cockpit, Julie fought the urge to continue gnawing her thumb as the engines sucked fuel from the wings and ignited it. Her teacher was only a few feet away but was unreachable and absent. She wondered how their situation was concocted and contemplated the body hidden in the lower deck. *Six hundred and five miles.* She ceded and brought her finger to her teeth. Only once in her career had her skills truly been put to the test like tonight and she let her mind escape to her early training.

■ ■ ■

"Okay, Julie," said her instructor, "it's all yours!" The lieutenant, not much older than herself, popped the canopy and crawled out of the ejection seat with the engine still running. "It's time for your first solo as an Air Force pilot," he yelled over the propeller. "I'll be on the radio if you need me." Twenty-two year old Julie beamed. It was her first month at US Air Force Undergraduate Pilot Training and she had studied endlessly for this moment.

With twelve hours of instruction in the T-6 Texan II Air Force trainer under her belt, she taxied the trainer to the end of the runway. The humid air of Columbus Air Force Base, Mississippi was a long way from the University of North Dakota's flight training program but today it smelled sweet. *You're an Air Force pilot, Julie.* A proud new member of the Air National Guard, she moved from Grand Forks only weeks before to complete her military flight training.

"Columbus tower, three eight four alpha ready to go runway thirteen left," she called over the radio.

"Three eight four alpha, cleared for takeoff, runway thirteen left," called the controller back.

She exhaled and tested the breaks. *I can do this.* She pushed the throttle forward on the single, turbo prop Texan and felt the engine come alive. *Like an animal wants to be free.* Rolling down the runway, she sensed the eyes of her squadron mates watching closely.

The airplane became lighter as wind began to lift the wings. *Nice and easy, Julie.* The nose wheel accelerated down the center of the runway and the airplane felt spirited and agile. She ignored the tickle in her belly and heart beating in her throat.

*85 knots.* She applied light back pressure on the stick and the airplane lifted itself off the runway. *Accelerate to 140-180 knots and climb.* She executed her training by the books.

The world was so vivid in that moment. The smells, the sounds, the views were detailed and complete. Every cell in her body was energized because there was no better seat in the world than exactly where she was.

*Six hundred feet off the ground.* The forest beyond the field was green and abundant. She exhaled and was calm. Beautiful.

*What?*

A wrenching thud of a falling weight clawed her from the view. *Shit.* The engine quivered. *No.* It sputtered and coughed but then it stopped. *Silence.* It only took seven seconds.

The air whispered over the wing and the airplane slowed. Julie leveled the nose and she considered her options amidst utter fear surging through her body. *Holy shit.* She thought back to her training. *First, fly the airplane.*

Her airspeed indicator showed one-hundred and twenty-five knots. *Not enough speed to turn back to the field.* Over the instrument panel, she saw trees and swamp. *No good options.* Searing hot fear bit into the tip of her tongue. *Stay calm, think.*

*I don't see any flames.* She ran the checklist.

```
Fuel Selector                    BOTH

Mixture                          RICH

Engine Ignition                  ON
```

She flipped the ignition and the engine began to rumble. *Four hundred and fifty feet.* The tops of trees were growing closer.

Julie considered ejecting but instead reached for the engine starter and activated it. *Come on.* She held her breath and came close to praying. *Please.* She could hear it winding up and click. The engine came to life. *It's working!* She pushed the throttle forward and the airplane was pulled ahead. *Thank God.* She began to climb. *First, fly the airplane.*

Five seconds passed and her stomach squeezed. *The engine.* It growled and again protested. It grinded to a halt and the airplane began to sink. *Five hundred feet.* The swamp below was looming and the cars along the highway could be seen in more detail. *One hundred and twenty knots.* The silence in the cockpit was disturbing and she was running out of options.

*One more time.* She pulled the throttle back and flipped the ignition in desperation. She held her breath. *Come on, please.* Pistons compressed, magnetos fired, and fuel exploded below the hood. The engine groaned as each cylinder and lever worked in concert to bring the engine back to life. *I just need to swing back to the field.*

It engaged but only idled. *That's all I need.*

She cautiously pushed the throttle forward, intimately listening to its tune, but found a bitter growl beyond thirty percent power. She decided not to push it. It was just enough to stop her descent.

"Mayday, mayday, mayday, three eight four alpha," she called over the radio. "I had an engine failure on take-off but it's holding at," she looked at her instruments, "at eight hundred RPM now," far lower than the two-thousand, three hundred revolutions per minute required to climb.

"You can do this Julie," it was her instructor over the radio. "Just focus." *First, fly the airplane.* "Do you have enough power to come back to the field?"

"I think so," her hands were shaking.

"Good, make a wide left turn and closely watch your airspeed," his voice was calm. She dipped the left wing just below the horizon and the engine quietly purred. A mist of sweat speckled her upper lip and her eyes were sharp but wide. She fought the urge to shear nail off its bed with her incisors.

The long, shallow bank brought her just where she needed. The nose was lined up with the runway and she ran a final checklist.

*I'll turn the engine off immediately on the ground in case the plane starts to burn.* She picked her thumb nail with her index finger. The world felt like a movie. She popped the door latch two hundred feet off the ground. *To escape if this flight ends in impact.*

Lieutenant Julie Sampers descended towards the runway as fire trucks began to line along the taxiway. An ambulance stopped at the far end and she prayed it wouldn't be useful. The airplane slowed but she altered the flaps and made it over the threshold. *Oh my god, I'm over the runway.* The large white runway numbers passed beneath her and she slightly pulled back on the stick just before the rear wheels to kiss the ground. *I'm alive. The* muscles in her neck relaxed.

The nose wheel directed the airplane off the runway and came to a stop on an adjacent taxiway. *Emergency shutdown checklist.* An explosion would make everything else moot.

| | |
|---|---|
| Fuel Selector | OFF |
| Mixture | OFF |
| Engine Ignition | OFF |
| Master Electrical | OFF |

She popped the canopy and crawled out. *Air.* Her world was spinning in growing relief and eventually there was bliss. A dozen people were running towards her, cheering and a fleet of vehicles followed. *I did it.*

With only twelve hours of flight training, the lieutenant negotiated an engine failure on takeoff, brought the airplane back to the field, and landed successfully. *I didn't eject!* The exceptional performance won her swift recognition across the fleet and a new call sign: *Lucky.*

The accolades were exciting, but her true satisfaction came from discovering within herself the strength of character to approach challenges with bravery and skill.

■ ■ ■

The metallic ring of the galley phone summoned Julie from her thoughts. It was Shari, "The passengers are getting anxious, I think you should say something." Tonight, she was being put to the test again.

"Of course," she probably should have said something sooner, but the thought was lost in the disarray. Her eyes searched for the moon, but she knew it was veiled in the clouds. "Have you briefed the other crew?"

"Yes, I only told them the captain became ill, which caused the turbulence. As you can imagine they're worried," she said. "I told them the airplane seems to be okay."

"That will do for now. Are any other crew injured?"

"Just bumps and bruises."

Julie considered her options. She too would've been anxious in their shoes and now hoped they didn't know how fast her heart was beating. The GPS showed high cloud cover over the Pacific skies and calm air before Hawaii. "It should be smooth for the next hour or so," she was thinking, "Do you think the crew would be up for serving some drinks or something to help keep calm?"

"Honestly, it's a mess back here, Julie," she sounded weary. "When we tipped, so did every meal tray in this plane." The line was unfilled for a moment, "but it may not be a bad idea." The night's action occurred in the midst of dinner: there was gravy on the walls, chicken in the aisle, and red wine in the laps of many. One unfortunate passenger was caught in the restroom and his shoes had filled with contents not yet flushed into the septic tank.

"I'll make an announcement, you update the other crew," Julie ended the call. Her voice buried her uncertainty and she knew it was required. *Focus, think.* It was clear her decisions tonight would be thoroughly dissected, and her actions would be a defining moment in her career. At twenty-nine years old, she was in command of the wide body airliner and every person aboard was looking to her.

Julie exhaled and flipped on the public addressing system, "Ladies and gentlemen, this is the first officer speaking from the flight deck." She was poised and paced herself. "I want to start by saying, the airplane is functioning properly, and I assure you we will be safely on the ground in Hawaii in a few hours."

She wanted that to sink in before she went on. *I've trained for this my whole life.* "There is a medical emergency onboard that is being dealt with by a physician. I know others are injured and medical services will be available immediately when we are on the ground." She looked out to the stars just beginning to peek through the nighttime sky.

"I apologize for the unanticipated cabin movements you experienced," she swallowed. "Perhaps these were frightening but there is no reason to believe this will happen again." The sentences flowed naturally despite knowing she was likely being recorded by a dozen cell phone cameras.

"I have asked the flight attendants to serve some refreshments in the meantime," she had nothing else to tell them and her mind dwelled on the body in the hold. "I'll get us to Hawaii as quickly as possible." She ended the announcement and picked at her nail again. Her finger pulsed with an electric ache to the beat of her heart. *Now to update the airline.* She rubbed her temples.

■ ■ ■

Still buckled in the forward galley, Captain Robert "Mac" Frank stared vacantly. *How did I let this happen?* The spinning continued to plague him, and the crashing waves of nausea persisted. He was submerged in Julie's announcement and remained perfectly still. The medical emergency was sitting in his chest. His impenetrable stare was locked on the satin pool of blood a few feet from his shoes and he knew who was to blame. To consider a stroke was the culprit of their predicament instead of an aeronautical emergency was still too much to bare, but the towering walls of reality were inching closer.

The erratic beating in his chest was uncomfortable but not unfamiliar. He tried to purge the memory of the previous morning from his consciousness, but it ricocheted back with growing intensity. *Chaotic beating.* He was at home. *I woke up and couldn't move my arm.* He didn't go to the hospital. *It was fine by the end of the day.* He would've lost his pilot's license if he went to the emergency room. *I have nothing else in this world.* He had sacrificed so much and wondered how much more he would be willing to give.

■ ■ ■

Six hundred miles away at Honolulu International Airport, news of the battered flight quickly spread. Controllers dispatched medical crews and fire trucks to the runway and the airline sent an army of gate agents to local hospitals to meet incoming passengers and families.

With passengers reaching out to friends and family from the airplane, news agencies caught wind and reporters made their way to the terminal. Cell phone footage would be a hot commodity, and many aimed to be the first with their hands on it. *Airplane emergencies make big news.*

# Chapter 15

March 1989 | Washington, District of Columbia

Mac paced Washington's National Airport Terminal One, parading a union made sign:

GOOD PAY
FOR SAFE
TRAVEL!

The heavy afternoon clouds sagged in the sky and his dress shoes beckoned aching in his feet. Banned from picketing inside airports, dozens of pilots marched outside the terminal among passengers shuffling between taxis and the ticket counters. Their future looked bleaker with every passing hour. Not a single Eastern Airlines flight had taken off in over two days and negotiations were locked.

Mac followed the line of pilots lumbering the long corridor trying to make their pleas. He marched bitterly, knowing this was not what he wanted.

Signs about low pay, cut benefits, and poor management papered the crowd, but many knew low-cost carriers and a tired business model had sealed their fate long before. After only two days, their resolve was fading, and bleak faces painted their skulls.

Out of the sea of taxis and exhaust fumes, a brown suited man in a fedora approached the crop of pilots. He shuffled around passengers swiftly and bounced with each stride. A stack of envelopes appeared from the inside of his blazer and he began passing them without a word.

"What are these?" asked one of the pilots, ripping it open. The man continued as if nothing was said. One made it into Mac's hand, and he studied the blue company seal on the front. He shook his head and tore it open, wishing he didn't already know what was enclosed.

One of the pilots cursed and another began tearing up the paper. Mac read it once then let his arms fall to his sides. He muttered something to himself and he read it again amongst the shuffle of passengers entering the terminal unaware of the history being made. It was hard to believe, and he didn't want to know the consequences. The slow and unceremonious arrival of the moment was visible for hundreds of miles, but Mac didn't want to believe it had arrived.

```
Dear valued employee,

We regret to inform you...

...Eastern Airlines will file for bankruptcy...

...your    position    is    terminated    effective
immediately.

                              - Management
```

Mac read it a final time. *How could this happen?* His legs stood frozen in the concrete and the roar of an airplane taking off from National Airport riled him. A central institution in American aviation began its long descent into the history books. *What am I going to do?* His left hand reached into his greying locks and ran his fingers into his coarse hair. The company was gone, and from the billowing Washington skies, fat raindrops began to fall. Mac wanted to cry but there was nothing inside. Life's spoon scooped him empty and the contents were scorched and dried. He didn't want to strike – it was the union. He simply wanted to fly and had sacrificed so much to do it.

The aviation giant, once the largest in the world, was falling from high and the wreckage would bring everyone down with it. The man in the fedora took one last look at the pilots and nodded his head like he wished there was something left to say. Instead, he disappeared into the crowd as enigmatically as he came.

■ ■ ■

The rain seeped heavier into Mac Frank's uniform, but the pilot didn't bother seeking cover. The weight pressed him further into the concrete and sunk him into a new despair. Life felt senseless and it was hard to know what to do. Families with kids and business people scuffled around the pilots indifferently while two taxis honked at each other from a few yards away. The residue of car exhaust and the sweet smell of jet fuel seemed to mix, and a dying fluorescent light flickered its final affair. The airport's momentum remained steady and undisturbed, but Mac's world was crumbling. His sense of self was propped up by the wings and engines of an L-1011 Tristar but now any remains were artifacts of the past.

He threw the picket sign into his pick-up truck and slumped in the driver seat. It took him almost an hour to insert the key because there was nowhere to drive.

*How could the company do this to me?*

He thought of his empty suburban house, echoing and apathetic, and the life that didn't fill it. News like this warranted an urgent phone call but who the recipient would be remained elusive. Water from the Washington's skies oozed through his blazer and now onto his skin. He let his head sink back on to the truck's headrest and he closed his eyes to ponder what was left. Carved like a pumpkin, his guts were trashed. He thought about Mel boarding a plane in Los Angeles and Susan in some basement operating room at Georgetown. Loneliness flooded him like typhoon rains on an impermeable desert floor. He felt himself drowning but he didn't try to swim. The water pooling around his exposed eyes and open mouth was welcomed.

■ ■ ■

Beaten and wet, Mac pulled his pick-up into his driveway and let it idle. His eyes were fixed forward, focused on no particular point, while the house stared back devoid of life. It was a wooden rambler with a three-stall garage, five bedrooms, and a porch across the front that stood as a shrine to the life he didn't have. He finally found the strength to turn off the engine but didn't open the door. Instead, he thought about the story that was supposed to be written on these hallowed grounds. The sticky door handles and the fridge with sack lunches. The Christmas tree in the living room and the Thanksgiving turkey in the oven. Birthdays and thunderstorms. The yard where he'd coach and the bedroom where he'd make love. Now, the bedrooms collected dust, the fridge was empty, and the backyard had weeds.

Inside the house, Mac let his uniform blazer fall on the floor. His white dress shirt and slacks soon followed. After opening a beer from the fridge, he sat heavily at the kitchen table under the weight of the culmination of his life's decisions. He would have to tell Susan but what it would mean to her remained uncertain. It had been over a week since their paths crossed, but the time didn't really seem to matter. His wife was a stranger.

Countless nights were spent staring at the ceiling trying to understand, but he knew the source of their indifference was neither complicated nor mysterious. It was simple but shouldered a pernicious truth. Two people made a life together only to find the product to be contrived and afflicted. Often, Mac persuaded their loss was the product of two people who stopped trying, though he now wondered if they even started with anything at all. Perhaps there was someone else, or worse, she too filled the hollow cavity that companionship was to occupy with career and achievement. He couldn't be upset. He tried to fill the chasm in his heart with an affair, but the space was too vast. Though the misfortune of their predicament was trying, the reason she didn't leave him was often the most excruciating to bear.

*It was just easier not to.*

In his shirt and underwear, he took another swig. Susan was away at the hospital for the night. *She'll know soon enough.* At thirty-six years old, she was one of the youngest associate deans at the School of Medicine and her professional momentum seemed to grow. Mac knew it was a notable accomplishment, but they had exchanged no more than a few words about the promotion.

*"Congratulations, Susan," he said when she coughed up the news.*

*"Thanks," she was sorting her mail. "By the way, please park further on your side in the garage. I can't get out of my car when you park so far over." She went into her room and closed the door.*

He finished his second beer and the rain continued. Flying was the only thing he had left in the world and an unaddressed envelope and generic letter changed that. Now, he only wanted to be numb.

■ ■ ■

Over the coming days, Mac descended into new depths. He couldn't sleep at night but laid in bed aimlessly through the afternoon. He didn't bother turning on the lights so the house remained drab and somber. If not in bed, he occupied space in the living room, listening to the silence of the house. The newspaper headlines announced the end of Eastern Airlines and its thousands of layoffs, but he didn't bother with the articles. He wondered when the last time he showered was, while his temples thinned and eyes brooded. Another sleepless night came, and he stared at the ceiling through the afternoon like morning never arrived. *What part of my life is worth living?* He was exhausted but restless, shackled by demons and regret. Mac hadn't left the house for four days.

He heard the backdoor open and he ambled into the kitchen.

"Jesus, Mac," Susan's arms were full.

"Hi, Susan," he wandered into the kitchen and brushed absently at the front of his shirt.

"Aren't you supposed to be on a trip?" she unloaded on the counter and rummaged through her purse. The garage door was closing.

"Yes, I am," words took all his strength.

"Okay then," she looked up then kept rummaging, "why are you here?" Her voice was moments from boiling over the caldron.

"Haven't you heard what happened to Eastern?" he sounded airy and anemic. He wanted to crawl back into his bed.

Susan looked up, "Mac, I've been in an OR for days and hardly slept," her voice was sharp. "So, forgive me for not following the news." She found it in her purse.

"They filed for bankruptcy," he watched from his drooped perch on the opposite side of the kitchen. "I was laid off."

She pushed her bag away, "Eastern Airlines is going under?"

"Yes, Susan," he felt defensive, "and I got laid off."

"I heard you got laid off, Mac," her fist pressed against her hip, "What are you going to do?" She pointed at him.

"What do you mean 'what am I going to do?'" he could feel himself sinking into his skin.

"I mean are you just going to sit at home, Mac?" she gestured at him. "You look terrible."

"I lost my job, Susan, what do you want me to do?"

"I don't know, Mac. *You're* the pilot." She tried to massage a headache from her temples. "You'll have to figure it out," she grabbed her backpack and filed up the stairs. He wanted to say something but instead merely watched her retreat. She strode into her room and the closing door echoed throughout the house with symbolic finality.

■ ■ ■

Early the next morning, Mac heard the house empty and garage door close, but he didn't get out of bed until well after two in the afternoon. *She won't be back for a few days.* He wandered from room to room when he finally found the strength, searching for something. *"You've got to find what's missing in your life, Mac because it's not me."* He missed her. Hours blended to days. He didn't shower and his pants were loose. Every cell in his body was cracked open and their contents evaporated. *I loved you, Susan.* He didn't know what day of the week it was and it didn't matter. He was bored and restive and wondered if it was worth it to even go on.

Sometime after the sun rose, but before it peaked in the sky, Mac's fingers split the blinds in his shadowy living room.

He watched an airliner climb into the clouds, wondering if it was the third or fourth day he remained alone. If he sat perfectly still, he could hear the engines humming. *What used to be.* The sky was pure and blue, painted only with the wispy lots of cirrus clouds. Mac regarded the craft's majesty like he would a symphony or waterfall and permitted himself a moment to feel inspired by its beauty. He used to sit in the nose and make decisions, a master of his craft, but no longer. He closed the blinds and turned away.

*When was I last happy?* The sun set on another day and Mac watched the walls. He remembered his first flight at UND and the recruiting fair in the Student Union. He reminisced walking University Park with Susan and their wedding day. He could feel the moment he kissed her on the National Mall and fell in love with her all over again. *That was a lifetime ago.* His mind filled with imagines of red hair and a freckled nose. *Mel, I wasn't enough.* He hadn't spoken to his parents in years. He remembered his first flight with Eastern Airlines and his promotion to the Tristar. *A dream career.* His mind looped all the things that were gone.

*Dennis.*

He thought of all the promises he made but never kept. *My friend.* Beyond the occasional holiday card, the two had not spoken in over ten years. He wished he would've called him but knew he pushed him away. What he had was elusive until it was gone.

It all seemed gone. *The loneliness would fade.* There would be no more search. *The restlessness would finally calm.* He wouldn't hurt anymore.

It surprised him how quickly he made his decision. Nearly forty years of life, it took him only a few seconds to decide to die. Though he'd thought about it before, it now made sense. The excuses to stay were meek and limited and the rational to go piled like avalanching snow. It would be easier, there would be relief. It would be today.

The truck would start and it'd be pulled into the garage. He'd close his eyes and breathe. The door would lower and he'd relax. *It's all going to be okay.* The pick-up would run and sleep would slowly swaddle him into deeper slumber.

*Relief.*

Mac's feet stood lighter on the floor. He lifted the window shades and he began to move with purpose. *The loneliness will be gone.* Mac underwent the strange phenomenon many experience after deciding to end one's life - *I feel better.* He sat at the kitchen table with a yellow legal pad and wrote:

```
- Call my parents
```

   *...was it last Christmas...?*

```
- Mow the grass
```

   He laughed. *Who knows when Susan would do it.*

```
- Donate my clothes
```

   *...at least I'll do some good.*

*Dennis.* The pen hovered over the page. For some reason, his old friend pecked at his mind. He wondered what he would say to him. Their lives had diverged, and so little seemed to remain. *He's happy, he wouldn't want to talk to me.*

```
- Dennis (?)
```

*Calls for a toast.* Mac stood from the table and found an unopened bottle of Cognac above the fridge. He slapped a cup on the counter and poured himself a healthy fill. Never much of a drinker, today seemed like an appropriate day to indulge. He tilted his head back and let the woody liquor fall down his throat. He grit his teeth against his body fighting the delivery and poured himself another. It was harsh but resuscitating.

The list occupied his mind. He sifted through his closet and trimmed the bushes with a new grace. *Last time I'll do it.* He mowed diagonal stripes into the lawn and got the mail. The Cognac wet down smoother with each sip. He pushed the lawn mower into the garage and the final drop of the next glass fell on his tongue. He went back for another.

*Dennis.* His old friend echoed in his mind like a cave. *I want to call him.*

His veins were warm and everything didn't seem so bad. If he focused hard enough, he could keep the truck between the lines all the way to the Good Will three miles away. *Hope someone can use these.* He brought his clothes to the counter and retreated again to his pickup. Back in his kitchen table, he inspected the list:

- Call my parents

- ~~Mow the grass~~

- ~~Donate clothes~~

- Dennis (?)

*Dennis.* He thought it over. *What would I say to him?* He had two young kids and a second wife. *I got laid off, have a broken marriage, and I'm about to end my life.* He took another sip. The warm embrace of the auburn malt surged through him and he looked into his glass like a crystal ball, wondering if he had the courage to go through with it. *It'd be the only brave thing I've done in my life.* He decided he did.

*Dennis.* He stood beside the phone holstered on the wall in the kitchen. *What do I have to lose?*

The phone number remained locked in his mind after all these years, though the knowledge wasn't called forward in some time. The atonic beep of the digits came through the receiver while Mac wondered if the number dating back to Dennis's start at Northwest remained.

It rang. *What is there to say?*

It rang again. *Shit.* He didn't know who would answer and debated hanging up.

A final time. *It's probably the wrong number.*

Answering machine. *Thank God.* Mac listened absently and recognized the voice on the other end. *Dennis.* It started recording with a beep.

"Oh, hi Dennis," Mac's words were slippery and bulky, "just calling." His voice trailed and he scratched his head. "Hope you're doing well, so, thanks." *Jesus Christ.* He positioned the phone back on the receiver while he tried to evade from his mind berating him. Leaning back, he filled his lungs and poured himself another glass. He wanted to go back in time and erase the message but instead stood embarrassed and alone. There were two items left on his list and he put a line through the first. If he couldn't handle Dennis, his parents would be out of the question. Like a video, his mind transported him back to his dorm room floor watching Dennis page through *Flying* magazine. He wished he had done things differently.

■ ■ ■

The stove clicked as Mac flipped on the gas burner and a raw steak and bag of carrots appeared from the fridge. *Ribeye and candied carrots.* He let the oven warm and oil sizzle in an iron pan. There were few things he knew how to prepare in the kitchen, but his favorite meal was one of them.

A lone plate rested at the head of his formal dining room beside a burning candle. Sulfur from the lit match smelled sweet and the steak steamed on the plate. The cup held the last of the Cognac in his hand and blood seeped from the cut of meat.

*My final feast.*

He draped the napkin across his lap and handed his fork and knife. The five empty chairs around him stood testament as he cut into the flesh. The first bite was a moment of sadness but also relief.

*Ring.* It was his phone from the kitchen. He hesitated. The mechanical chime rang through the house again and he debated.

*Ring.* He slapped his napkin on the table and walked into the kitchen.

DENNIS CULLEN

The caller ID was a new technology, curious and innovative, and illuminated in green. He wanted to ignore the call but each of the block letters allured him. His mind criticized the bothering of his old friend but the possibilities stirred curiosity.

DENNIS CULLEN

*...maybe the only one who knows me.*

The floor swayed like a ship and Mac had to shuffle his feet to maintain his sea legs. Much of the world felt inconsequential and, before he cognized his actions, the phone was palmed and held to his ear.

"Hello?"

"Holy shit," a familiar voice cracked through the line. The worlds were drawn out and zest with anticipation. "It's about time you called, Mackie."

He didn't know what to say so he didn't say anything. He was drunk and was buried in the sudden urge to cry.

"Mac, are you there?"

"Yes," his voice was greasy. "I'm here, Dennis."

"It's been a long time, my friend." Mac looked at his feet and absorbed every syllable. "Say, I'm sorry about Eastern." His voice felt lighter than it should have.

Mac swallowed. "Me too..." his voice trailed.

"Are you hanging in there?" he could feel his energy a thousand miles away.

"Trying too," Mac said. His mind tumbled and he begged it to focus.

"I'm sorry I missed your call," he said, "I was outside shoveling the driveway when you called. I'm getting tired of this damn Minnesota winter," his laugh was round and easy. Mac could hear the muffled sounds of activity in the background.

"I'm sorry I didn't mean to interrupt," Mac said, falling again into contrition.

"You're not interrupting anything new," Dennis laughed again and hushed off the line. "My kids had a snow day from school," he shushed again, "and they've been cooped up all day."

"Who decided you could be trusted with kids?" the words fell out of his mouth in slick disinhibition.

"There he is!" his friend chuckled cheerfully. "I'm glad you called." Mac wasn't sure if he was and neither said anything for a moment. "Say," Dennis cleared his throat, "If you can believe it, I actually start a trip tomorrow and my first overnight is in DC." Mac felt a tickle like he was falling. "I'll be there overnight," he hesitated. "I mean, if you're around..." his voice tarried.

"Tomorrow?" he wished his head wasn't reeling. It was unexpected and Mac felt vulnerable knowing the sun wouldn't rise for him after tonight's dusk.

"I know it's short notice so if you're busy..."

"...have you been here often?" Mac asked.

"Well," he swallowed," I've been there a few times."

"You never called?" said Mac. His words came faster than his mind could think.

Dennis exhaled and Mac could palpate the taxing distance between them. "I guess I just figured you were..." he hesitated, "busy." Mac rubbed his forehead. "Listen," Mac wished he could take his words back and his weight fell against the kitchen wall. "Let me know if you want to have dinner tomorrow night. I land around five thirty." There was another uncomfortable silence and the words felt forced.

"Thanks, Dennis," The alcohol's numbness faded and now he throbbed. "I'll let you know." They ended the call.

The house was quiet. Mac's mind was spinning as he pulled the phone receiver from his ear. He looked back into the dining room and at the corner of flesh speared on his fork. The house echoed in emptiness as he paced back to his seat. At the head of the table, he lay the napkin across his lap again and propped the fork in his hand. He thought of all that he had accomplished, though there was little triumph. Feeling small and insignificant, Dennis's words reverberated in his mind. There was someone in the world that wanted to see him, though the seductive thought of reprieve was alluring. *I'd drift off the sleep.* He wanted the loneliness to fade and for the torment to vanish. *Five o'clock tomorrow.* His wife, the physician, would find his cold lifeless body. *It could all be over.* He tried to bring the steak to his mouth, but he couldn't bite. Something told him it wasn't over yet.

Mac rose from the table with a new firmness and brought his plate to the kitchen. Opening the trash can, the beef slid off the plate and slumped to the bottom. Poised, he picked up the phone and dialed the number he knew by heart.

"Yes, Dennis. I will pick you up at five thirty."

# Chapter 16

April 1989 | Washington, District of Columbia

The sun seared into Mac's retina after a night of restlessness. His head pounded in cadence from the previous day's poison and his nausea was robust. He stared at the ceiling, hot and swollen, and his hamster wheel ran again:

*What am I going to say to him?*

He thought of the late-nights concocting dreams and plans together.

*We've lost so many years.*

I owe my career to Dennis.

*I wish I wouldn't have called.*

He thought of the family holiday card, *they looked so happy*.

The North Dakota prairie and a brilliant sunrise.

*I'd drift off the sleep.*

*What happened?* Perhaps he didn't want to explain who he had become. He considered the strength it would take to face someone who knew him at his core. Dennis changed his life and it felt unfair to meet him under these circumstances, but he was desperate. Today would be a crossroads and a decision to turn.

Mac arose from bed and popped something to quiet his aching skull. He hoped a blistering shower would seep the alcohol from his pores, but his blood felt viscous inching through his pipes. The hamster wheel ran again while the steaming water poured over his shoulders and collected at his feet. Yesterday replayed in his mind while the steak rotted in the garbage can. The option was still on the table and it gave him a sense of control in a life where he had none.

He paced the house until four o'clock in the evening before realizing he had to go out and get some clothes.

■ ■ ■

Mac cut through traffic at National Airport's Terminal A. The ornate, Roman style building was part of the original airport construction in the 1940s but increasing flights and growing passenger numbers left the terminal congested and chaotic.

Mac parked his truck in the '*Arrivals*' section and waited for Captain Dennis Cullen. He pulled his watch out of his pocket and regarded the hands. *Five after five.* He'd have some time to let the hamster wheel run again while each second ticked along, protracted and stale. The airport he considered home was the product of Franklin D. Roosevelt unilaterally reallocating $15 million to its construction because he was "tired of waiting for Congress." It was lobbied to be part of Virginia instead of the District of Columbia to clarify liquor tax revenue, and construction was completed as the US entered WWII. The 1970s brought a new metro rail to the growing airport and talks of new terminal buildings were in the works, though remained years away. The dull ring of yesterday's headache lingered but his uneasiness called for another drink.

He looked at his watch again. *Quarter after five.* His shoulders were tight and contracted with every passing minute. Foot tapping on the truck floor, he kept his eyes locked on the terminal exit. *I could tell him I'm sick.* The triple engine rumble of a Northwest Airlines 727 cut through the dusk and loose moisture rested on his forehead. *Five twenty.* He watched a family of four emerge through the sliding doors, rolling suitcases behind them and a crop of uniformed pilots passed by. He hadn't always been an anxious man, but today turmoil kindled its grip.

The glass doors opened and Mac's eyes locked on an aged face he recognized. The sharpness of his jaw had dissipated and his black pilot uniform with four golden captain's bars fit snug about his waist. Pulling his suitcase behind him, he smiled at Mac in a big way. Mac stood by the headlights after opening the passenger door reluctant but present.

"Mac, you son of a bitch!" Dennis wrapped his arms around him without reluctance. "How the hell are you doing?" He shook him by the shoulder before getting a good look at him.

"It's good to see you, Dennis," Mac smiled but felt weary. He put Dennis's suitcase in the bed of the truck and they both climbed into the cab. "So, you're ditching the rest of the crew tonight?" Mac put the truck in drive and tried to make his voice sound light, though the effort was draining.

"I've traveled with these guys before and they're boring as shit," the truck navigated through parked cars and goodbyes. "The copilot never wants to spend a penny and the flight attendants just go back to their hotel and sleep."

"Are you hungry?" They pulled out of the airport and drove north along the Georgetown Washington Memorial Parkway.

"You bet I am, I don't eat that shitty food in the airport anyway." Unhurried waters of the Potomac River passed on their right, over which erected the pearly white stone of the Washington Monument. Rows of Arlington National Cemetery tombstones stood in perfect interval on the left, glowing in the District's moon.

Words came gradually easier and they spoke like the old friends they were as the truck rumbled over the Arlington Memorial Bridge into the District of Columbia. *"...and then you puked out the back door?!" Dennis could hardly contain himself. "I'll never forget it!"*

The brilliant white hue of the Lincoln Memorial grew as they neared the classic Greek-style temple at the entrance of the District. The radiant Yule marble of Colorado sparkled in the moonlit sky and the thirty-six Doric columns towered high above the traffic honking and sputtering around the memorial circle. "It's beautiful," said Dennis.

"The columns represent each of the states in the union at the time of Lincoln's death," said Mac. All the effort he put in his sanguine façade was gradually replaced with genuine spirit. He pointed to etching lit along the top of the temple, "the forty-eight states that were in union when the memorial was finished are inscribed along the top." Dennis leaned forward off the seat and struggled to soak in the entire scene.

"I've been flying into DC for years, but I've never really taken much time to check out the city," said Dennis.

"Should we do a little driving tour?" asked Mac. He let himself fall into the moment and be pulled along its momentum. Dennis agreed and the truck made a quick turn off the Parkway and headed towards Constitution Avenue.

Taxi cabs darted between lanes as they drove along the National Mall, filled with spectators relishing the cherry blossom trees just starting to pink in the springtime air.

"The Washington Monument was built in two phases," Mac spoke as Dennis's eyes were locked on the soaring silver edifice on the right. "They started in 1848 but stopped in the midst of the Civil War," Dennis opened the window to get a better view. "Abraham Lincoln ordered construction to continue as a symbol of a preserved union twenty years later." His finger pointed at the base, "if you look close enough, you can see where the brick color changes from the two periods of construction."

"I'll be damned," Dennis squinted and looked back across the cab. "You know a lot about this stuff, Mackie." It had been years since he'd come down to the National Mall and he was recollecting what he loved about this city.

"When it was completed, it was the tallest structure in the world," he added.

Dennis's head was again nearly out of the window, gazing up at the pyramid on the memorial's pointed tip. "Amazing how things have changed."

*Things have changed so much, my friend.* It was the first time he had been with Dennis in the city since moving over fifteen years before. It didn't take long for Mac to recognize the person who changed his life and the warm hug of nostalgia soothed.

■ ■ ■

"To Doctor Bet's shitty weather course," said Dennis ceremoniously. They raised their glasses high over the white tablecloth lit by the velvety light of a candle and clinked glasses.

"Here, here," Mac laughed. The red oak paneling and the swanky green carpet made the restaurant feel cozy amidst the troves of DC elite conversing over dinner.

*The Monocle* was an iconic restaurant nestled on D street in the Capitol Hill neighborhood only a few miles from Congress. Historically frequented by heavy hitters like John F. Kennedy and Richard Nixon, it was Mac's favorite restaurant in the city. He used to bring Susan downtown to enjoy the sweet smell of baked salmon or buttery Maryland crab, but it had been years since they'd come. Now, he sat across from Dennis among muffled laughter and the misty sounds of wine falling into crystal.

"So, how are things going, my friend?" asked Dennis. The red wine was half out of his glass and in his body.

Mac adjusted his fork, "things are going pretty well here actually."

"I heard what happened to Eastern Airlines, Mac. It's terrible."

"Yes, it was a pretty big blow," he exhaled. Dennis waited while Mac looked at his hands, "I was laid off a few weeks ago."

"That's what I figured," he leaned back on his seat. "I heard from some buddies at Northwest that they laid off most of the pilots at their Washington station." Dennis watched his friend while Mac tried to disappear. The thoughts conjured a familiar mood. "It looks like you've lost some weight."

"Really? I haven't noticed," said Mac.

"Yes, it looks like that shirt is about to fall off you," he smiled. "Are you eating?" Mac shifted in his chair.

"Apparently not as much as you," Mac raised his eyebrows.

Dennis's eyes brightened. He slapped the table and bellied a round laugh. "Well, you have me there!" Mac admired the novel roundness of his face and wondered where the waitress was, even though food sounded burdensome. "So, what have you been up to if you're not flying, Mac?"

Mac hesitated, "I've been keeping myself pretty busy around the house," his words were glib. "Working on projects I haven't had the chance to do."

"I never really fancied you much of a handyman," he pressed.

"You know," he stumbled over his words, "just reading books I meant to get to and what not."

"And how is Susan?" *Please, let's not.*

"Susan is," he paused. A waiter balancing a tray stacked with plates shuffled by. "Busy with work."

"I'm sure she is, a high-class gal like that!" Mac tried to smile but looked away. "Maybe you can be a stay at home dad after all," Dennis said playfully but it hurt more than he could know.

"I guess so," their momentum began to sputter and Mac wondered what else there was to say. Muffled laughs came from a woman a few tables over and a host escorted an elderly couple in a tailcoat and evening gown to a table past them.

"Listen Mac," Dennis's elbows pressed into the table, "I know you're probably in a tough place but," he hunched his shoulders forward and leaned over his plate, "I would be happy to try and get you plugged in at Northwest."

Mac felt his face get red and his chin came to his chest. A hefty man in a blazer too small shuffled past their table mumbling some pardon. "It's okay, Dennis," he didn't look up. The cloak of humiliation draped over him and he wanted to fade into the busy Washington street. "I didn't mean to..." his voice lingered, "this wasn't about a job."

"It would really be no problem, Mac." Dennis's teeth were a light shade of red from the wine and the air was thick.

"It's okay, Dennis, I will be fine," he looked out of the window and felt insignificant. "I'm not sure if I'm ready to go back to flying anyway."

"What else would you do?" Dennis gulped down the last of his wine, fueling the impetus. "All we know how to do is shuttle people around."

"I just don't know if I'm ready to go back." Mac studied the subtlety of his hands and let his jaw swing open in anticipation for the words to come. "Honestly, things with Susan have been pretty hard lately," Dennis stroked his round face with a finger and thumb. "I just don't know her anymore."

"It wouldn't be the first time a pilot's marriage fell on hard times, my friend."

"I know but it's different, Dennis," he looked up. "She hardly talks to me anymore…" his voice fell. "She's cut me out of her life."

"How long has this been going on?" his fingers were interlaced, propped up on his elbows.

"It's been years."

'Do you want to leave her?"

"Of course I don't," his eyes shot up. "I love her." Dennis studied across the table but didn't say anything. Mac didn't know if it was honesty or a wish, but he wasn't surprised by his defense. "I'm not sure how much longer I can go on like this."

A waiter appeared beside their table, "Looks good!" she had a plate in each hand. Her hair was greased back tight out of her face and the whites of her eyes were clear and round. "Now, who ordered the chicken?" Her voice was high and animated, and Mac wanted to vomit. He didn't try to smile and simply waited for her to go. They began to eat in the restaurant's symphony of clanging silverware, popping corks, and muffled conversation.

"What are you going to do, Mackie?" There was only silence until Dennis mouthed his third bite. Mac pushed some potatoes around his plate and wondered why he agreed to see him. He felt tired and couldn't stomach the salmon.

"I'm not sure," he thought about the garage and his truck waiting for him. *I'll drift off to sleep.* "I'm not sure what I'm going to do."

Dennis took another bite and slapped his fork on the table. He chewed openly and rubbed his round chin. "Listen, Mac. I don't know what to say. Jesus, I mean look at you," he raised his hands. "You look like shit!" Mac looked up but didn't smile. He didn't know what he wanted from him, but it wasn't this. Dennis raised his brows. "Maybe it's time to find something new."

"What do you mean new?" The words came out reflexively and sharp.

"Maybe a new job or a hobby," he leaned forward unfazed and shoveled another bite. "Something that will bring you *joy.*" The meat jostled between his teeth. "When's the last time you felt that?" he pointed with the prongs of his fork.

Mac took a sip of water.

"Volunteer or something, Mac. Maybe work for the Boy Scouts and bring them flying." Mac tapped his fingers on the table, thinking. He wasn't sure if there was anything left for him to give. "You're still a flight instructor, right?" he asked.

Mac's eyes furrowed and he crossed his arms on the table. "I haven't flown a small airplane in years," Mac's mind percolated. He had earned his instructor credentials in college but was hired by the airlines so quickly he never used the training. The teaching license never expired but he was nowhere near ready to jump into a two-seat trainer and teach someone how to fly. "What does that matter?"

"If you're not ready to go back to the airlines, why don't you do some flight instruction?" said Dennis as he picked something out of his teeth. "Go fly around with some people who *pay* to do it because what we do is *fun*. Remember?"

Mac sat back in his chair and looked out the window into the busy Washington night. Bundled office workers were scurrying home with briefcases and honking taxis swerved between cars trying to maximize their tip. He thought of flying over the snowy North Dakota countryside when things were simpler. The exhilaration of being freed from earth's pull for the first time was something he'd never forget.

"Go to a local airport and apply for an instructor job," he said. "You can do it for a few months and then apply into the airlines when you're ready." Dennis mopped up everything on his plate with a piece of bread. "You won't have trouble getting back into the airlines."

"There is a flight school not too far from my house," said Mac distantly. He considered the idea for a moment, but it felt senseless. He was an airline pilot and hadn't flown in a Cessna 172 since he graduated from UND.

"There you go, pal. Give it a shot," said Dennis. He spoke with a coolness he used in all matters of life, but Mac sensed he recognized the consequence of the moment. "Things will look up, man. Know I'm always on your side." His words meant more than he could know.

■ ■ ■

Mac drove Dennis over the Francis Scott Key Bridge into Arlington while the moon was full in the sky. The towering spires of Georgetown University passed on their right and the ivory marble of the Kennedy Center for the Arts was nestled along the Potomac on their left. Something previously dormant stirred inside Mac.

"Thanks for picking me up," said Dennis as he climbed out of the truck under the hotel awning.

"Of course," Mac pulled the suitcase out of the bed of his truck and passed it to the pilot.

"Gain some weight, okay?" Dennis's blazer was draped over one hand and his wheeled pilot cap sat atop his head, "you look sick."

"Only if you cut back on the snacks out of the cart," Mac wedged. "You're looking a little round." Dennis laughed and they embraced.

"Good luck, Mac and stay in touch," said Dennis. *Thank you, my friend.*

As Mac pulled the pickup away from the hotel, Dennis stood waving one final time. Traveling west out of Arlington on Highway 66, Mac smiled.

# Chapter 17

February 2016 | Pacific Ocean

"There are no other pilots aboard, Julie," said Shari into the cabin phone. She had paged through the passenger manifest hoping there would be a company pilot heading to a Hawaiian beach vacation among the passengers. "I guess it's just us."

"Appoint someone in the cabin to take your role," voiced Julie. She was chewing her pinky nail as she spoke into the phone. "You'll assist me into Honolulu." Shari acknowledged and the call ended. This was part of the lead flight attendant's job as third in command. If things went south, she was to maximize life.

The first officer called the airline to inform them the purser would be assisting in their approach. *Do what you need to do, Julie,* said the chief pilot, *just get that plane on the ground.*

The doctor came into the flight deck and gave a detailed list of the medical needs for the injured over the phone. "We have one deceased on board," she said to Hawaiian controllers, "the captain will need immediate transport to the nearest stroke center." She knew if too much time passed, he would not be eligible for the medication. "An ambulance must be ready immediately when we get into Honolulu." Every second counted.

"Megan, why don't you sit on the crew seat in the galley with the captain when we land," said Julie. *Crew resource management.* Now in command, her charge was to ensure each member of her team was in the right place doing the right job. "If anything changes, let me know immediately over the galley phone." The doctor agreed and Julie hoped her sturdy face masked her apprehension.

Shari sat in the captain's seat and walked through the checklist as they approached Oahu. *Twenty minutes out.* Shari called out each line item on the approach checklist and her cadence granted Julie ease. *We can do this.* The massive ship descended out of the clouds and made for the pulsing lights of the runway. *I'm about to land a wide-body airliner with a flight attendant as my co-pilot.* She wished there was someone to reassure her but knew the buck stopped with her. *First, fly the airplane.* Her heart thumped with resolve knowing the culmination of her intentional studying and training prepared her for this moment.

The low roar of air catching the extended flaps reverberated in the cabin and three instrument lights turned green. *Landing gear down.*

"Jet Stream one forty-four heavy, Honolulu approach. You're cleared to land runway 8 right," the controller broke through the radio.

"Cleared to land, runway 8 right, Jet Stream one forty-four heavy," Julie responded. Responsibilities are typically split during a complicated approach like Honolulu's International Airport. While one pilot flies the aircraft to the runway, the other will operate the radios, navigate, and monitor the engines. *Tonight, I do nearly everything.*

"Call out the before landing checklist," said Julie without looking at Shari. *Focus, breathe.*

The senior flight attendant was strapped in over her shoulders and a pair of yellow reading glasses were perched at the end of her nose. The greying crew member's eyes peered over her glasses when she looked to the sea.

Shari started at the top:

"LANDING GEAR..."

"...down," Julie responded mechanically.

"AUTOPILOT..."

"...off."

"AUTOTHROTTLE..."

"...off."

"LANDING SPEED..."

"...one hundred and forty-five knots." They continued.

The hue from Honolulu grew closer in the ocean darkness. Lights purred from the skyscrapers in downtown and highlighted the white sandy beaches crashed by rolling waves. To their right, the Pacific Ocean extended thousands of miles to South America while the looming summit of Diamond Head thrust from the horizon off their nose. Hawaiians knew the peak as Le'ahi because the ridgeline resembles the shape of an ahi tuna dorsal fin, but British sailors mistook calcite crystal as diamond and gave the mountain the name it retains today.

"We're ready to land," declared Julie. *We can do this.*

The vast landing gear hurtled through the salty air over one hundred and sixty miles per hour and descended closer to the earth. Cars motoring along Highway H1 came into focus and the masts of battle ships ported in Pearl Harbor towered into the night. Vacationers milled Waikiki Beach lit only by the moon and a golden hue from incredible hotel super-structures off the Pacific.

Julie exhaled and pulled the wing flaps back to full deployment. The flashing lights of emergency vehicles were positioned along the north end of the field marking the end of their target. *We made it to Honolulu.*

The twenty-nine-year-old pilot guided one of the most complicated machines humans have created over the beach and the airport boundary fence. *Touchdown speed one hundred and forty knots.* Over the runway threshold, she pulled the throttles back and lightly pulled the nose up just above the asphalt. Like a wilted flower peddle, they were back on earth.

"Jet Stream one forty-four heavy, turn left onto taxiway Kilo contact Honolulu ground on 121.9," said the controller. The engines screamed in reverse and the wing spoilers pulled Bernoulli's lift off the wing. "Contact Honolulu ground 121.9, Jet Stream one forty-four heavy," Julie confirmed the controller's direction.

Shari took off her glasses and brought her forehead to her hand. Her exhale filled the cockpit and she seemed to sag into her seat. The muscles and tissue holding her bones and metabolic stew together relaxed and she shook her head subtly. Julie pressed the left rudder pedal and pulled onto taxiway Kilo with a deep sigh. *We made it.* The flight attendant eyed the pilot and smiled but Julie knew their work was far from over. Controllers vectored the 767 to the terminal with emergency vehicles following closely behind. *We need to get the captain off this plane.* With glowing orange wands, the ground crew guided Julie into the gate and she quickly ran through the run-down procedures by memory. The engines began to whine down while Julie pulled her headset off and leaned back in her seat.

"You did it, Julie," Shari's eyes were tearful, and directly pointed to her, "You should be really proud." The copilot pulled the harness off her shoulders and laughed nervously. It was hard to believe. *Tonight, I was tested.* She had a reflexive urge to call her Mom and purge every detail of their dire tale, an outlet she'd depended on often in her life, but knew the night was only beginning.

"We all did it, Shari," said the pilot. Julie felt a human yearning to comfort her for the loss of a friend. "We should all be proud." Shari gave her more strength tonight than she could possibly know. *Three strong women together.*

"Ladies and gentlemen, this is the first officer speaking," Julie spoke into the public-address system curtly before climbing out of her seat. "Please remain seated until directed." *My work isn't over yet.* She unlocked the cockpit door to find the gate already pulled to the plane and the boarding door open. In the mouth of the jet bridge, half a dozen person army stood at attention and ready for orders. They waited for her to speak.

"Medical personnel first," she directed, and the group jumped into action. Captain Robert Frank was still strapped into the crew seat in the galley and Dr. Delaney sat beside him.

"Can you walk, Mac?" asked the doctor. The captain nodded as the paramedics stepped into the galley.

"This is a physician," Julie said to the medical crew. "You will follow her direction."

"Yes, ma'am," said the brawny medic. "Sir, allow me to help you to the ambulance." The captain stood unsteadily on his feet with Megan at one arm and the medic on the other.

"Mac," Julie lowered her head to meet her superior's eye as he got to his feet. "I will find you in the hospital," she said. She recognized an agony only another pilot could understand in his eyes. "I'll take good care of your airplane." The captain and doctor filed through the door and into a different world, now fouler and more complicated.

*One emergency down.* She collected her thoughts and turned to face the cabin and its occupants. Looking down the aisle, over five hundred eyes stared squarely back at her.

No one moved. It was perfectly silent.

Shari came up from behind her and rested a hand on her shoulder. *You saved us, Julie.*

The first officer held her breath. *What do I do?*

A woman in the second row brought her hands together and another passenger followed suit. The third and fourth row trailed along and soon every seat in the first-class cabin was clapping. The sentiment spread like wildfire. Within seconds the entire ship erupted in ovation.

*You saved us, Julie.*

For an instant, her heart didn't ache, her shoulders relaxed, and she breathed easy. *We did this together.* She waved and smiled amidst the high-octane joy.

■ ■ ■

The ambulance rocked like a ship riveted in storm. Mac's head lay on the stretcher and the movements magnified his disorientation. *It's louder than I thought it'd be.* He grit his teeth against ferocious nausea. *There's nothing left to throw-up.* The wailing sirens accompanied the harsh fluorescent lights and cuff squeezing above his elbow. He always wondered what it was like inside an ambulance but the only thing he could think about now was escaping this torment.

*What have I done?* His mind was reeling. In command of a wide body airliner only hours before, he was now an indentured patient. *It finally caught up with me.*

"Let's give him some Zofran," said Dr. Delaney beside the medic. The siren was sharp and pervasive. "Try to relax Mac, this should make you feel better." *She didn't have to come but she did.* Mac was grateful for a familiar face and closed his eyes to let them work.

*I killed someone tonight.*

. . .

"Julie, you have to go directly to your hotel room," said a union lawyer. He had been dispatched when the airline was notified. "You'll be stampeded by the press," his thumbs hooked into his belt and he paced in a private office in Honolulu International Airport. "There is already cell phone footage out there of what happened tonight." He was uneasy and she wondered what part of tonight she was most anxious about.

"I need to see Mac," she said. She picked at her fingernail and looked exhausted.

"This is a big deal, Julie," he pointed at her. "This is going to make news." Julie didn't say anything. "Someone died and there is going to be an FAA investigation." Recollecting, the night felt dreamlike and abstract. "It is my professional opinion you do not speak to the captain," he stood squarely.

# Chapter 18

September 1999 | Washington, District of Columbia

Standing on the taxiway with an aeronautical radio in hand, Mac cupped his eyes from the sun. At the north end of the runway, he watched the single engine, high wing trainer wait at the foot of the runway. The sky was painted with vast wisps of clouds high in the troposphere and a warm breeze sifted between each strand of his hair. He pulled the watch weighing in his pocket and checked the time, his body buzzing in anticipation: 1:15 pm. It was the perfect day for flying.

The engine purred and the Cessna 172 pulled onto the active runway. "Leesburg Airport, Cessna four papa three eight departing runway three five, closed traffic," the familiar voice of his 17-year old student broke through the radio. He had grown to admire her during the dozen hours of her flight training and today, her diligent study and practice would be put to the test.

Her instructor backed his pick-up truck beside the taxiway and stood on the bed to follow her every move. His anticipation swelled with hers. *I have given the gift of flight.* Like a symphony growing into its peak, the engine roared and the craft accelerated down the runway. Today, was her first solo.

Mac met a turning point in becoming an instructor at Leesburg Executive Airport at Godfrey Field. He formed intimate connections with dozens of students and lit up alongside them as they discovered the magic of aviation. The lush green fields of southern Maryland and the rolling farms of northern Virginia were a breath-taking backdrop to guide new pilots to their wings. Students of all ages sat beside him: a stay-at-home mother of three, a twenty-five-year-old airline hopeful, and even a sixty-seven-year-old retiree. Despite the thirty new pilots he'd trained over the past few years, there was something special in this student. It seemed he was unlocking something that enabled her to evolve into the person she was supposed to be.

The forward wheel navigated down the centerline of the runway and her speed grew. An abundant woodland lay beyond her wings and a busy highway bustled to the south of the field. He peered through the cabin window and could see her broad smile as she passed him along the runway. *Elation.* It was a feeling he recognized. The nose slowly came off the ground and the airplane rose into the air. It was a central moment in the journey of a pilot.

Mac was quick to become a respected instructor in Leesburg. After a handshake deal with the flight school owner, Mac signed on and was surprised to find no shortage of students interested in flying. Within a few weeks, his schedule quickly filled, and the airport was soon to feel like a second home. The field was originally built for radio personality Arthur Godfrey to access his personal DC-3 but was later purchased by the city in response to growing aviation demands in the Washington region. Its proximity to the District of Columbia offered remarkable airplane spotting and its location in the rolling hills of the Virginia countryside brought stunning views from the air.

As he watched the Cessna soar into a left bank on its return to the field, Mac tried to put his finger on what it was that made this student so unique.

The high schooler's aptitude for flight was obvious and her encyclopedic knowledge impressive but, importantly, working with her demanded he be the best pilot he could possibly be. It was hard to not notice her jitters manifested as occasional nail biting, but she remained focused and curious during each step of her training. Every day of his career was spent around aviation but there was something special about teaching her that reignited a spark within him that once was a flame. While fostering something in his students, he was nurturing something within himself. The opportunity to teach her was a gift.

"Leesburg Airport, Cessna four papa three eight turning downwind for runway three five, closed traffic," her voice was calm over the radio. She piloted the airplane parallel with the runway one thousand feet above the ground. The sky was so pure it begged to be reached out and touched. Mac exhaled and smiled. *Peace.* Teaching brought new purpose in his life and he found the space to experience the same awe and wonder he had years before.

His student lined the Cessna up with the end of the runway, her wings gliding over the trees. The flaps extended from the wing's aft, slowing her speed and increasing her lift, as she neared the earth. The engine rumbled and she floated just above the runway until the squeak of the wheels announced her safe return. Mac waved his arms high above his head, signaling his congratulations. Pride ran through his veins.

"Leesburg Airport, Cessna four papa three eight departing runway three five," the crackle of the radio broke through his excitement as she announced her departure again. The engine reared in full force and the airplane accelerated down the runway until she again leapt into the air. There was no better moment for an instructor in the world.

■ ■ ■

She was committed to earning her private pilot's license before going to college in a few months and he worked to see her dream come true. He sat his kitchen table early each morning closely reviewing the material he would teach her while they flew.

The pace at which she consumed knowledge pushed him and she didn't falter with his increasing rigor. The challenge was exciting, and the work consumed him. Before long, the next milestone in her training approached with much anticipation. Cross country flying signaled an evolution in training, from the early fundamentals of air field work to the freedom of flying across land and water. Mac transitioned from lecturing about maneuvers and airfield operations to distance navigation and weather. It was one of his favorite phases of a student's expedition because it enabled the chance to discover thousands of regional airports and their many attractions. With a new type of flying came new challenges and the opportunities for a student to demonstrate their skill.

They agreed that her first cross country flight would be to Williamsburg, Virginia, a historic Victorian town nestled between the York and James River just off the Atlantic Coast. Views from the sky revealed stunning rows of colonial, brick structures dating back to the Revolutionary War, bounded by rolling hills of rural Virginia life. When Mac made it out to the region, he made it a point to show students the campus of the College of William and Mary just outside of town. With its sandy brick academic buildings and pristinely manicured grounds, it stood as the second oldest institution of higher learning after Harvard University and was easy to recognize from the sky. Importantly, Mac liked Williamsburg for Charly's Airport Restaurant, certainly a local favorite. Airplane parking right on the field allowed for a quick break and the opportunity to feast on a notoriously massive double cheeseburger. It didn't take much to convince his student to make a stop.

■ ■ ■

Cirrus clouds whisked across the Saturday morning sun on the day of their flight. He reviewed her flight plan in detail and was impressed with the preparation. He quizzed her contingency plans for changing weather or an engine failure but, as he had grown to expect, she came prepared to fly.

"Tell me about our weight and balance," said Mac. Calculating the distribution of fuel and passenger weight often challenged students and it was a favorite assessment.

"With full tanks of fuel, we're 2,100 pounds with a moment arm of 41 inches, putting our center of gravity within the normal limits," she said smiling. The nail of her little finger came to her mouth, but she pulled it away and blushed when Mac smiled. She loved the challenge but today would push beyond her comfort.

"Good," he tried not to give too much, "and tell me about our route." They sat at a table in the pilot-lounge overlooking the tarmac. Several single engine trainers were tied down beside the fuel pump beyond the windows and the muted smell of burnt popcorn from the machine imbued the room.

The student pulled out her aeronautical sectional chart, a detailed depiction of visual landmarks used for navigation, and pointed out a pencil line charting their route. "Williamsburg is one hundred and twenty-seven miles to the south of the field at a heading of one hundred and sixty-six degrees," she referred to a three hundred a sixty-degree compass. "Winds are from the west at twelve knots at our altitude, so I calculate we'll need to fly a heading of one hundred and seventy-four degrees for one hour and twenty-five minutes." Mac raised his brows and nodded. Her hands pointed on the map, "and if you were going to ask, I have two diversion airports in mind if things get hairy up there," she smiled. "Or if you need a bathroom break."

They ran the checklists, started the engine, and soared. She flew with a precision he had seen in few and an intensity that was infectious. After pointing out campus landmarks and blocks of brick buildings in the Victorian downtown, she glided the Cessna over a winding river and wooded marsh into Williamsburg airport. Adjacent to the single runway, Mac treated his student to a famous hamburger and before long the two were back in the air returning home.

■ ■ ■

Five thousand feet above the ground, Mac gazed across the rolling hills of the southeast Virginia countryside. Trees just beginning to change painted the landscape and the edge of the Blue Ridge Mountains grew out of the lush valleys below. It was no mystery why so many songs and poems tried to capture its splendor. Abundant, green fields of hay connected with wooded brooks and streams intertwined by twisting farm roads and old tractors between them. The familiar hum of the roaring pistons in the engine was a peaceful accompaniment to the scene before them.

Time between airports in cross country flying provided prime opportunity for new pilots to critically think through simulated emergencies. The cabin was quiet, and his student was also admiring the stunning Virginia landscape. Without disrupting the silence, he reached to the instrument panel and pulled the engine to idle. Both pilots were pressed into their harnesses as the airplane slowed and began to glide.

"This is a simulated engine failure," said Mac flatly and the student's eyes expanded as if awoken from a daydream. She hesitated a moment longer than Mac expected but ultimately reached for the checklist.

"We're at five thousand feet," she began to pick at her thumb nail with her teeth. "Let's get through the engine checklist and attempt a restart." Mac nodded, satisfied with her plan. She brought the Cessna into a slow constant descent and passed him the laminated paper to begin calling out each line.

"AIRSPEED, SIXTY-EIGHT KNOTS," said Mac.

"Sixty-eight knots," she responded in tempo.

"FUEL SELECTOR, BOTH," he continued, and she followed in time. Her actions were gaining momentum.

The airplane drifted towards the earth as he ran through each line, "AUXILIARY FUEL PUMP SWIT…" Air immediately stopped blowing through his vocal chords. There was a precise and acute moment where everything changed, and he felt suspended in time.

*What the hell is going on?*

The checklist fell out of his hand and he clasped his palm over his chest. Crushing fear enveloped him and his chest squeezed. It was a sensation he had never before endured.

His heart suddenly began to fire with the relentless cadence of an automatic machine gun. *Can I breathe?* He pushed his fist into his chest. Dread oozed from each pore, feeling powerless and bound.

Several seconds on unyielding discharges left him stunned and the final beat was powerful and terminal. Nothing came after it. The silence filled him with terror. *Am I dying?* He wanted to cough or slam his fist into his chest, hoping it would act again. It finally conceded but the pattern continued.

*Boom, boom, boom, boom….*

*Pause… Pause…*

*Boom, boom…*

*Pause…*

*Boom, boom, boom, boom, boom…*

The feeling was alien and unwelcome but did not recede. His abdomen roiled and he held his breath while the student studied his colorless face.

"Are you okay?" the airplane continued to descend amidst the purr of the idling engine. Mac was so aware of the chaos in his chest that he couldn't get a word out. The heat of flames engulfed him and his skin misted.

*Is this when I die?*

"Mac," she elbowed him. "Are you okay?" She reached to the panel and pressed the throttle forward, bringing the engine back into full roar. His vision blurred like a dream and he forced himself to inhale.

*Boom...*

*Pause... Pause... Pause...*

*Boom, boom, boom, boom...*

*Pause...*

*Boom, boom...*

He strained to focus his thoughts and mind. *Do I feel pain?* Its void was filled with terror.

"End the exercise, Mac," her voice cracked. "What's going on?" The high schooler brought the airplane into a climb and kept the wings level. She used the nail of her index finger to tool at the skin around her thumb.

"Let's head back to the field," he said searching to find the beat of his pulse on the inside of his wrist.

"Are you air sick or something?" she tried to lighten the mood, not knowing the gravity unfolding. Her eyes showed her concern as her nail began to bleed and she leaned forward into the straps.

"Something like that," he pulled out the map and searched for their location on the route.

*Boom...*

*Pause... Pause... Pause...*

*Boom, boom, boom, boom...*

*Pause...*

*Boom, boom...*

"We've got about twenty minutes before we make it to Leesburg," she said. She studied the sectional chart and pointed to their location. "Do we need to find somewhere to land before that?"

*I hope I'm still speaking in twenty minutes.* A man of faultless health, his body surged with bewilderment and terror. It was impossible to ignore the knocking in his chest but he strained to focus his mind on the task before him. Fear exacerbated his heart already pumping out of control.

"No, we will make it to Leesburg," he said trying to hold his voice steady. His student reached out and pulled back on the throttle into a cruise setting but Mac came behind and returned the power into the full position.

"Let's get back as quick as we can," he avoided her glance. She looked at him from the corner of her eye and let her teeth take over picking at her thumb nail again. They cruised with a compassionate tail wind and eventually entered the flying pattern around Leesburg's field. The student completed the pre-landing checklists and flew competently while her instructor was quiet. A few hundred feet above the runway, sweet reprieve swept over Mac's entire body. Without notice or proclamation, something again changed. The muscles clenching in his back relaxed and he let his weight fall onto the back of his seat.

*Boom...*

*Boom...*

*Boom...*

*Boom...*

Order was brought to the electrical system of his heart. Beneath his leather jacket, plaid shirt and sternum, Mac's beating heart again squeezed with the timing of a grandfather clock. He popped the window and wallowed in the cool air as his student pulled the airplane onto the next taxiway. The cockpit was quiet until the engine finally sputtered to a stop on the ramp. Mac didn't wait to unlatch the door and ducked his head under the wing to egress out of the trainer.

"I feel better," he said before she could ask any more questions. "I must have been just a little airsick or something." He lied and needed to leave.

"Do we need to bring you to the hospital?" she asked. She climbed out of the plane and threw yellow chalks under the wheels. "You didn't look very good up there, Mac."

"Everything is fine," he barely let her finish. "Let's get the plane cleaned up so we can sign your logbook." She looked up to reply but instead followed his directions.

Mac felt his body go through the motions of packing his headset into his flight bag while his mind raced. *What the hell was that up there?* For the moment, no damage seemed to persist other than lingering uneasiness. It had come and gone so quickly and with such might it left him stunned and confused. There was no explanation. *Should I go to the emergency room?* He was sinking in the pace of his own thoughts. The possibility of seeing a doctor was crushing. *What do I do?* He zipped his bag and could hear the beat of his heart in the cadence he had always known.

*Boom...*

*Boom...*

*Boom...*

*Boom...*

*I can't go to the doctor.* He thought about his student and all the things that could've happened in the air. *I will lose my pilot's license.* He knew regulations required him to stop flying until he was assessed by a doctor, but he also knew what seeking care would mean.

Flight doctors are cautious, always erring on the side of safety, and this report would certainly conclude one way. There would be immediate grounding, maybe the end of his career. The fleeting thought of life without flying seared through his mind and the prospect harbored implications far worse than any palpitations. *Nothing would be left.* There was a responsibility to do the right thing, yet his retort seemed unclear. *It was just a fluke, right?* He grabbed his bag and walked into the hanger tall, compensating for the prowling sense of vulnerability. *A pilot with a heart condition?* Another job with the airlines would forever remain a dream.

■ ■ ■

Mac drove Highway 7 silently and ate dinner at home that evening perturbed. Lying sleepless in his bed, he contemplated the consequences of what happened. The thoughts about his empty house and the child he didn't have soon followed. *The right thing would be to report it no matter the consequences.* His breathing quickened and he tossed in bed. *My broken marriage.* His students and a stunning sunset over the rural Virginia countryside eddied. *It was probably nothing.* He knew too many pilots whose careers ended with such a misstep. *What would be left if I couldn't fly?* He decided he would wait while his heart throbbed beneath the sheets. *It won't happen again.* He would fly again tomorrow.

*No one can know.*

# Chapter 19

February 2000 | Washington, District of Columbia

"Listen Mac," spat Susan and he recoiled, "I honestly don't care what you do with your life but it's time to grow up. You need to stop sulking around this house and that airport and get a real job."

"You don't care what I do with *my life?*" he said trying not to manifest his wound. "Susan, what about *our life?*"

"What do you mean?" she stood across the kitchen with her arms crossed over her chest. The two discorded like water and oil sharing a vessel.

"Don't try to tell me you don't see what's happening," his voice cracked. "We have completely fallen apart, and I don't know what's left to pick up." He tried to swallow but the muscles were tight. His skin was hot and his fists clenched.

"Are you just realizing this now, Mac?" she leaned forward and pointed as she spoke. "We have been for years." Each syllable cut through him like a hot knife. It was the first time he'd heard her acknowledge what chewed him.

A bitter stiffness filled the cavity between each opponent and for a moment he thought the unbridled pluck of tears would follow. Susan had returned home after a two-week unexpected absence and Mac woke the growing beast between them when he inquired.

"Of course, I've known, Susan," he tried to abate his peeling voice. "Because I *love* you and I've always wanted to glue the pieces back together." He looked at her desperately. *Please, Susan.* She rolled her eyes and turned away.

"Mac, you have no idea what I do every day," her back was towards him. "I save people's lives and watch people die. You've never understood that."

"I've tried, Susan, but you've pushed me away," he moved closer to her but kept his distance. "I tried to be what you wanted."

"Don't give me that bullshit, Mac," she flipped around and cocked her head. "Is that why you were fucking that flight attendant for all those years?" Her pointed finger was like a bullet. "Don't even try to tell me you tried." He was stunned.

"Susan, I..." his voice weakened. He stepped back against the counter, astounded and overwhelmed.

"You what, Mac? You're different than all those other pilots?" her eyes were fiery red.

"Susan, I..." he couldn't finish. He wanted to explain but emotion clawed at his throat. What was there to say? He felt precariously stuck in the simultaneous states of rejected sufferer and unscrupulous offender. Ultimately, it was she he wanted, but his provisional fill for her inescapable void had only driven her further away.

"I...." he tried to get a word out, but the vertiginous flurry of nihility suffused.

Leaning against the counter, his focus shifted as a familiar sensation enveloped him with a new, spectacular grip. Shame and loneliness faded behind a dreadful, careening awareness that was tearing its way forward. *No.* He could hear his heart beating in his ears and he squeezed his fists. An acute and finite moment changed everything and nothing else mattered.

*Boom...*

*Boom...*

*Boom...*

A familiar pressure grew in his chest like something trying to escape through his breastbone. *Please, no.* His breathing quickened and his vision greyed in the corners of the room. Doused in boiling water, his skin ailed and his pupils expanded. The urge to run surged but there was nowhere to hide. He leaned heavily against the kitchen counter and stared vacantly. If his pulse clipped at any faster rate, it may have ejected through his chest.

"Mac, calm down," she faced him but scowled. He didn't say anything because it had started again.

*Boom, boom, boom....*

*Pause...*

*Pause...*

*Pause...*

*Boom, boom...*

*Pause,*

*Boom, boom, boom, boom...*

"Mac," her tone abated, and he fell into one of the kitchen chairs a few steps away. Barrages of contractions were followed by deafening pauses. They lasted a second or two before the cycle began again. *It's here.* It was a sensation he would never forget.

"My heart," he said still holding his chest, "I feel like it's beating so quickly." He gritted his teeth and ached with the mayhem below his ribs. Susan approached, her eyes indifferent and annoyed, and pressed two fingers inside his wrist. It was the first time he had felt her touch in years.

"Do you have any chest pain, Mac?" her tone was automatic and she stood over him.

It took him a moment to focus on her question, but he finally organized his thoughts. "No, I don't have any pain," she continued to feel his pulse.

*Boom, boom...*

*Pause,*

*Boom, boom, boom...*

"Do you feel light headed?" she didn't move her hand.

"What the hell is happening?" Mac stirred in his seat. Fear was flowing in his veins and he could feel the blood squeezing through the capillaries behind his eyes. *Chaos.* She asked him the question again with a sharper tone and he shook his head. He looked up at her, alarmed and tenuous, "Susan, tell me what is happening."

"Your heart is beating so irregularly," with pursed lips, her voice drifted. Time stood still as she postured above him. "Has this ever happened before?"

*Yes.* He looked away and considered what to say. Her presence was onerous, and she finally moved her hand. He lied.

"Mac, I think you may be in atrial fibrillation," though the anger dissipated, her cold voice remained. *Atrial fibrillation?* He tried to repeat the words. She rolled her eyes, "It's a problem that causes your heart to beat irregularly." The tautness in his neck grew knowing his nightmare had returned. "Mac if this goes on much longer, you need to go to the hospital."

He supported his forehead with his hand. *Go to the hospital?* Collections of his brain's neurons fired vigorously to make sense of the disarray. *Why was this happening again?* "If I go in there, you and I both know what will happen," he didn't look up.

"You won't need a pilot's license if you have a stroke, Mac," she stepped back and propped up her hands on her hips.

"What do you mean a stroke?" leaning back to expand his lungs, he tried to concentrate on his breathing.

"You have to get this figured out Mac," she was annoyed. "If you don't, you're going to have a stroke."

"Why would this make me have a stroke?" the frenzied thumping kept veering his thoughts.

Her lips snapped and she collected her papers off the counter, "blood flow can slow down in the heart and cause a clot to form," she shifted her weight. "It can break loose and shoot into the brain." Her apathy made him sink. "If you have it long enough, you'll need to be cardioverted or take blood thinners."

"You mean I'll need to be shocked?" his eyes darted to her reflexively. She stood in the kitchen as Mac sat below her. *I have always been healthy.* Everything was happening so quickly.

"It's possible," she paused. "And even if it goes away this time, you will probably have it again." She lifted her chin slightly with an arm full of papers. *It's already come and gone.* "Certainly, you will not fly until you get this figured out."

Mac thought about his student and a future at the airline. The rolling Virginia countryside and the searing fear. Reality felt numb and he looked down at his feet, offering nothing.

"Mac, you will *not* fly again until you get this figured out," her eyes were indignant, "Do you understand?" She was bent over him slightly, but his eyes were still away and dejected. *I will lose my license.* He couldn't imagine a meaningful life without his work, and he wondered who he would be if it was ripped from the fleeting seize of his fingers. Mac remained reticent.

She coughed in disbelief and stormed away. He knew his silence said something. "If you fly again, Robert, I am leaving you for good," she spoke over her shoulder as she doubled up the stairs. "I will not be affiliated with someone who will knowingly put people in harm's way." Her eyes scorched and she yelled from the top of the stairs. "Be a man for once, Mac!" she slammed her bedroom door.

Sometime in the night, Mac's heart paced back to its steady beat and he woke up the following morning alone.

■ ■ ■

His student passed her private pilot's check ride with high marks the following Monday and the festive tone was a welcomed distraction. She would be graduating from high school in May and Mac beamed with pride knowing she would be attending his alma mater in the fall. She would follow his footsteps in the commercial aviation program and even mentioned joining the Air National Guard as a military pilot. She would pursue her lifelong dream of being a professional aviator and it brought him more joy than she could know.

As she climbed out of the Cessna for the first time with a certificate in hand, she wrapped her arms around her instructor.

"I'm so proud of you, Julie. You will make an incredible pilot," he said, pride and furor swelling. "It would be my privilege to one day fly with you again."

■ ■ ■

Mac returned home that evening to find Susan's room empty. The closet doors were open and the medicine cabinet cleared out. The bed was made, though the pillows were gone, and the window shades were drawn shut. A note rested on her made bed with two simple words written in red pen:

It's over.

# Chapter 20

June 2011 | Seattle, Washington

Mac gazed through the train window at the vast form expounding from the earth. The clear day was a treasured reprieve from weeks of overcast barring view of the evergreens and purple stone. It was the first day one could appreciate how the warm days of spring had receded the snowy white caps and filled the streams and rivers flowing into Puget Sound. Though it often hid in the clouds, Mac found Mount Rainier's endless presence a source of inner peace and he regarded its majesty with reverence.

The Link Light Rail rocked lightly as it clicked along the track heading south out of the city. The new metro rail connected Seattle's downtown near Elliot Bay to Seattle-Tacoma's International Airport, just under fifteen miles to the south. After decades of turmoil about its construction, the city finally approved the purchase of nearly three hundred properties in the Rainier Valley to build the track that would eventually exceed twenty miles. The project was finished only a single year earlier and Mac rode along its course towards the airport on schedule to begin a week-long trip.

At fifty-seven years old, he'd returned to an early passion during his commutes: reading. As the stunning scenery of the upper Northwest passed beside him, his mind danced amidst pages of fiction. When not on the train, he sat beside stacks of books on an overstuffed chair in his apartment on Capitol Hill, wallowing in rousing lines of war novels and stirring prose of romance. The escape was a meek gift in his new and quiet life. His apartment building was just north of downtown Seattle, nestled between a grimy bar that opened at nine in the morning and a small grocer that sold individual cans of beer. There was one bedroom, no elevator, and hot water that usually worked, a marked change from his suburban house outside of Washington. Regardless of how meager, it was home. He walked his block with caution at night but there was something genuine about the neighborhood. Living with the good and bad in plain sight fostered an authenticity he found both daunting and laudable.

A metallic voice called out each station as the Link Light Rail traveled away from the Puget Sound. A suited businessman read the sports section of *The Seattle Times* across the aisle and a young mother fussed over her baby tucked into a stroller. The warm scent of Chinese take-out provoked his nose, but unlike his neighborhood, the cabin was impeccably clean. Mac had made the trip to the airport from Capitol Hill countless times in his twelve years since moving to the city. He had seen the city grow as new people arrived and evolve as the demographics shifted. Though he lived a private life, he found the energy of the city infectious and the mountains breathtaking.

His stomach grumbled, demanding calories to replace those burned at the weight bench earlier that morning. Massaging his achy thighs, he worked the lactic acid accumulating in his quadriceps. He had become accustomed to starting his day with his heart rate elevated over the past few years and he diligently worked to maintain his routine. *The new me.* Whether in the dark morning hours of a hotel or at the small sports club near his apartment, Mac felt his physical strength grow and his emotional vigor follow suit.

The symptoms hadn't returned since Susan left in 1999. He had spoken to his wife only a few times over the subsequent years, mostly details about selling their house and dividing up furniture, but the period was more trying that Mac could have ever known. When Susan mailed Mac their divorce papers, he signed them without struggle. There was nothing to fight for and the only option that remained was to start a new life. He transitioned his students to other instructors and looked for work flying with the airlines, longing for the only identity that ever felt true. The path back into commercial aviation would likely be difficult, with low seniority calling for flights on holidays and weekends, but it didn't bother him much. There was no longer a reason to be home and he ultimately hoped for the contrary.

The train came to a stop at Columbia City Station in an industrial part of town, south of the city. He watched the mother pack up her child and scurry off the train and onto the platform. The doors slid closed again and the car launched back onto the track. Like the metronomic nodes of the Link stations, Mac's life was static in routine. He expected he was happier, though what that meant was not always clear to him. In the solemn moment of contemplation, unwelcomed scenes from the day he spoke to Dennis replayed in his mind. *I haven't been in that place again.* He could quickly swallow them down.

The Link slowed and Mac slid a hardcover book into his briefcase. He excused himself around a family pushing a half dozen roller bags off the train at the Seattle-Tacoma International Airport Station and strolled towards the terminal. The station was bright and freshly constructed, with vaulted white ceilings and colorful tile portraits sprawling across the floor. The terminal's double doors pulled open and his roller bag hummed behind him. A roaring engine passed overhead, and passengers stood one behind the other at counters or within security cordons. *Home.*

The opportunity at Jet Stream Air was certainly one of being in the right place at the right time.

Mac began looking for hiring airlines in early 2000 but found that most of the heavy hitters were looking for pilots to work their small regional lines. He assumed as much in an industry where years with the company determined pick of schedule and size of airplane, but he was desperate to get out of DC. If flying a puddle jumper out of North Dakota was what it took, he would've signed the dotted line.

In the midst of his search, he stumbled upon a new, Seattle-based investment airline flying 767s into the Pacific in an attempt to target a new market. The opportunity to fly wide body airliners was exceptional and he flew out to Washington State to interview. He fielded questions about aeronautics and flying that he answered with ease and alacrity. It became clear he was a prime candidate, though select details of his story remained concealed. The meeting was brief, and they couldn't offer much pay, but he accepted the job on the spot. With their house sold, he moved to a new city across the country to begin at an airline uncertain to succeed. Like so many in the United States, the infant company struggled after September 11, 2001 but seemed to fill a niche that permitted it to not only persist in an industry lull, but to grow. With profits came expansion and Mac was quickly promoted to Captain, where he soon became one of the most senior pilots in the fleet.

With his eyes pitched slightly above the horizon, Mac buzzed through the terminal. His shoulders were back and he breathed easy. *Here, I am king.* Families shuffled between the ticketing counters and passengers gazed up at signs with passports grasped in their hands. He moved with the momentum of the airport and the energy of the travelers. Windows traversed from floor to ceiling, permitting sunny warmth through the complex and views of Mount Rainier towering beyond the tarmac. Massive airliners floated across the asphalt and another growled into the air. He thought of the intricate inner workings of an international airport like a coral reef and he lived to be the stony, calcium foundation that permitted the spectacular array of marine life. There was something comforting about being a stranger among strangers in a bustling airport. He was both anonymous and known and could meet the world's expectations without a word.

Mac's captain's uniform was crisp and pressed, and his shoes clicked on the floor as he walked. He strolled among crops of people ambling along open storefronts or running towards gates. Sequestered by his thoughts amidst the energy of the airport, he was pulled by the eyes of someone staring from across the terminal. He kept his head forward but caught her eyes as she approached his path. The woman wore a simple black dress and a red scarf that danced off her shoulder. Years had greyed her hair, but her smile was spirited, and gold name tag sparkled in the sunlight. When he finally looked over at her, she met his eyes with a growing smile. He cleared his throat and scrambled to place her. *Shit, what is her name?* Her black suitcase trailed behind, and a long raincoat was draped over her left arm.

"I thought that was you," she spoke with the fullness of a church choir. Mac stopped and tried to smile. Her slight southern drawl was immediately disarming.

"Hi there," he finally got out. She wore the uniform of his airline but didn't seem to recognize her face. "How are you?" passengers wheeled around them shuffling to their gates. He was embarrassed of his poor performance trying to conceal his confusion.

"You must be Robert Frank," she let her bag rest with the handle straight up and swung her weight to her left hip. "But you go by Mac if I recall."

He tried not to look surprised, "yes, you are correct." He laughed uncomfortably and propped his bag up.

"Come on, people don't stop you all the time since they put you in the company newsletter?" she opened her hands.

"The newsletter?" he racked his brain.

"Well, are you so famous now that you can't remember being featured in the company newsletter?"

Her casual ease lowered Mac's guard but it took him a moment to recollect a brief conversation with a marketing intern some time ago. It was the first day of a trip and he was waiting in the pilot's lounge when a twenty-something asked to do an interview with him. *Cheap marketing labor for the airline.* The intern said something about a new corporate culture thing, efforts Mac preferred to distance himself from, but he agreed. It drifted from his mind after hearing nothing back for several months.

"Was that actually published?" he let his hands fall into his pockets.

"Just yesterday," she said, "but I work with the union and got an early read."

"People actually read those things?" he laughed.

She grabbed the handle of her suitcase and tipped it forward, "well I hope they do because I sure as hell didn't do it for any extra pay." She smiled. "Where are you headed?"

Mac had to think for a moment. All the cities melded together during his trips and it felt less about travel from city to city and more about flying from one food court and public bathroom to the next. "I'm headed to Anchorage tonight."

"I meant which gate," she laughed. Her grey hair was tied back in a wild bun and a bright orange pair of reading glasses were perched on her head. "I guess we're both heading to B10 because I'm going to Anchorage tonight too."

They walked together through security and their conversation cultivated through the terminal. The sun was setting on the west coast and the infinite span of cold fluorescent lights began to illume the expansive stone floor.

"I read you left the airlines to flight instruct for a few years," she walked with a slight limp. "What brought you back?"

He thought about the day Susan left and his first night truly alone in their empty house outside of Washington. "I was ready to get back on the road," he said. "I missed being on the go." He pretended to look at an airport sign.

"It seems like most people like this lifestyle less and less as they get older," she prodded.

Their conversation danced in the three-four time of a waltz and it felt like remembering a friendship many years old. "If us old folks still do this every day," he took off his cap, "there must be something special about it." She was kind and he surmised she was only a few years his senior.

"Who the hell are you calling old, you old man?" she pushed him at the shoulder.

"I wasn't... I..." Mac blushed.

"I'm giving you a hard time," she laughed easily. It felt natural, like siblings. "My name is Shari Phillips by the way," she said extending her hand.

"Pleasure to meet you Shari," Mac took hers and smiled. "I'm a local newsletter celebrity."

■ ■ ■

The rear landing gear connected with the runway amidst a puff of white smoke just after midnight in Anchorage. The blue hue of the taxiway lights glistened off the Boeing airliner and snow powdered the expanses of the wings. The jet bridge parked next to the boarding door and the engines spun down as hundreds of people disappeared into the airport.

Mac stood at the open cockpit door in his black-billed uniform cap and blazer fit snug around his broad chest. The four gold bars embroidered around each sleeve clearly indicated his rank of captain and he didn't hide them. Continuing a habit from Eastern Airlines, he greeted each person who disembarked off his airplane. He figured people had a right to put a face to the person responsible for their life and he didn't mind the occasional quick smile or "attaboy" handshake that often came with the task. Shari came through the cabin besieged by the aftermath of a full flight as the final passengers disembarked.

"Captain Frank, your work tonight was just stupendous," she pulled her shoulders back and held her hands cupped just above her waist in jest.

Mac smiled at her formality, "why thank you, Ms. Phillips, likewise." His golden skin pulled in a smile and the two began to laugh. Thousands of hours in the air was seen in his greying temples and the results of his focused exercise wasn't hidden beneath his uniform.

"Say, we don't leave tomorrow until two in the afternoon," she spoke easily, "What do you say we grab a beer tonight?" She began picking up a pile of newspapers on a first-class seat but quickly sensed a brewing excuse.

Though he admired her effortless charm and enjoyed their amusing exchange, he wished to be alone. *I just want to go to my hotel room.* It was what he did nearly every night and it was a routine he liked. "I'm not sure, Shari," he shifted his weight, "I was thinking about calling it quits early."

"What are you going to do tonight, watch a rerun of CSI Miami and eat some shitty room service?" Her southern inflection seemed to make cutting to the core more palatable. She crumpled up the paper and waited.

"I was thinking about getting a workout in and…"

"There must be something else about this type of life besides an empty hotel room and a suitcase that you find special, Captain Frank," she interrupted. Mac scratched the back of his neck. "Why don't you just tell me what that might be," the side of her mouth curled up, "over a beer."

■ ■ ■

The two met for a drink at a sleepy bar a few snowy blocks from their hotel. It didn't take long before they conversed with momentum and Mac laughed easily. Shari was amiable and storied, which made their time pass with little effort. They occupied two seats in the nearly empty, Monday night bar and spoke of trips they've reveled in, the cities they've explored, and the life that eclipsed them while on their road.

"You're kind of a beefy guy," she took another sip. "Have you always been like this?" her pint was nearly empty.

He looked down at the veins in his arms and the muscles pressing his undershirt self-consciously. "Not really, it's something I started when I moved to Seattle."

"Were you fat before?" she asked. "I knew a guy who was fat before he moved to Seattle but then lost a bunch of weight after living there." She signaled the bartender for another. For a moment, Mac wondered if it was a developing romance but instead saw a friend with a life not so different from his.

"No, I was never fat I guess. It was just something I felt like I should start doing."

"Would other people say you were not fat?" her eyebrows arched, and she smiled with cheeks full of beer.

"You're right," he tapped his chin with the hint of a smile. "I never asked anyone if I was fat."

"I knew it!" she said, "bartender, get this fat boy another beer!"

Shari told stories about early flight lessons and a career that was disrupted by an unintended pregnancy and a single motherhood as a stewardess. She spoke about the struggle of working in cabins during the 1970s, *"I had my ass grabbed by more horny businessmen that I care to count..."* and the instability of an industry fraught with decades of tumultuous change. Mac spoke of the loneliness in his marriage and life on the road. Sharing intimate details of his inner monologue was a peculiar feeling but being heard conferred some coveted vindication. To commiserate with someone so much akin to himself felt good for once and a novel sense of fellowship seemed to flourish. As they walked back to their hotel, dissonance within seemed to ease and he walked lighter.

■ ■ ■

Coffee meet-ups near Pike's Place and walks in the city turned into holidays together and abiding companionship. Their friendship grew as weeks turned to months, and one afternoon on a walk around the Sound, Mac realized the cast of his life was one-member fuller.

# Chapter 21

February 2016 | Seattle, Washington

Mac lay in bed with the blanket pulled just below his chin, hiding his body in the warmth of sleep. The early morning sun shone through the shades and the muffled sounds of car horns bled through the walls.

*Searing hot fear.*

Mac's eyes were pried open in a reflex of defense. *Please, no.* The disorientation was staggering. His pulse ticked violently in his ears and was the only stimulus his brain could focus on. He was carved out of the warm cocoon of sleep and a vague new awareness grew. His skin buzzed and his pores wept. Fatigue was central and the fog left him dazed. Quarter to five read in red block letters on the alarm clock. Each beat bulged behind his eyes. *Make it stop.*

*Boom, boom, boom…*

*Pause…*

*Pause…*

*Pause…*

*Boom, boom, boom, boom…*

*Pause…*

Like a nightmare clawing out of sleep, it was back. Mac felt his heartbeat erratically in every cell of his body while his mind whirred in growing consternation. The rhythm came so rapidly and out of control he thought his heart would rupture and prayed the organ wouldn't cough to a stop. *My eardrums are going to burst.*

*Boom, boom…*

*Pause…*

*Boom, boom, boom…*

*Pause…*

A familiar foe from years before, it now returned with a renewed and stunning power.

Mac took his right hand and pressed into the crease along his trachea. A degree of shock and fear prodded his body at a level he had only experienced in dreams. Satin red blood pulsed through the artery under his finger in a frenzied gallop and the acid in his stomach burned at the bottom of his throat. *Why is this back?* All those years he pled it would leave him alone, but it had resurfaced in full debut. Adrenalin poured from his glands and bathed his body. Each of his muscle fibers, from between his shoulder blades to the arches of his feet, squeezed in preparation for the fight of his life.

With his right hand, he freed his body from the blanket and contracted his abdomen to rise from the pillow. If not for his cautious movements, his unsteadiness and the daze would have thrown him to the floor. He sat on the side of the bed and brought his left elbow behind him to prop himself up, but the movement was confounded.

*What the hell?*

His left arm buckled under the weight of his thorax. The arm lay motionless and limp behind him. Laying across the bed, his legs dangled over the edge and panic raised. The thumping in his chest was staggering and he fought to sit up. Any command he made of the arm was naught and instead it lay defiantly indifferent. His eyes thrashed around the room, searching for something to orient to, but instead growing alarm ensued.

Rolling to his opposite side, he managed to prop himself up and garner enough strength to swing the inert limb into his lap. He studied it with curiosity but germinating alarm. *What is happening?* It felt swollen and numb and remained perfectly still. His ears clapped with each contraction and he felt sticky and claustrophobic. It all seemed like a cruel trick, but reality pressed with each passing second.

Mac hoisted his left wrist with his right hand and found the mass of muscle and bone to be heavy and dead. It fell apathetically onto his lap when he let go, and he watched with both awe and dread. The arm was warm and muscular, but Mac had little control over it. His brain told the left to make a fist, but the fingers were slow and hardly complied. The extremity was foreign and didn't feel like his own. In so few seconds of consciousness, he was in near hysteria.

*Boom, boom, boom…*

*Pause… Pause…*

*Boom, boom…*

Breathless, he sat frozen over the side of his bed and his mind raced. In his chest, each component of his heart worked as an orchestrated symphony to pump nearly two thousand gallons of blood through his body every day. The ensemble was usually conducted by a precise series of electrical discharges but now the signals were anything but regular and rhythmic. *I'm in atrial fibrillation.*

A single bead of sweat journeyed down his forehead and his jaw ached in tension. Mac looked towards the Seattle sunrise out of his window but saw nothing. The pandemonium felt like a paint brush fiercely slapping caulk on the inside of his chest. He tried to slow his shallow breaths but made little ground against the concentrated catecholamines flowing through his blood. His arm was completely inert, and dread filled every ounce of his body as he realized the possibility...

*Am I having a stroke?*

Susan's words had stuck with him all these years. She was the only doctor to name it. *"Essentially, slow blood in your heart can create clots that shoot them into your brain."* The dreadful condition seemed to be completing the cruel circle that began years before. *Should I call an ambulance?* Time was vicious and brash. *I need to go to a hospital, right?*

His mind experienced going to the emergency room while his body remained in bed.

*...the cold fluorescent light of the hospital, the sterile smell of disinfectants, the hustle of dozens of nurses and doctors around him, the scans and beeping. I would let them do their work. Enduring the tasteless food and the sleepless nights, I would stay in the hospital. They would give me medicine and maybe I would get better...*

His eyes were wide and he again inspected his arm. The squeezing below his sternum was merciless and unruly.

*...athletic clothes, a physical therapist, and resistance bands. Maybe my strength would return. I could use my hand again. I would transition back to my apartment and perhaps life would go on with a new normal. Or maybe it wouldn't. Certainly, they could give me a medicine for my heart. Perhaps this would never happen again. I would never have to think about it again.*

Though the thought of eliminating dysrhythmia and its loitering fear would be a cherished reprieve, seeking care would cause something to be lost forever. Atrial fibrillation, let alone a stroke, would certainly engender the end of his pilot's license and the single remaining source of joy in his life. He pictured Susan doubling up the stairs years before, *"I will not be affiliated with someone who will knowingly put people in harm's way..."* The words cut through his core, tearing through fascial planes and organ capsules. Before every take-off over the past twenty years, the words dwelled in his mind along with the luring demon that started decades before. *If I would've turned myself in, my career would've ended.* He thought about the palpitations and panic over the fields near Williamsburg, Virginia. *I've put hundreds of people in jeopardy every day I fly.* With nothing left, there was nothing to lose. He kept flying because it was a risk he was willing to take. *Flying is all I have.*

It wasn't about the pride or prestige, and neither money nor benefits mattered. His life lay in the rubble that his work left behind and flying was the beacon that let him traverse the terrain. The failed marriage and enduring loneliness, the children that were never born, and the lost connection with Dennis were the culmination of his life's work and it was a sacrifice he made willingly. It was the man he was, and if he lost it, there would be no reason to live. It was something he learned about himself years before.

*Boom...*

*Pause... Pause... Pause...*

*Boom, boom, boom, boom,*

*Pause...*

Staring at the floor, his mind bustled. *It resolved before.* He would wait. *It will resolve again.* He had already sacrificed so much and perhaps there was no limit. *If I go now, I will lose my life forever.*

Mac struggled to his feet and shuffled through his faintly lit apartment into the bathroom. *No weakness in my legs or feet.* He flipped on the light and turned the shower knob as hot as it could go. He looked at himself in the mirror as the shower began to steam. *What has happened to you, Mac?* The life dimmed in his eyes and his face looked haggard and old. He struggled to undress with only his right hand and was careful not to slip on the white tile floor.

The water was blistering hot as it fell over his face, but it felt good to feel something new. Steam swirled in the air and he thought of the many things he wished the water would wash away. The hand continued to lay limp by his side, like the duty he abandoned. *Was it worth ending my career?* It had been over fifteen years since it first showed its ugly head. *No one was hurt under my watch.* It felt irrefutable but he wondered how much more he was willing to sacrifice. *Who do I call?* He longed for a friend and thought of Dennis. It had been years since they last spoke in the restaurant on Capitol Hill, but he'd left his life as swiftly as he reappeared. He thought of Shari, and the feeble prospect of clemency, but he knew there was no one in the world he could call. *No one can ever know about this.* He would wait and hope.

■ ■ ■

*Boom…*

*Boom…*

*Boom…*

*Boom…*

By mid-morning, his heart returned to its regular cadence. Beats were neither spared nor added.

Just after eleven, his arm gradually regained its strength.

By three in the afternoon, he opened a jar.

He sat at his computer:

```
google.com
```
[enter]

```
atrial fibrillation and weakness
```
[enter]

*'Increased risk of TIA and stroke in Atrial Fibrillation' @ mayoclinic.org*

[enter]

### Overview
Atrial fibrillation is an irregular and often rapid heart rate that can increase your risk of stroke...

...the heart's two upper chambers (the atria) beat chaotically and irregularly — out of coordination with the two lower chambers (the ventricles)...

Mac's laser attention was fixated on the screen.

### Types of Atrial Fibrillation
...paroxysmal (par-ok-SIZ-mul) atrial fibrillation. You may have symptoms like palpitations that come and go, lasting from a few minutes to hours and then stop on their own...

### Complications
Stroke: Blood flow in an artery in the brain is disrupted...
Transient Ischemic Attack: ...

He read it again. *TIA.* He skimmed the page faster, knowing the verdict was declared. *This is it.*

...chaotic rhythm may cause blood to clot in your heart's chambers...

He flexed his left fist open and closed as he read.

**…these can dislodge and travel to your brain causing blocked blood flow… symptoms last less than twenty-four hours…**

*I had a TIA.* Again, the words seared into his retinas. The symptoms came and went over a few hours, leaving only lingering turmoil and anguish.

**…weakness, vision loss, even a sensation of spinning….**

He didn't need an emergency room to confirm what he knew. The laptop clicked shut and he fell back into his chair. He tried to wrap his mind around the proposition and the implications, knowing a TIA was a warning sign for worse to come. *It won't happen to me.* He wasn't ready to risk seeking medical care because every element of his existence in this life was on the line.

■ ■ ■

Mac Frank tossed in bed through a sleepless night and arose to the sound of his metallic alarm in the early morning hours. He showered, shaved, and packed his black suitcase as he had for the past twenty years. Finding comfort in his routine, he fought disruptions from recollecting the previous morning. He opened and closed his fist with clumsy dexterity, and he had to concentrate when he pulled on his black slacks and white undershirt. His left hand stumbled over the buttons on his uniform shirt but eventually made it to the top. *It was temporary and won't come back.*

■ ■ ■

On the Link Light Rail headed south, Mac watched the sun peaking over Mount Rainier.

The oranges and reds dancing on the snowy white peaks contrasted the purples and greys of the cliffs and valleys below. He took a sip of coffee from his mug. *Am I doing this?* Towering evergreens folded into the mountainside and fine, wispy clouds blanketed like frosting on a cake. Mac wondered what choice he had. He'd always thought the world was most beautiful from the sky but today it was beautiful being within it. *It may be my last.* He was ready to risk it all because it was already on the line.

■ ■ ■

At Seattle-Tacoma Airport, a fully loaded Boeing 767 pushed back from the gate. Some passengers excitedly chattered about vacation plans while others prepared for business meetings or reunions. Mothers comforted infants, honeymooners held hands, and weary travelers slept. The engines whined, and the airliner shuttered down the runway and into the air.

In front of the passenger compartment, ahead of the galley and behind a locked and reinforced cockpit door, Captain Robert "Mac" Frank sat at the controls of the aircraft bound for Honolulu, Hawaii hoping and waiting.

*I am in command.*

# Chapter 22

February 2016 | Queen's Medical Center
Honolulu, Hawaii

Mac's body was wrapped in an oppressive cocoon of plastic like a coffin. Two blocks of padded foam pressed the sides of his head making movement nearly impossible. Only his eyes could peer around the body-length tube, four inches from his face. He focused on his breathing. A plastic cage covered his face like an animal and his back ached on the rigid board.

"Don't move now," said the technician's metallic voice over the speaker. He scrutinized through the window of his enclosed control booth. "When the scanner starts, you're going to hear some loud banging," the microphone scratched off.

No more than a few seconds passed until lurid racket blasted the tube. Mac cringed, underestimating the noise. Five construction workers hammered the MRI scanner with metal mallets. The nurse warned the space would be tight, but he misjudged how claustrophobic he would be and questioned if the air was circulating fast enough. The nurse had offered something to help him stay calm and he regretted declining it.

"Mr. Frank," said the voice again, "Do not move or it will blur the images." Mac apologized but couldn't have been heard over the clatter. *How did I get here?* The past five hours in the hospital replayed in his mind.

■ ■ ■

When they pulled into the gate at Honolulu's Daniel K. Inouye International Airport, the jetway pulled to the fuselage and the boarding door hinged open.

*"This is the first officer, please remain seated until otherwise directed,"* Julie cracked over the PA system. Six medics bolted onto the plane and dispersed into the cabin.

*"The captain is here!"* barked one medic as he and his partner knelt beside the pilot. *Everything happened so quickly.* He was strapped to a gurney and rushed into downtown Honolulu under lights and sirens. The spinning was relentless and riding every crack and pothole from the back of the ambulance worsened his plight. *Does this thing have suspension?* The jostling fueled his nausea and he prayed for relief. The medic cut him out of his shirt, placed heart monitor stickers across his chest, and inserted an IV needle in his arm. The back of the ambulance cracked and shifted over the road and Mac was silent. A healthy man for much of his life, it was surreal.

*"Gurney on the left!"* yelled the medic as they pushed around obstacles in the busy emergency room. *"On your left!"* Staff in blue scrubs and white coats lined the walls with contraptions and needles in their hands. Mac was pushed into a small room with three walls, a sink, TV, and a mess of equipment. *"Intake!"* The room glowed with a sterile hue and beeping muffled exchanges between the hospital staff. There was a constant ebb and flow of people filling and emptying the room and the confusion was dizzying. The fluorescent lights glared his view and someone put another needle in his arm. The noise was like static on a stereo, but the commotion could not distract him from the chaos in his chest and relentless rotation of the room.

*"Step aside!"* Two technicians allowed a short, stout man in a long white coat beside the bed. His round glasses magnified the plump eyes studying his clipboard. He had stubble that sagged on his gullet and an irate looking pimple on his left forehead.

"Who is this?" his voice was nasally, and he didn't look up.

"Sixty-two year old male presenting to the emergency department with acute onset dizziness and vomiting that started about two hours ago while he was flying," said the medic.

The doctor looked up, "that sounds dangerous..." his voice trailed, and a nurse laughed. Mac remained silent while he was being connected to wires and machines.

"Has this ever happened before?" He stood with feet apart and a clipboard in hand, not animated by the chaos in the slightest. *"This is a code stroke..."* a nurse murmured in the corner.

Mac said nothing for a few moments. *Has this ever happened to me before?* He thought about the previous day and tried to ignore the gyration. *You mean the sudden weakness in my arm?* The sweat made the sheets stick to his skin.

"...no, this has never happened before." The walls were inching closer and he tried to remain perfectly still. Consequences were trailing him and he didn't know where to run.

The doctor squinted, "can you tell me *exactly* what happened?" He was no more than two feet taller than the bed.

*Everything I say counts.* He thought about the years of lies, the hundreds of flights he's commanded since this first started. They would figure it all out soon enough. "Well..." he clenched his teeth against another wave of passing nausea, "I was flying and suddenly I felt the airplane begin to spin," he sounded small.

"What type of airplane are we talking about here?" the doctor looked tired.

"A Boeing 767," Mac said but the doctor didn't react. Mac closed his eyes but nothing seemed to relieve his plight. "A large airliner," he followed, and the doctor muttered something.

"And *was* the airplane spinning?"

Mac opened his eyes and heeded the doctor for relief. He thought of Susan bounding up the stairs years before… *"you'll have a stroke…"* and tried desperately to end yesterday's episode playing on loop in his mind. Nurses scurried around the room and the monitors bleeped and belled, "I…" he searched for the right words, "I'm not sure, I guess."

The paramedic interjected, "According to the other pilot on the scene, the airplane was not in a spin, sir."

"Do you still feel the spinning now?" the doctor looked at the clocked.

"Yes," *God, please don't vomit again,* "I do." Mac pressed his head into the pillow as a bead of sweat fell into his eye. He had given his life to his work but was now left digested and discarded.

"Doctor Jensen, here is the EKG," offered a nurse. He studied the thin piece of paper for a moment without expression.

"Do you feel your heart beating funny, Mister…" he shuffled through his clipboard, "Frank?"

The color drained from Mac's face, "How do you mean?" *Buy some time.* He was being backed in a corner and haunted by the years of lies. *Dawnis.* Now he'd killed someone.

"Skipping beats or beating rapidly?" he scanned the EKG strip again. "Perhaps you've felt lightheaded?"

He could play dumb or get the help he needed. *They're going to figure out anyway.* He had been flying with it for almost a decade and the façade now seemed moot. *They'll say I lied and put thousands of people at risk.* He had a duty to report it years ago and now the doctor's eyes were oppressive. *Judgement day.* Perhaps the doctor already knew, and he wondered what his sentence would ultimately be. Susan's voice tormented. *"You have to get this figured out Mac… you're running the risk of having a stroke…"* Her voice was cold and indifferent. If they learn the whole story, he would probably go to prison. The cruel circle was tracking along the bottom of its loop.

He'd take the middle ground. *No one can know how long this has been going on.*

"Mr. Frank?" the doctor waited as another monitor emoted a routine alarm.

"Yes," he was mum and looked at his hands, ailing. "I have been feeling that." *I was in atrial fibrillation before my world started spinning.* Every ear in the room seemed to weigh on his words and he felt vulnerable and weak. It was catching up to him. He wouldn't tell them about the previous day's weakness. *To have flown would be considered negligence.*

"You're in atrial fibrillation, Mr. Frank," the doctor shifted his weight. "Have you ever been told that before?"

*Lie.* Mac shook his head. *"…you're in atrial fibrillation, Mac…," the knife of Susan's voice.* The doctor was unfazed and moved on to some of the same maneuvers the family doctor did while aloft over the ocean. There was no clear weakness, but his incoordination was staggering and the doctor scribbled some notes before taking a seat next to the bed.

"Mr. Frank," he pushed his spectacles up his snout. "It appears you've had a stroke and we need to give you a medicine to help bust up the clot."

Mac's world was crashing down while the doctor's eyes were sunken and his voice flat. *Bust up the what?* He wanted to wake up from this nightmare. "Atrial fibrillation severely increases your risk of having a stroke and your story and my exam seem to be consistent." He motioned for the nurse to draw up the medicine.

Everything was happening so quickly and Mac struggled to piece it together.

"Strokes can happen anywhere in the brain, Mr. Frank," he was signing a form, "I'm suspicious you've had one in your cerebellum, which is likely causing these exact symptoms." The circle had closed.

■ ■ ■

*A blur.* Speeding through the busy emergency room to the CT scanner. *"We need a picture of your brain before we can give you this medicine…"* Nurses and doctors parted as he rolled through the department. *"…this will only tell us if you are bleeding in the brain."* The machine was shaped like a human sized donut and clicked for only a few seconds. *"No blood!"* Rushed back to the room. *"On your right!"* Moments later, bags of medicine were hung and Mac was signing a consent document. The doctor called out the time and emptied the syringe into his veins. *"Medicine in!"*

Tissue plasminogen activator propelled into his brain. *Make the spinning stop.* The battle against the clot began.

The excitement calmed, the staff thinned, and he settled into a hospital room. *What time is it?* Mac was disoriented but the nausea medication seemed to help. In the wee hours of the morning, Mac found himself amidst the awful hammering of the MRI machine taking detailed pictures of his brain. *This board is killing my back.*

. . .

As the magnetics constructed a precise depiction of his brain, Mac thought about the flight. His heart clapped in his chest and he tried to remain still. *We were in danger, I had to save those people.* He thought about turning off the autopilot. Shari's voice played repeatedly in his head, *"we have seven passengers in serious medical condition and one crew member is dead...."* Weakness from the prior day haunted his mind. *Could I have prevented this?* Guilt collected at his feet as he futilely evaded contemplating the risk he took flying. *I'm a liar.* He was drowning under the weight of his burden.

The crushed cockpit and the dripping blood of the Grafton crop duster seared through his mind. *Dawnis is dead.* It could've been him.

. . .

"Good morning, Mr. Frank," Mac woke up from a restless sleep the next morning in a hospital room partitioned from another patient by a thin drape. "Or perhaps, Captain Frank?" the man wore a long white coat with a manicured grey goatee. He appeared older than Mac but looked like the kind of guy to run a 10k every morning.

"I see you met my resident physician last night, Dr. Jenson." His words were calm, almost melodic, and he rubbed his hands together. "My name is Doctor R. J. Fickelson and I am the attending stroke neurologist," they shook hands. A blue dress shirt and patterned yellow tie lie beneath his long white coat. "So tell me, what do you understand about what happened last night?" He pulled a chair from along the wall and sat.

"Well..." Mac propped himself up in the hospital bed, tired and disoriented. "I guess I had a stroke."

"Right," his head nodded slowly, "What else?"

"I was flying," his thoughts were cloudy, "and I felt the airplane begin to spin." The doctor's warmth was like speaking to an uncle. "I tried to recover from the spin, but I guess…," he had to reconnect the dots every time. "There wasn't a spin…" his voice trailed and he scrutinized the doctor's face.

"Captain Frank, did you feel your heartbeat differently before this all began?" his chin pitched up.

"Yes," he decided. "I did feel my heartbeat change." *Proceed with caution.* The fabrication didn't come naturally and he struggled to maintain his story.

"Has that ever happened before?"

Mac had decided his answer amidst the hammering of the MRI the night before. *This could be a criminal offense.* He was submerging in his own lies.

"No, it has not," he broke the doctor's gaze and Dr. Fickelson remained stoic.

"Right, well let me tell you what we know," he crossed his legs and sat back in the chair. "After Dr. Jenson heard your story and saw your physical exam last night, he felt you were having a stroke. He gave you a medicine called, 'tPA,' to help break up the embolus," he said each letter individually.

"I still feel like I'm spinning," Mac lifted his head off the pillow but let it fall back down. "It is better than what it was but…" he didn't finish his thought.

"You bring up a good point," he held his finger extended. "This medicine sometimes can help people right away, but the real benefit is in long-term recovery." Mac's eyes widened, lingering on the notion of long-term. "When we looked at the results of your MRI scan, we see that in fact you *did* have a stroke in the superior cerebellar artery within the posterior circulation of the brain." Mac understood the words slowly and the doctor waited.

"Right, the cerebellum," his crossed legs exposed red socks above black Oxfords. "This is in the back of your brain," he planted his hand on the back of his own neck, demonstrating the location, "it manages coordination, speaking, balance, and visual harmonization, and so on. When a stroke occurs here, symptoms can be profound: spinning, nausea, imbalance, discoordination, double vision, et cetera," the doctor continued.

He accounted for each of his symptoms like looking into a crystal ball.

"Now that's part one," Dr. Fickelson gestured. "Now for the next." He transitioned in his seat and Mac held his breath. *Jesus, part two?*

"In further studying your MRI, we can see evidence you've had other small strokes in the past," he spoke slowly, and Mac hung on every word. "These may not have been symptomatic but tell us you've likely had atrial fibrillation for some time."

They knew. *Atrial fibrillation and old strokes.* It would all come out soon enough.

"Some time?" Mac didn't move but he knew the damage was already done.

"The MRI gives us a very detailed view of your brain. We can see if there have been strokes and whether they are old or new," he crossed the other leg. "It appears you have both a new stroke in your cerebellum and several smaller old ones in other parts of your brain." Mac wished he wasn't alone and handed the thin sheet draping his body. "The most likely cause is several small clots being launched into the blood vessels of your brain from paroxysmal atrial fibrillation." The arrhythmic beating periodically showed its ugly head, only to later be disguised and out of view.

"Well, I can assure you I've not felt any afib before..." Mac felt defensive and the doctor raised his hands in concession.

"Often people can go out of rhythm and not even know it," the doctor said, and Mac let his mind go. "You could've had it for years without knowing," Mac's stomach squeezed. "It's just unfortunate this happened when you were flying."

The pilot said nothing. He'd given up his marriage, his romance with Mel, and meaningful friendship to fly, and now it was ripped from his fingers amidst his costly decisions. "Is this spinning ever going to get better?" It was decelerating but persistent.

"The body has a remarkable ability to recover function from an injured cerebellum," the doctor's pressed shirt crackled with movement. "I presume you'll make an excellent recovery over the next few days to weeks." The doctor planted his feet on the ground. "You'll start with our therapists today."

"And my heart?" Mac brought his palm to his chest and a nurse hung another bag of fluid.

"Ah yes," the doctor leaned forward. "I am quite certain your stroke came from your heart. When the heart beats so atypically, such as in 'a-fib,' your blood has enough time to sit in a chamber and form a clot. When the ventricle finally contracts," the doctor clapped his hands together, "the clot can shoot out of your heart and into a place like your brain."

*The weakness in my arm yesterday.* This wasn't new information to him. "So, this can happen again?"

The doctor slid a sheet of paper out of his white coat pocket and studied it for a moment until he demonstrated it to his patient. The entire sheet was a checkerboard of little squares, outlined with thin red lines. Four horizontal squiggles painted across the page that looked like a piece of abstract art.

"This is your EKG from last night," the doctor pointed with his pencil. "Each of these peaks are contractions when your heart squeezes blood," he pointed out the peaks. "Do you notice how some contractions are so close together while others are so far apart?"

Mac nodded. "There's a different amount of space between each beat."

"Exactly, and the space in between represents time," he lifted the pencil off the page. "This is a textbook EKG of atrial fibrillation." He slid another page out of his white coat pocket and covered the first. "Now, this is another tracing from this morning," he looked up. "Completely normal." The doctor permitted silence while Mac processed. "You have what is called paroxysmal atrial fibrillation. Your afib comes and goes." *I've noticed.* "It's actually a common medical condition."

The pilot felt his body slowly sink into a murky swamp of despair. *Medical condition.* "Am I going to be able to fly again, doc?"

Dr. Fickelson rose to his feet and stashed the papers in his coat pocket. "Well Captain Frank, let's just take it one day at a time," the pilot hung on every word emitted from the doctor's mouth. "You will need to go on blood thinners, which we will start today," he cut towards the door.

*If I'm not a pilot, who am I?* "Doctor..." the tone in Mac's voice cracked. The physician stopped under the door frame and looked over the shoulder of his white coat. "How are the passengers?"

The sparkle in his eye faded and his lips squeezed, "Unfortunately, I can't say anything due to patient privacy," he gestured towards the television in the corner, "but perhaps there are other places to start." The pilot descended deeper. "I'll order the blood thinners and we can talk more tomorrow."

# Chapter 23

February 2016 | Queen's Medical Center
Honolulu, Hawaii

Mac worked up the courage to pick up the remote. *"…there are other places to start."* The device felt oppressive in his hand. *I don't know if I'm ready.* The past twenty-four hours had been hardly believable, and he longed to wake up in his North Dakota dorm room in a simpler time. Dennis would be reading an issue of *Flying* magazine and they would get breakfast together in the cheerful chatter of the dining hall. *This is my new reality.* He thought about his new label and how everything would change. *I killed someone.* The TV sprang to life and he turned up the volume.

"A nightmare at sea," a male and female reporter sat beside a color photo of the airplane he flew. The male spoke crisply, "A wide body, Jet Stream Air 767 landed at Honolulu International Airport last night after a near disaster in the sky."

A shaky cell phone video filled the screen. The lens captured the view of an aisle seat passenger looking over a sea of occupied coach seats.

Passengers were reading or engaged in their devices, while a flight attendant stood beside a beverage cart. A middle-aged man struggled with his bag in the overhead bin and the roar of the engines cracked through the gruff and scratchy audio.

"This is actual footage from a passenger aboard Jet Stream Air flight one forty-four last night. The flight departed from Seattle-Tacoma's International Airport destined to Honolulu," narrated the male voice. The flight attendant in the video began to pour a cup of coffee as the reporter spoke.

"It was a routine flight across the Pacific until the unimaginable occurred two hours from land," said the female reporter before she paused. The TV engrossed Mac's complete and total attention. A private man, the world was crowbarring into his life.

The camera began to shudder, and the flight attendant swiftly passed the steaming coffee to a seated passenger. She looked over her shoulder to someone out of view and voiced something inaudible. Mac sustained the same surprise of a suited man across the aisle, as he braced himself on the seat in front of him. *Growing cabin movement.* Passengers began to mumble, and the flight attendant stepped back to prop her weight against the cart. The volume grew and stacks of empty cups and bottles started plunging onto the floor. The camera shuttered as the flight attendant's eyes darted. She pushed deeper into the cart, while the foreboding noise grew. *The airplane is in a dive.* The standing passenger threw himself in his seat before he could close the bin and two bags crashed onto the floor.

"*Everyone fasten your seat belts!*" the flight attendant began to shout and the audio cracked. The video rocked with the airplane's movement. "*Remain seated!*" The engines whined and a passenger began to scream. The cart fell against a seat on the right side of the aisle, causing ice and a pot of coffee to fall into the passenger's lap. *The airplane is banking.* Fear and panic pumped through the cabin in burgeoning tumult.

A passenger popped into view, bolting down the aisle and hurdled into an open seat. *The seat belt sign is off.* The dive grew deeper and the young flight attendant battled with the cart. *Don't let it go!* The noise was staggering, and the airplane cracked and moaned. "Oh my God!" a passenger began to scream, and the camera began vibrating with the accelerating airplane. *"We're going to crash!"* Mac wanted more than anything than to look away from the screen, but couldn't

*I did this.*

Bags and bottles slid down the aisle as the nose plummeted. *Hurtling towards the sea.* The video paned to the left, showing passengers in the seats across the aisle pressing their heads against the seat in front of them. A young mother pulled her baby into her chest, tears running down her face, while another passenger held a cell phone to his ear. The camera panned back to the flight attendant's arms quivering against the cart. Her eyes were clasped shut as she strained. *A bank and dive.* The cart wouldn't hold much longer. *It's going to roll.* She gritted her teeth until it finally happened.

*The cart broke loose.*

The flight attendant succumbed to the gravity pulling her into the row of seats and the cart accelerated down the aisle. "Oh my god, watch your arms!" *Get out of the way!* Terror boiled in the cabin. Another young male flight attendant ran into view, chasing after it. *"Everyone, fasten your seat belts!"* The camera trembled as it captured the mayhem. Another baby began shrieking and another luggage bin several rows ahead popped open. The high pitch whine of the engines rang in a chorus and the cart trundled out of view.

*It's going to hit the cockpit door!* The video didn't capture it, but Mac knew it was only moments away.

A deafening boom dwarfed the already horrible cabin noise. The cart collided with the forward wall of the airplane.

"Mom and Dad, I love you so much," said a boyish voice out of the image. Fear was bleeding through each word. The camera panned around and showed the teenager with moppy hair under a Seattle Seahawks baseball cap. "I'm sorry for everything," his eyes were swollen and red.

The video abruptly concluded.

*Breathe.* Mac couldn't move. *What have I done?* The two reporters appeared again on the screen.

"The airliner was flying at altitude, with the seat belt sign off, when it began moving violently in the sky," said the female reporter.

"One crew member is confirmed dead and many are presumed injured after the airplane leveled out and made a safe landing in Honolulu," said the male reporter. The screen switched to the terminal entrance of Honolulu International Airport with a microphoned man standing among shuffling passengers. Traffic honked and automated glass doors cycled amidst the crowd. The bottom of the screen displayed a blue banner.

## TOM JOHNSON, PASSENGER

"The airplane began to move all over the place," his hands gesticulated wildly. "People were up walking around and stuff but then we were flying straight for the ocean," he looked away from the camera. "Bags were falling and a drink wagon almost killed someone!"

"What was that moment like for you?" a local reporter stood just out of view and flipped the microphone back.

"What was it like?" the passenger was in a daze. "I thought I was going to die."

The screen split with the field reporter on the left and the studio reporters on the right. "Our field correspondent, Kahili Akela, is at the airport speaking to the passengers who endured this shocking story," said the female. "Kahili, tell us what happened tonight?"

"Thanks, Chelsey. Shock, fear, anger, and more characterize the sentiment here at Honolulu Airport," the reporter spoke with emphasis. "Passengers describe how the massive airliner suddenly dove in a steep bank for nearly two full, heart wrenching minutes before the airplane leveled again."

"Unbelievable," said the studio reporter. *They're really selling the story...* "And tell us what's happening there now?"

"Passengers are trying to determine their next move," a suited man with a roller bag passed behind the reporter. "As many as twelve passengers were taken to local hospitals, where they are being treated, and one crew member is confirmed dead," she looked at a notebook. "Representatives from the airline are taking contact information from passengers and say further direction will be provided in the coming days."

"Is there any sense of what happened?" asked the male reporter.

"It's not clear what happened tonight in the sky, Brian," she pressed her earbud. "We'll be watching closely for statements from both the airline and investigators in the coming hours and days."

"That's our field reporter, Kahili Akela. Thank you Kahili," the studio filled the screen. "Stay tune to channel seven for more on this unfolding story."

Mac extended the remote and the TV went dark. *Jesus.* His head fell back on the pillow and wished he could exhale the toxicity fuming his body.

*Julie.* He thought about his copilot. *My student.* His voice was harsh. Without her action, they would've been in the Pacific. *I'm sorry Julie, it's more complicated than you think.*

# Chapter 24

February 2016 | Queen's Medical Center
Honolulu, Hawaii

Roving nurses and aides came in and out of his room and, to evade exchange, Mac pretended to sleep through the day. *"Nightmare at sea…"* The news repeated in his mind like a destructive habit. He wondered about Shari and what he could say to her. *Will she come back?* It was impossible to know what she could know and what she couldn't. His friend was the only person in the world that cared for him but now he wondered if there was anybody left.

A knock at the door. *Please leave me alone.* Mac opened his eyes, lifted his head from the pillow and permitted entrance. *Doctors and nurses don't knock.* The clock read eleven in the morning, but time didn't seem to matter in his zero-privacy state. Sleep was impossible and staff fumbled around his room at all hours of the day. He needed to keep his story straight but if he'd slept, he'd experience it all over again anyway. *"Well, I can assure you I've not felt any afib before…"*

"Captain Frank?" a woman in a grey blazer and knee-length skirt stood at the foot of his bed. The cloth blended with her golden skin and hugged her youth. She had blonde hair cut in a bob and a briefcase strapped over her shoulder, "I'm Lori Burkett."

Mac pushed himself up in bed but blushed in his thin hospital gown. She was attractive and professional, and her heals clicked as she walked.

"Hello," he offered extending his hand. The business suit was at odds with the baggy scrubs that everyone else seemed to wear in the hospital.

"It's a pleasure to meet you, Captain Frank, though under unfortunate circumstances." The harness from her black bag fell off her shoulder and she placed it on the ground. Mac nodded and rested his hand back on his belly. "I am an attorney with the pilot union," she monitored his reaction closely. "Do you mind if we speak for a moment?"

*A lawyer? That didn't take long.* "Have a seat," he was uneasy and spoke cautiously. He gestured towards the chair in the corner and she sat with her knees pressed together. *And so, it begins.*

"Captain Frank," she was down to business. "It is routine for someone from the union to come see a pilot involved in a serious incident," she took out a notebook without looking down. "In addition to providing you legal advice, I am here to talk you through the investigation process."

Mac couldn't believe it. The air in the room became salty and heavy. "Legal advice?" He wanted a shower before this conversation, though no soap was strong enough to clean his narrative.

"I don't mean to alarm you, Captain, it is only a precaution." The pilot pulled the bed sheet higher up on his chest and his jaw tensed. "I know a lot has happened in the past twelve hours. How are you feeling?"

Mac tried to let out a laugh but simply exhaled air. "That's a good question," he said. *Do they already know about the heart condition?* "I guess okay given the circumstances."

"I'm happy to hear that," Lori gave a calculated smile. *As long as I don't talk to the press, right Lori?* "Let me start by saying that you do not need to say anything to me about the specifics of the incident," it felt rehearsed. "I am here if you have questions and to be present if you need me. Because there was loss of life during the incident, the FAA will be investigating. I'm here to guide you through the process."

Mac's stomach turned and a fresh wave of nausea concocted with shame and fear. He suspected she was there for damage control and to curb any additional expense to the airline. "How many people are hurt?" he asked flatly.

"I," she was not prepared for her routine to be interrupted, "I am not sure."

"Listen, I understand you have your job, but I also have mine," he searched for resolve as he spoke. "I am the captain of that airplane and I don't know what's going on with my crew or passengers." *They were my responsibility.* The irony was metallic in his mouth.

Her hair didn't move as she spoke and she remained square on the chair, "I am here on your behalf, Captain Frank. A representative from the airline is on his way now and I assume he will be coordinating that effort."

From the fourth-story window, Mac looked out into the Hawaiian sky from his hospital bed. Palm trees waved in the easy breeze and the sweeping ocean waters looked serene and grand. He was the captain of that airplane, the party responsible for hundreds aboard, but now he was in the dark. Perhaps he lost the privilege to know, but the rapid transformation was hard to stomach. "So, you're here to tell me not to talk to the press," white-capped waves crashed onto the beach. "Am I correct?"

"Captain, I can't prevent you from doing anything" Lori was unfazed by the question. "I *can* give you my advice." She paused with emphasis. "This incident will be investigated closely." Her gaze was locked and seemed to emphasize that point. "If the news coverage and social media are any sign of what is to come, it's clear people will be closely watching what happens too." She spoke like a midterm paper. "It is my professional opinion you should speak to as few people as possible," she gestured, "including the press." *You fucked up once, Mac, don't do it again.*

Naked in a glass hut, thousands of eyes criticized his every millimeter. Loneliness had set in and the future loomed with a vague anguish. Mac heard about the isolation a pilot endures after an accident, but now he was beginning to understand it fundamentally. His house of lies was going to collapse. *Trust me, I won't talk to the press.*

"A rep from the company and your chief pilot will be coming to see you when they land in Honolulu," she continued. "While they are on your team, everything you say to them can be used in an FAA investigation."

"You make it sound like I've done something wrong here," Mac snapped back at the lawyer. He wished his voice wasn't so defensive. *That's because you did.* He knew he shouldn't fight because it would all be over soon. *"...it looks like you've had atrial fibrillation for some time..."*

"I have a duty to give you all of the information, Captain. I am not suggesting anything." She took shrapnel without a glitch, "like I said, I am on your team." The machine beeped indifferently on the other end of the room and Mac's shoulders rested on the bed. "Investigators from the FAA will likely come and see you today and want a statement," she was succinct but icy. "Captain Frank, so I can be fully prepared," she paused, gaging his face. "Is there anything I should be aware of?"

*The walls are coming closer.* The skipped beats and weakness in his Seattle apartment replayed in his mind. *"…you will not fly until this is figured out, Mac,"* Susan's voice bounced around his head. He couldn't lie to himself and he wondered how much longer he could lie to others. The hospital room smelled like cheap disinfectant and the air was stale. He thought of Julie's first solo flight. *If I am not a pilot, who am I?* His divorce, the lies, and empty house with nothing left.

"Where is the co-pilot?" he said to no one in particular.

Another knock at the door.

"Hello, hello?" more knocking and a familiar voice came into the hospital room. "I'm not interrupting a rectal exam, am I Mac?" Shari's oversized hoodie came down to her knees and her chaotic lot of grey hair was pulled out of her eyes. "I brought you some food," she held a paper bag stained with grease from a nearby fryer. She looked exhausted and stopped after noticing the woman in the grey suit.

"Hi Shari," a familiar face was sweet reprieve. "Please, come in." It was a fleeting moment of joy to see her.

The flight attendant had aged overnight and came to the side of his hospital bed to wrap her arms around him for several long seconds. "Jesus, Mac. What is happening?" she spoke into his shoulder and it meant more than she could know. Mac didn't reply and she leaned back, resting one hand on the side rail and the other on his knee. "Are you alright?" Her face was tight with emotion.

"Thank you so much for coming, Shari," his tears welled. *What have I done to her?* "They're taking good care of me here."

Shari eyed the women sitting across the bed from her, with her legs professionally crossed. "I'm sorry," she said but didn't step back away from the bed.

"This is a lawyer from the union," Mac didn't look over.

"They think you need a lawyer?" she searched for answers in Mac's eyes. A pair of blue glasses was buried in her hair.

Lori Burkett stood and introduced herself to the flight attendant. "Don't worry Shari, it's only a precaution," said the pilot. Shari shook her hand but was disinterested, though Mac knew Lori would likely be more helpful than he wanted.

The flight attendant tried to swallow the lurking tears, "Mac, what happened last night?" A nurse passed through the room silently and Mac felt Lori's watching eyes.

"They tell me I've had a stroke," he paused, "They think it gave me the spins while I was flying yesterday." *I knew it was coming, Shari.*

"Captain Frank," she interjected. "It is my recommendation you do not comment on the incident yesterday."

Shari scoffed, already raw and uninhibited. "Excuse me?"

"It is standard procedure," the lawyer was unperturbed. "This is to protect you both."

Shari didn't acknowledge her. "Mac," a tear was bubbling over the cusp of her eyelid, "Dawnis is dead."

Mac looked away, knowing she wanted answers. "What about the others?" his voice was distant.

The lawyer interjected robotically. "Again, I would recommend you not make any statements about the incident prior to the investigation."

"You know what?" Shari shot back, "I don't give a damn about your opinion!" her voice grew and words accelerated.

*It's catching up with her.*

"Something happened to this man and now someone is dead. He was the *captain* of that airplane and he needs to know what happened to the people he was responsible for!"

The lawyer didn't recoil but said nothing. Her attention was back to Mac, "five others are in the hospital and a few others are banged up," her voice softened. She waited for him to offer more but instead he sat silently.

Mac suffocated under his own weight and wondered if he'd ever rise from this bed again. He couldn't bear looking at his old friend, and it was hard to receive her naive concern and love. *You don't realize what I've done.* He rested his forehead on his hand, closed his eyes, and hoped shame would dissipate like the hot air blowing from his mouth. Shari's open palm rubbed his back like a son. *My only friend.*

"This isn't your fault, Mac," she said softly.

*I flew because I didn't want to lose my job.* The price seemed microscopic now.

He released his grip and buried his face in his hands. "You don't understand, Shari," he struggled to keep his voice steady.

"You had a stroke. How could you have known?" she continued to rub his back. "You did the best you could."

"How do you know I did the best I could?" his face rose from his hands and his eyes were red like a pressure cooker. There was something about lying to her face that was too agonizing to tolerate. "You have no idea what happened," his voice was sharp and her compassion made him cringe. She stepped back, surprised.

"Perhaps we should discuss this at another time," the lawyer rose to her feet.

"Jesus, can you just give us a minute?" Shari shot across the bed.

"I fucked up, Shari," he buried his face back in his hand and a tear came.

"You can't control a stroke, Mac." she paused and ached with him. "This is not your fault," the room rang with silence. The beeping hustle of the hospital seemed to quiet and the world seemed calm for a moment. "You were sick and Julie was there to help, that's why there are two pilots."

*Julie.* His pupil. *She saved us.* "No Shari, you don't understand," he wondered if he could ever look at her again, "This is *my* fault." He didn't deserve forgiveness.

A short tap at the door broke their rapt stare. "Excellent," the lawyer shot up and walked to the door. "The company rep and the chief pilot are here to see you, Mac," she was visibly relieved. *Everyone seems to want a piece of my hell.* There was so much he wanted to say to Shari, but he couldn't. "If you wouldn't mind, I think it would be best for Mac to have a few moments alone with his team." The two middle aged men stood against the wall and Lori Burkett held the door open, waiting for the flight attendant's departure. *They're isolating me.*

Two friends, each other's central link to the world, were torn apart in twenty-four hours and now simply stared at each other partitioned and confused. *I'm sorry, Shari.*

"We'll be in touch with you soon," Lori said.

# Chapter 25

April 2016 | Seattle, Washington

*Silence.*

The light pattering of rain percussed the window overlooking the shuffle of people on the sidewalk below.

*Isolation.*

A car forced a prolonged horn as a woman pushed a stroller across the crosswalk. The driver yelled something from his window.

*Shame.*

Mac leaned his forehead on his apartment window overlooking the city below. *I'm empty.* His life replayed in mind like a work of fiction.

*Waiting.* His cell detained him until his decree. *FAA investigation.*

Mac roused from his daze, a common past time recently. He turned back towards his kitchen to the buttery scent of coffee dripping into the pot.

He had never been one to drink coffee this time of day, but the clock didn't seem to matter. His sleepless nights became days and evasive fatigue made the days into nights. With no appetite, there were no meals and with no interest, there was no action. He was a shell walking in a trance.

He sipped from a steaming cup and looked back over the Seattle streets. The roads seemed more congested and the sidewalks busier in a city growing at a rate faster than its infrastructure. Though Boeing Aircraft Manufacturing had been the longtime life blood of the city, the influx of new tech companies like Amazon and Google heralded a vast influx of people into the bursting metropolis. With the millions of new jobs came increased rent and a strain on the system not designed for the number of new residents. *It's a zoo.*

Days were spent gazing through the window and nights in front of the TV, though recently he couldn't impel the energy to lift the remote. The hours blended into days like an unwinding roll of twine and the disorientation made the origin and termination equal and unimportant. *Without flying, there is nothing.*

The sole light in his apartment was sourced from the grey sky, growing dark in the overcast of the late afternoon. Mac took another sip and watched the sidewalk below. A man and a woman walked in the center holding hands. He seemed to say something, and she smiled. A businessman in a black suit and raincoat scurried pass them, jabbering his mouth wildly into his phone, and a woman with a young child in each hand walked a few steps behind him.

He found himself wondering about these people more and more. *Where are they going?* He questioned whose lives they were in and what it meant. *To where does a man rush?*

Mac's eyes settled on a man squatting on the opposite side of the street, leaning despondently against a vacant building. He was covered by a blue tarp structure, presumably to combat the endless drizzle. Mac had watched him for weeks now, always holding a cardboard sign: HOMELESS VET. Each day of passing rain made the words more difficult to read, and he often wondered which of life's injustices drove the forgotten man to this dejected moment. *So much we have in common.*

Mac hadn't left his six-hundred square foot apartment in two weeks. *My prison.* He walked into the bedroom to peel off his clothes after days of doing without. The effort weighed on him and he had to lean against the wall to catch his breath. He wondered if it was the months of apartment dwelling that left him deconditioned or it was the toll of his life. There was only one pressed dress shirt in his closet and he took it off the hanger to pass an arm through each sleeve. Each button was an insurmountable challenge. The shirt felt like a parachute and its redundant cloth enclosed his sunken circumference. Perhaps he should've showered, though he saw little purpose. He pushed his hair out of his eyes but didn't bother to put socks on. He tucked his shirt into his pants but left the belt. His movements were slow in the grey light and the ordeal was something he had to recover from. *I'm a murderer awaiting trial.* It was time to take his blood thinner again.

After his discharge from Queen's Medical Center, the airline put him in a first-class seat back to Seattle beside a union representative, who said no more than a dozen words. They directed him not to wear his uniform, so he donned a wrinkled polo and a pair of slacks. A black Chrysler picked him up at the airport and drove him back to his apartment where he was told to wait. *I've been waiting for two months.* His time was restricted to his apartment, most of it in the thirty-five square feet of his bed. His stroke took him off flying status and atrial fibrillation terminated his aviation medical certificate.

There was no reason to leave and his days were spent both waiting and taking his blood thinner. He attended a few follow-up appointments with doctors in Seattle, but it seemed inconsequential. He wasn't sure how much longer life would persist.

*"Don't talk to the press,"* they had told him. *"It's in your interest to not talk to anyone until the investigation."* Shari needed her job. *"I only have a few years until my pension…"* They agreed to stay apart.

Countless nights he woke up in a cold sweat. *"We're in a spin! You have to do something."* The airspeed warning horn clicked wildly as he fought to save the airliner barreling towards the sea. Every muscle in his body contracted as he pulled back on the yoke. The ocean would come closer every night until he was thrashed from sleep just before the airliner shattered into the water.

Julie and the rest of the crew returned to the fleet, while Mac did not. *Even if I don't go to prison, I will never fly again.* He preserved his lie. *"I didn't know I had this condition."* The awareness awoke only him at night. *No one knows.* He wondered how much longer it would last.

A single knock at the door echoed off the walls of his silent apartment. Mac's brain told his body to shuffle to the door, but his legs were slow to comply. *I'm coming.* He couldn't remember the last time he wasn't alone. Another harsh series of knocks came only a few seconds after the first. "You finally dead in there, you old man?" a muffled voice spoke through the door.

Mac unlocked the latch and, after opening the door, took a moment to get a full look at his friend. The man was a greying version of the person he once knew. *Dennis.*

"Jesus, Mac you look like shit," his voice was ironic when he looked up. Mac gave a weary smile and let him pass through the door. *You showed up.* "Have you been wandering the desert for 40 days?" Dennis threw his coat on a chair and fell into a seat in the living room. He pulled a bottle of beer out of a brown paper bag and passed it to Mac. "Looks like you could use one of these," he waited for him to grab it. "And maybe a steak too." He cracked one for himself after Mac.

"Thanks for coming Dennis," he said quietly. He reached for the remote and held it in his hand. "It was good to hear from you."

"Have you been eating? I mean seriously you look like the walking dead." Mac had noticed his sunken cheeks and eyes falling deeper into his skull, though thought little of it. Food was onerous and tasted like sand.

"Yes, I've been eating just fine," he pretended to study the beer label.

"How have you been holding up, man?" The piles of dirty clothes and cluttered garbage seemed to answer the question. Taking another swig, he felt Dennis taking stock.

"I've been holding up," said Mac. It was the first time he noticed the mess. *Isn't the only one.* "I was surprised to see your call."

The beer splashed against the glass. "Of course, man, when I heard what happened I knew I needed to come," he spun the bottle in his hand. "Plus, I was flying to Seattle anyway."

"Bullshit," he looked over. "I know your airplane doesn't fly to Seattle."

"Alright," he smirked. "I jumped on a plane out here. I figured you could use a friend." The room fell silent and Mac set his beer on an end-table unopened.

"We haven't spoken in a long time," Mac's voice trailed.

"Life is busy, Mackie," said Dennis. "Time got away from us."

"I guess so," Mac thought. Decades had passed since their dinner in Washington and it felt like a lifetime ago. Dennis couldn't have known how he'd changed his life. "Why did you come after all of these years?" So much had changed since then.

"If I was in an accident," Dennis swallowed the rest of the bottle, "you would've done the same for me." His words were again a chief influence in his life. *If only it was an accident, Dennis.* They had missed out on so much time together, but Mac knew it was he who created the distance. Dennis seemed better off without him, but chiefly, interfacing a man with everything Mac longed for in life was too much for his precarious state to endure. He never reached out after their dinner together and remained an arm's length from most of the world.

"I think it's going to start," Mac pointed the remote to the TV and the screen lit into color.

"Are you sure you want to watch this?" asked Dennis.

"I think I need to," he turned up the volume.

The iconic tune sung, and an open-faced clock ticked. A few seconds passed and the music faded into a trim, female reporter sitting before a fiery red backdrop. Mac felt his throat contract. *Coming full circle.* He considered flipping the TV off but couldn't move. *I need to see this.* The volume grew.

"This is 60 minutes, I am Tamera Goldstein," one captain shifted in his chair while the other remained perfectly still. Mac was a fawn crawling into the predator's jaws.

"Tonight on our show, Jet Stream Air flight one forty-four left Seattle-Tacoma International Airport on a clear evening nearly three months ago, in February of 2016. The airliner was fully loaded with passengers making their way to Oahu," said the reporter with the cadence and inflection of an experienced newsperson. "Passengers enjoyed dinner and drinks far over the Pacific Ocean when the nightmare began," the camera slowly zoomed into the reporter. *People love a good airplane story.* "Without any warning, the airplane began to move violently," her eyes peered directly into the viewer.

The video that played millions of times on social media and news outlets across the country busted from the screen. The images haunted Mac's dreams but he couldn't look away.

The flight attendant pouring a cup of coffee at the drink cart. The passenger getting a bag out of the overhead bin. The camera shudders. Eyes widen. The noise. *Don't let go of the cart!* The dive. *"Oh my God!"* The bank. *Panic.* The crying mother. *"Everyone fasten your seatbelts!"* Unbearable collision. *Look at the bags falling down the aisle.* The engine screamed. A passenger cried. *"I'm so sorry Mom and Dad..."*

Dennis looked over at Mac and speculated he was holding his breath. The video was visceral and stunning every time Mac watched it. *I knew I was going to have a stroke.* Even to a senior pilot, the scene was awful, but to Mac, it was also shameful.

The video had over one-hundred and fourteen million views on YouTube. *People love a good airplane story.* A GoFundMe page raised almost seven thousand dollars for the young boy with moppy hair. *"I'm so sorry Mom and Dad..."* He was flying to a band trip along with forty-one other students from a rural high school in Iowa.

The video abruptly concluded, and the blond reporter appeared again on the screen.

"Well if that isn't at attention getter," Dennis tried to lighten the mood, but Mac didn't hear a word. His anemic face was sunken and pale. *What have I done?*

"Tonight, we review the terrifying moments on Jet Stream Air flight one forty-four and try to piece together what caused this routine flight to turn into a deadly ordeal," said the female reporter. Her hair was short, above her shoulders, and her lipstick shimmered in the studio lights.

"Jesus fucking Christ, Mac," Dennis spat, "how can they do a story of this already? There hasn't even been an investigation yet," he opened another bottle.

Mac re-lived every moment in his mind. *I was weak.* Mac said nothing. *I'm a liar.*

"Are you okay, Mackie? You look sick."

"Just minutes before near certain death, passengers report the young co-pilot entering the cockpit and gaining control of the aircraft," the reporter continued. "Later, passengers report a physician was called to care for the captain," the words conjured nausea, "and the airplane made a safe landing in Honolulu." A photo appeared beside the reporter that plagued Mac's mind. "Dawis Woods, a flight attendant for 23 years, a wife, a mother of three, and grandmother of five, lost her life on that fateful night while dozens of others were hospitalized for non-fatal injuries." *Dozens.*

Mac's hands would shake if he extended them. He thought back to Julie's first cross-country flight and the rolling hills of Virginia. The harrowing day it all began replayed in his head in a relentless loop.

"Was it a pilot error?" the reporter pitched her head.

"Was it a mechanical malfunction?" her voice elevated.

"Was it negligence?" Mac tried not to flinch.

"Tonight on 60 Minutes, we will talk to aviation experts, passengers, and airline professionals to better understand what happened that tragic night." The camera zoomed out as the music began to grow. "We hope to bring light to a situation that *you* could face in the air."

The ticking clock filled the screen before the first commercial played.

Dennis finished his second beer and Mac's eyes were glazed over. *What is there to say?* It was a pilot's worst nightmare.

"Don't worry Mac, this shit is just to stir people up," his gulp didn't go down easy. "You look like a ghost man, you didn't do anything wrong."

"I killed someone, Dennis," Mac stared vacantly.

"You had a stroke. It could've happened to any of us, Mackie." He turned his body towards him and spoke with a cool ease. "You couldn't have done anything about it."

"I turned off the autopilot and put the plane into a dive," his voice wasn't his. *My life is empty.* "Someone died, Dennis." This is not who Mac wanted to be.

"You thought the airplane was spinning. You did what you thought was best," Dennis leaned forward and rested his elbows on his knees. "You can't beat yourself up about it." Mac knew he didn't know what to say. "You're going to get through this investigation," Dennis lowered his head trying to catch Mac's eyes. "Tell them what happened, and your name is going to be cleared."

"What if I knew it was going to happen?" Mac said flatly. The distance between them grew.

"What do you mean?" Dennis held the second empty bottle in his hand. Mac couldn't bare it alone any longer.

"What if I knew I was going to have a stroke?" His fate was sealed when he crossed the threshold of the boarding door three months ago.

"What the hell are you talking about, Mac?" Dennis tried to laugh and reached for another bottle, though the change in his voice was palpable.

"Dennis," he looked at his thumbs, "I should tell you something."
*This is where it ends.* He felt like a criminal.

"Fucking Christ, Mac," he took a deep gulp of the third beer. "Are
you sure you want to do this?" The character of his voice grew inward,
and he leaned back in the chair, looking away.

"I knew this could happen before it did," Mac continued to avoid his
gaze and his bones ached with the years he hadn't yet lived. "But I didn't
tell anyone."

Dennis's lips tightened. "What do you mean?"

"For years, my heart has been flipping into unusual rhythms," Mac
came to his feet and ambled to the window beside the TV. "I never said
anything, Dennis." The city streets below looked small and trivial.
"Susan told me years ago she thought I had atrial fibrillation."

"Jesus, Mac," his voice trailed.

"You know as well as I do, they would've grounded me and I would
never fly again," he didn't turn around. "It happened only briefly, and I
figured it wouldn't be a problem." *Another lie.*

Dennis stood to pace the room but settled on facing opposite the
wall. "Fuck, Mac," he covered his mouth in the room's perturbed milieu.

"I had nothing left, Dennis," he pleaded to him. "If I lost flying, what
would there be left?"

Dennis didn't turn around. "You had a fucking responsibility," each
syllable was curt and hot.

Mac felt each passing moment unfold like a dream and nothing felt
real. His unscrupulous plight, long in the making, was being freed but
the worst was yet to come.

"The day before the flight, I woke up in atrial fibrillation with weakness in my arm." Dennis turned around and Mac let the words purge from his mouth like half-digested feed, "the weakness got better, and I flew the next day." Mac was surprised to see the rage in his eyes but the pressure within him was releasing.

"You're telling me you had a stroke and you flew?" The disgust was surging, the shock budding.

"I didn't know for certain at that time, but I had a stroke later that night that caused me to become so dizzy I thought the airplane was in a spin." The words were erupting and it was real now. He hadn't planned to disclose the truth tonight, but it unveiled itself along with the culprit as its broker.

"Jesus Christ Mac!" the anger boiled, and his face was red. "I don't want to hear any more!" There was silence and he took a moment to compose himself. *I know, Dennis.* Finally, the burden wasn't his alone. "Who else knows?"

"No one else knows." Individual atoms in the air were hoisted in place.

The patter of rain came onto the window and Dennis walked beside his friend to gaze onto the street below. *You've stood by me for years.* "What are you going to say at the investigation?" He wondered how much longer.

"I don't know," Mac's voice was battered and tired. "I have to make an opening statement."

Dennis picked up his jacket from the chair and slid on each arm. *What is there to say?* Mac watched him from his perch by the window and remained static. "I think you know what you need to do." Each movement was slow and thoughtful, like Dennis didn't want the next to come. Time was cruel, life was unforgiving, and Mac wondered if he were a better person for saying it or a worse.

Dennis stood at the door, trying to recognize a friend from a lifetime ago, while Mac thought of all they've shared. Their trip to St. Paul during their senior year swooned his mind in a momentary flash of nostalgia. Dennis had pulled him into life, abided his isolated course, and rescued him from critical moments adrift. He shepherded him to a career that defined his life, stirred his sole romance, and furnished strength when there was none. They lived detached and parallel lives, each with different characters and plots, but Dennis had always remained a key cast member in the narrative of Mac's story.

Dennis compelled so many moments that made life worth living but now he stood on the stage prepared to take his last bow.

"You'll go to prison for this." Mac wanted to stop him, but he could feel the curtains drawing closed. Dennis stepped into the hallway and closed the door behind him.

# Chapter 26

June 2016 | Seattle, Washington

"I, Captain Robert J. Frank, pilot in command of Jet Stream Air flight one forty-four on the second of February 2016 would like to make a formal statement," he paused with emphasis. Mac sat squarely at the head of his kitchen table, freshly bathed and cleanly shaven. "I am solely responsible for the death of stewardess Dawnis Woods and all other injuries aboard." The investigation would be tomorrow, and the sun was setting in the calm before the storm.

"I was the sole pilot on the flight deck at twenty forty-eight Pacific Standard Time when the Boeing 767 was nine hundred miles from the coast of Hawaii. The co-pilot had taken her relief break and I was in command of the aircraft." He had to admit a shower felt good after weeks of foregoing it. A silver voice recorder, the size of a dollar bill, sat on the table with wheels slowly turning. He thought about the questions he would face in the morning.

"I began to experience severe and prolonged heart palpitations that my doctors later diagnosed as atrial fibrillation," he paused and tried not to wonder about the people who'd hear the tape. "I did not call for the first officer to board the flight deck at this time to relieve me of duty despite this medical emergency."

His shoulders barely filled his black uniform blazer and the four golden bars around his sleeves showed while he read the paper scribbled with notes. *They want me to explain myself.*

"These palpitations went on for several moments without reprieve until I suddenly perceived the airplane spinning." Mac turned the page. The black uniform slacks and white dress shirt draped over him like a tarp, no longer feeling like his own. *Decay.* Weeks of his absent appetite was evident. "I incorrectly deduced this sensation was a structural or functional failure that caused the aircraft to actually enter a spin."

He had walked to the hardware store earlier in the day to purchase the recorder, wrote the script and pulled his uniform out of the closet. *"You know what you need to do…"* He ironed, shaved, and dressed in the mirror. He recited the script endlessly until it could be recalled without fault. *The circle is nearly complete.* Now it was time to perform.

"I wrongfully determined a true emergency was occurring and I intervened in what I thought was appropriate," the page cracked. "I turned off the autopilot, pitched the nose down, entered full power in both engines, and applied full opposite rudder in hopes of recovering from this spin." *You killed someone.* Dennis hadn't returned his phone call. "After several moments of maneuvering, First Officer Julie Sampers relieved me of duty." Shari had kept her distance. *If I'm not a pilot, what do I have?* "I later learned I had a stroke that caused this false sensation."

Mac paused, feeling the weight of his burden being lifted with each passing word. Though the shackles of deception were slowly unlocked, the looming dissidence of penalty pervaded. It's *all nearly over.*

"First Officer Julie Sampers saved the two-hundred and sixty-three souls aboard Jet Stream Air flight one forty-four from near certain death."

Three other purchases were made that morning: a single cut of rib eye steak, a bottle of Jack Daniels Whiskey and a Glock 19 pistol.

"For FAA investigation number 4771D, I must make the following official statement," he coughed lightly and hesitated. "The atrial fibrillation and subsequent stroke I experienced while acting pilot in command of Jet Stream Air Flight one forty-four is not the first time an episode like this has occurred."

Mac tried to purge his mind of the angry and insulted faces that would stir in the hearing room, submerged in the recorded words of his testimony. *Reactions I will not be there to stomach.* He found the fortitude to claim his fault, though he would evade the endurance of consequence.

"I have experienced years of episodic atrial fibrillation," the words finally made it true. "I violated FAA regulation 14 CFR 67 by not only failing to report this medical problem but continuing to fly for Jet Stream Air." He waited for the statement to settle. "The day before the incident, I experienced an episode of atrial fibrillation followed by weakness in my arm that resolved in about six hours." The page cracked again. "This was likely a transient ischemic attack, secondary to atrial fibrillation," he spoke slowly and hoped he sounded stronger than he felt. "The next evening, I took command of the flight subject of this investigation." *There will be fury.* He couldn't bear to see Shari's eyes. Mac struggled to maintain his calm as his notes neared their end.

"I want to apologize to the friends and family of those my actions have affected," his throat tightened. "The public trusted me, and I selfishly violated that trust in my dishonesty about my medical condition." Mac pictured Dennis standing at the door, searching for what used to be. The prime source of joy in his life that remained was abolished along with the reason to propagate his lies. "My actions resulted in a needless death, a burden I cannot bear."

Mac waded in the deep crevasses of his memory. Heavy clouds blocked the setting sun outside of his window and a car alarm oozed through his walls. He made his decision and it all was almost over.

"I would like to commend the actions of the First Officer and my former student, Julie Sampers," the tape continued to roll, but he no longer needed his script. "Your quick thinking and action saved hundreds of lives," his voice became wet and gravelly. "I am very proud of you." It seemed to be the one difference he'd made in the world.

He turned to the final page of his notes where a single sentence was penned across the top. He composed his voice and spoke with a slow resolve. "The FAA policy needs to change," it was his plight and he knew the implications well. "Pilots need to feel comfortable seeking medical help and treatment so something like this will never happen again." The stakes were too high, and he knew he stood among many who felt their life's passion could meet certain end. Mac had given up so much, risked it all to fly, and now would pay the price.

He clicked the recorder off. The notes fell on the table and he sat back in his chair. *It's almost done.* Thoughts that haunted him for years were finally put into words and the weight of the moment fermented in the silence of his kitchen. Today, Mac would give one final thing for his career. *I am admitting to negligence.* The truth would finally come forward and he alone would bear the consequences.

Mac slid the voice recorder and a folded piece of paper into a large yellow envelope and fastened the top. Across the front, he wrote in large block letters and held it close to his body as he rode the elevator down to the lobby. *Dennis, I'm sorry.* He couldn't even meet his eyes when he left. Descending within the walls of the elevator shaft, he dwelled on the years of deception and wondered what his life meant. He had lost Susan to indifference and questioned what their marriage was. The molded cast of what their life could've been taunted him after all these years and, as he lost more, the stakes were too high to desist. Only one thing remained and he couldn't bare its loss.

The bank of mailboxes spread across an entire wall and Mac used his key to open one on the far right. The lobby felt small and the air damp. He slid the yellow envelope inside as a man eyed him from a few boxes away. It wasn't the first time someone stared at his uniform. There was once a time where he'd swell with pride, but today he felt dressed in a costume. The box locked with a turn of his key and its contents stood ready.

Tapping his finger on the front desk, he waited. A woman no older than twenty-five smacked a wad of gum and scrolled through her phone in front of a computer. She didn't look up for several seconds until he coughed and she stirred. He had seen her before but never without eyes on her screen. "Can I help you?" there were many things she would rather do than help.

"Someone named Shari Phillips will be arriving tomorrow morning and I have directed her to come get this mailbox key," Mac held up the ring. Her phone buzzed and she looked down again. "It's very important she gets this," he said a little louder.

"Name?" she didn't look up.

"Shari Phillips," he was growing impatient. "Can you guarantee someone will be here to give her this key in the morning?" She would think differently soon.

"We're very short staffed," he could see the gum rolling around her mouth, "but we'll try." He wanted to say something else but instead tapped his knuckles twice on the counter and headed back to the elevator. He was accustomed to the prestige of his uniform but boarding the elevator, he was reminded how it was no longer his. Not only was his license forever gone, but he would be a criminal.

He looked down at Shari's text message:

21 JUNE @ 9:42 am: happy to bring you in tmrw morning. be there at 8.

Hearing from Shari after the weeks of isolation brought some comfort. The agency had been investigating the incident for months now, and the time to question the crew had finally come. They should've just called it what it was: *an interrogation*. Not a single moment went by where the inquiry didn't weigh on his mind. *"I had never experienced the skipping beats before,"* he told his lawyer. He had been reassured he would be freed of guilt. *"The incident will be labeled pilot medical emergency…"* Perhaps policies would remain, the problem still thriving, but his name would be cleared. *I won't go to prison.* It would all be a another lie but he had already weathered a lifetime of it. He didn't think he was a bad person, though he realized much of his life was detoured in easy bypass. *What wouldn't you give for your passion?* To preserve what he had, he did what it took. Now weak and empty, it was unclear if he could tolerate more.

In compliance with the union's direction, Shari and Mac did not speak during the investigation but her text in the days preceding the hearing brought temporary calm in the storm.

17 JUNE @ 07:55 am: `let's go together. I'll drive you.`

*Thank you, my friend.*

Fourteen hours before he was to appear at the hearing, Mac stood in the elevator and clicked at his phone:

21 JUNE @ 06:41 pm: `front desk has key to mailbox 48 for u. pls review docs in the box before coming upstairs in the am.`

∎ ∎ ∎

An iron skillet seared the fat on a heap of cow muscle and Mac took back a long swig of dark liquor. He could feel it warm his throat and swell in his veins. He still wasn't much of a drinker, but he knew it eased the pain. By the time the cut of beef hit the pan, the world seemed calmer. *Soon it will all be over.* The loaded Glock sat at the head of the kitchen table beside a table setting for one. He tipped another swig back and grit his teeth. Today, it seemed appropriate to open the bottle just as he did years before. *It's time to finish something I started long before.* Dennis saved him once, but he wouldn't do it again. *"You know what you need to do…"*

The fat danced in the hot oil while heat changed each molecule before his eyes. He thought about Julie getting ready for tomorrow's questioning, which made his stomach squeeze. She didn't know the story, but she would defend him. *Death.* Dawnis's family waiting for answers in the audience echoed within him. *She lost her life.* Mac sat at the head of the table wondering why he still had his. He killed for his job and people wanted answers. Adorn in the uniform that defined his entire life, he took the first of his last bites. At eight thirty in the evening, water fell from the saturated clouds of the Seattle sky. *My last supper.*

# Chapter 27

### June 2016 | Seattle, Washington

Two blocks to the south of Mac's kitchen table, a woman with greying hair and heavy eyes shuffled in the rain. Urgency pushed her body at a pace it was no longer built for. *Where is the building?* Her breath was heavy as she strained to gain her bearings. She jogged another block north with a yellow pair of reading glasses pronged through her hair. The rain fell horizontally around the umbrella. *Please, no.*

The message came and she knew she had to find him. *The front desk has a key to mailbox 48…* Something didn't feel right. She put on a coat and dashed into the night. Adrenalin poured through her veins and her mind raced as she hurried through the congested streets. *I shouldn't have left him alone.* Her thoughts were with him each day. She permitted her friend's isolation for weeks, though she thought it was the right thing. Being the subject of an investigation was an unfathomable thought. Something within her tittered out of balance and time was fleeting.

It didn't take her more than a second to recognize the building. Time fogged the memory but her many visits left a lasting picture. Her pace grew until her coat dripped on the floor of the lobby.

She was grateful for Mac's friendship. Though she often struggled in life, Mac had made her last few years better and knew their companionship stemmed from many roots. Both lost souls, they were drawn to aviation in their perpetual search, and their friendship seemed to ease the loneliness of their solitude. After the accident, they called for an investigation and told her to keep her distance. *"For your own safety, I'd recommend you don't talk about the accident..."* Retirement was only two years away and the airline would look for any reason to pull her pension. She acquiesced, though abandoned her friend in the process. The story was propagated on news outlets around the country and she couldn't imagine the strain Mac was enduring. Something about his text affirmed her fear.

Shari collapsed her umbrella in the lobby and stood before a woman smacking gum and scrolling through her phone. *...review the documents in the box before coming upstairs.* A decision had to be made. She had to act quick, but something told her she needed to get the documents. Time was urgent but she hesitated. *Documents then upstairs.* Her ears rang, and her eyes were sharp.

"I'm Shari Phillips," her southern draw came through as she tried to get the receptionist's attention. "I'm supposed to pick up a key here in the morning..." she bent down, trying to catch her eyes but she didn't respond.

Without looking up from her phone, a key fell on the counter. *Thanks.*

Mailbox 48. The flight attendant limped across the carpet and found the door on the right side of the wall. *Hurry.*

The lock disengaged, and the door swung open. *An envelope?* It was heavy as she pulled it from the locker and her breathing quickened. All the reasons she should've come earlier swelled in her mind. Big, block letters written in permanent marker across the front:

## SHARI

## OPEN AND READ

Her heart bound and her hands began to shake. *What the hell are you doing, Mac?* Her fingers tingled as she unfastened the clip. The silver voice recorder fell into her palm and a piece of lined notebook paper followed. *Mac, no.* The contents scorched her hands.

■ ■ ■

On the fourth floor, cooked blood sopped around Mac's plate as the last chunk of meat fell down his esophagus. The cup was empty and its contents coursed through him, making the world seem warmer and easier. The Glock pistol stood at the ready as the night sky clouded the view of Mount Rainier. The deep hum of an airliner passed overhead and rain pattered the window beside. *This is how it will end.*

Four documents, made years before, were displayed at the end of the table facing the front door. Life after tonight seemed unimportant but he did want certain arrangements to be made. The money remaining in his account would go to the University of North Dakota's aviation program and everything else would go to Dennis. UND gave him everything he had and Dennis was a beacon throughout his life.

He washed and dried his plate, returned the pan to its cabinet, and wiped the counter clean. He unlocked the front door and returned to the table as memories of his first flight in North Dakota and the farm fields of Grafton replayed in his mind like a dream. It would be easier for police and emergency workers to clean up the mess.

■ ■ ■

In the lobby, Shari tried to hold the letter steady as she read.

SHARI —

PLEASE TAKE THIS VOICE RECORDER WITH MY
STATEMENT TO THE FAA. CALL THE POLICE. DO NOT
COME UPSTAIRS.

YOUR FRIENDSHIP HAS MEANT MORE THAN YOU WILL
EVER KNOW.

                    YOUR FRIEND,
                    Mac

She held her breath. *Mac, it doesn't have to end this way.* Beginning to sweat, her heart pounded in her chest. *I hope I'm not too late.* The silver voice recorder weighed in her hand as the tape began to turn. Her heart ached and she thought about all the times she wanted to reach out to him but didn't. *Do not come upstairs.* His text came only an hour before. *I don't have a choice.*

The audio cracked as the voice of a broken man began: "I, Captain Robert J. Frank, pilot in command of Jet Stream Air flight one forty-four on the second of February 2016 would like to make a formal statement..."

Shari's entire body began to vibrate. She didn't know if she would cry or if she would scream. *It's a suicide note.* She bolted for the elevator as quickly as her body would let her and keyed the fourth floor.

■ ■ ■

Robert Frank's world rested as he wished and he studied it one final time.

*So much has happened here.*

His new beginning launched between these walls. It was in this apartment he became an airline pilot again and started his life over. He could look at himself in the mirror again after he was back on his feet and began taking care of himself. *Memories with Shari.* They had so much fun in this city and loneliness's grip quelled. The bedroom door was open and he looked on from the head of the table. It was where he had a stroke and made a decision that would change his life and end someone else's. *I was investigated for murder here.* His life felt meaningless, but his decision tonight felt right.

He tightened the black tie around his neck while his uniform blazer weighed on his shoulders. His breath was fruity and ketonic but felt warm and calm. He took the Glock Pistol off the table. *Beautiful.* It was smooth and newly polished. Mac appreciated its clear orientation, where a bullet originated and where it discharged. He realized this would be the last thing he would do on earth.

■ ■ ■

Shari pressed the circular button again, desperate to rush the elevator. *Hurry.* She thought of bolting up the stairs but knew her worn joints couldn't outpace the machine. Her chest burned and eyes locked on the red block letters illuminating each passing floor.

*Beep...* 5

*Beep...* 4

*Beep...* 3

*Beep...* 2

She prayed no one would interpose on its descending journey. *Hang on, Mac.* She wished she would've come earlier. *I shouldn't have distanced myself.* She was his sole companion. Her hands were cold and damp. *Please!* The elevator rung like a church bell.

*Beep...* Lobby

The doors opened, and she clicked repeatedly to bring the doors together. She finally began to ascend.

1... She could feel her heart dancing against her breastbone

2... *I'm so sorry, Mac.*

3... The elevator slowed one floor below her target. *No...*

Shari wanted to pull the doors off their tracks. Third floor. The doors opened and a woman waited with a stroller on the other side. She pushed it towards the elevator as Shari broke past her. "Excuse me!" Shari bolted off the elevator. *One more floor.* Her eyes searched wildly.

EXIT

She ran towards the stairwell, her breathing staccato and body numb. *Mac.* Both hands pushed the door open and it clamored against the wall. Her shoes tapped up each step in the concrete stairwell and her breathing grew louder. CALL THE POLICE. DO NOT COME UPSTAIRS. She was running out of time. The hallway on the fourth floor looked just like the previous, a cold line of doors without a single window. The fluorescent beams made it feel like the middle of the night and a sense of dread conjured deep within her. *It can't end this way.* She ran down the corridor.

■ ■ ■

Mac cocked the Glock back and felt a bullet fall into the chamber. *Loaded.* Seven rounds were holstered in the magazine ready to file after the first, but he only needed one. He heard one's life replays in its final moments but the only thing that filled his mind now was regret.

■ ■ ■

*407... 409... 411... 413...* Shari ran wildly down the hallway as her breathing grew harsher. Seattle rain dripped through a ceiling tile as her organs sloshed in her abdomen. Her mind raced: their trips, the stories, and a connection in the world. *417.* She fell against the closed apartment door. The flight attendant's gasping breaths were audible down the hallway.

■ ■ ■

Mac took the pistol in his palm, his index finger on the trigger, and brought it to the table. *I will have the strength.* His world was soft and spun like water in a tub. He wondered if he would need more whiskey, but he was out of time. His left hand explored for the gun's safety switch and he flipped it to the 'off' position. It was a symbolic click.

THE WILL AND TESTAMENT OF ROBERT J. FRANK.

The stack of paper sat on the table before him. *What meaningful thing have I done in the world?* He thought about his life of flying. *It's over.* In his full uniform and empty apartment, he brought the pistol to his temple. *This will be the only brave thing I've ever done.* He was more anxious than he anticipated, and he wished more alcohol was running through his veins. *It will only hurt for a moment.*

# Chapter 28

June 2016 | Seattle, Washington

There was only silence.

Shari began wailing on the door with both fists. *417.*

"Mac, let me in!" she yelled hopelessly. The reinforced wood shuttered in its panes. "Please open this door!"

Nothing came from the other side. She battered the door again with more force. *Please, Mac!*

She tried the knob, but she stopped in a reflex of shock. *It's unlocked?* The knob turned without resistance and she hesitated for a moment before pushing the door. She didn't know if she was ready to see what was on the other side.

# Chapter 29

June 2018 | Federal Aviation Administration Investigation
Seattle, Washington

"Yes, sir. I was in the crew rest area when I felt the airplane begin to dive," said First Officer Julie Sampers. She sat in her crisply pressed uniform and fought the urge to gnaw her nail at the cuticle. Mahogany wood backdropped the dozen or so people sitting around the conference table, shuffling papers or watching passively. The room was cramped and the vaulted ceiling made every noise echo.

"And First Officer Sampers, is it your opinion the airplane was not in a spin prior to Captain Frank disengaging the autopilot as documented in the cockpit flight recorder?" asked a bald man in a grey suit. Various documents were sprawled across the table, also peppered with Styrofoam cups and a voice recorder.

Julie leaned forward. "That is correct." The morning sun was hidden behind heavy rain clouds descending off the mountain.

"Let the record note this is consistent with the flight recorder at zero four forty-eight Zulu time," he said referring to standardize aeronautical time. "Aircraft type Boeing 767 tail number November seven five eight alpha bravo was flying at flight level three two thousand feet when the autopilot was disengaged," said the investigator.

Julie sat opposite the questioner and beside the airline's chief pilot and lawyer. Dozens of reporters were waiting outside of the door like famished dogs. *Anything to get the story.* The public had been gripped by the cell phone video for months and news circuits touted the story every chance they had. *People love a good airplane story.* Social media was saturated with posts and theories about the incident, and daytime talk hosts agonized over every detail. *What happened on the second of February?* Reporters yearned for the details unfolding in the room and the country was waiting for answers, wondering if they would be the next victim.

"Is it your opinion it was the direct actions of the captain that caused the airplane to bank and dive?" A shutter of a photograph reverberated in the room.

Beneath her cool and even exterior, she was perspiring and uneasy. At twenty-nine, she hoped she would never find herself in this seat, let alone so early in her career. "It's possible," she leaned forward into the microphone. Every word that came out of her mouth would have direct implications not only on her colleague, but her teacher.

"If the autopilot was disengaged, how else would the airplane have entered the dive without the captain's direct intervention?" The voice was sharp and nasally.

Her mind transported her to the skies above Virginia and the basement classroom where he patiently taught her. "It is possible this occurred, yes," she said. She was living her dream and he had been the gatekeeper that made it a reality.

"What is your opinion, then, First Officer Sampers?" he pushed. Julie shifted in her seat.

It was still unclear what happened in the air, but she did know how much her life had changed since that day. The one liner in news stories explaining how the *"copilot went into the cockpit and saved the airplane..."* made her a hero among some while others questioned why she wasn't there in the first place. "It is possible this occurred yes," she didn't budge. All she knew was that she wouldn't incriminate him.

The investigator squinted at her for a moment and Julie battled the urge to bring her nails to her teeth. "And First Officer Sampers, is it true you had to relieve the captain of command in order to take control of the aircraft?"

Julie paused and looked at her lawyer who offered no guidance. "Well..." she paused again. "That is correct." Her nerves made her speak quickly and she yearned for it to be over.

"Is it true you had to request three times to take controls before the captain relinquished control?" the investigator didn't look up from his page.

"To the best of my memory, that is correct," Julie worried where these questions were heading. She was a pilot, not a lawyer, but knew every syllable that came out of her mouth could change things forever. The investigator began speaking again but she interrupted. "Sir, it is not my opinion that the captain was acting with the intention to harm. He was flying with the information that was available to him." That's all a pilot could do. The investigation had not yet formally disclosed the results of the captain's MRI, but Julie knew within a few hours of the scans. *His brain was lying to him.*

"This is not an investigation about intention, Ms. Sampers," the condescension was sharp. "Would it be likely for a Boeing 767 flying at cruise altitude and speed to enter a sudden spin without a known cause?"

She hesitated, "well, no." He cut her sentence and her pulse bounded.

"And if you felt the airplane *did* enter a spin, would your first instinct be to turn off the autopilot before gathering all the information?" he looked over the top of his glasses.

She was on the phone with her Mom just before walking into the hearing room and their exchange played in loop: *"...just tell them the truth dear, it's all you can do."* Her familiar voice was comforting but no one could truly understand what she was going through.

Julie wasn't sure if she knew the truth, or if she even wanted to know it, but she would not allow her testimony to be the sole evidence that put the man who changed her life so profoundly into prison. "It's hard to say what you will do until you're in the situation, sir," she said a little louder. She would not be steamrolled. "Perhaps it was not the right action, but he was trying to do something."

"The captain's actions are the reason someone is dead, Ms. Sampers." The reality was harsh, and Julie tried not to react. When they arrived in Hawaii that night in February, the airline put her on the first flight back to Seattle while Mac stayed in the hospital. *"...don't talk to anyone. Don't make a single statement."* Her union rep had said. *"You need to protect yourself. People are going to care what happens with this."* Her career was promising but it was now on the line.

"The captain did the best he could do in that moment and in that moment a part of his brain did not have blood in it," she said. It was hard to imagine what it was like to be alone in the cockpit with a malfunctioning brain. "It is my opinion it could have happened to any of us." She didn't confer blame to Mac but the thought of all that could've happened was unsettling.

"I have no more questions," said the investigator now piling his papers. Others began to shuffle, and the noise echoed towards the ceiling. Julie looked deflated.

"I would like to make one more statement," she eyed the chief pilot who watched her placidly. "The captain could not have known he was going to have a stroke," the investigators looked up. "He did not do anything wrong."

"This investigation will take a recess and reconvene at one this afternoon," said another balding man at the other end of the table. "This FAA hearing will next hear testimony from Captain Robert Frank."

# Chapter 30

June 2016 | Seattle, Washington

Shari twisted the knob and the door opened without contest. She fell through the doorway and onto the apartment floor. Her bulky clothes, wet from the rain, dripped on the carpet as she struggled back to her feet. She was in a daze and could hardly control her breath.

*Mac.* It felt like she was still falling.

Her old friend sat at the table. *Please, no.* He looked gaunt and his uniform was tented over him. His eyes were despondent and saturated with despair while a single tear journeyed down his cheek.

"Mac, please no," she whispered. The two locked eyes in the oppressive silence and she couldn't find the courage to move. Memories danced in her mind. *I pushed away.* Many emotions came to her, but sorrow seized the deepest grip. She slowly mounted to her feet without looking away.

The barrel of a pistol pressed into the captain's temple and it trembled in his hand. Each second lingered wholly and the world seemed to look on. *You have the next move, Mac.* She called her body to near him but her feet wouldn't submit.

"Please," her voice faded. She would fall into the gaping crevasse between them if she were to leap. His eyes told her his decision was already made.

"Mac, please put the gun down," she tried to steady her voice and her hands slowly raised. He looked through her. "We can get through this together." She hoped the words made it to him. "You didn't do anything wrong, Mac. This is not your fault." He was moments from his end and she didn't know what to say.

"You don't understand," his voice splintered with a bullet seven inches from his brain.

"I do understand, Mac," her hands were opened towards him. "You're hurt but we can make it okay." She ached with him and could see his mind was screaming.

"I lied, Shari," the amplitude of his tremble grew. "I killed Dawnis." His shoulders began to shake, and the tears began to pool like saturated clouds moments from opening. "I had a stroke the day before," his words occupied the space between them but the pistol remained in place. "I flew anyway, Shari."

"Put the gun down, Mac," her voice was calm and stern.

"I have had atrial fibrillation for years, Shari but I didn't tell anyone. I kept flying," years of decay left him weak and now he was beginning to crumble. The apartment was dim, and the only light came from a lamp glowing in the corner.

"Mac, please. Put the gun down," it was the only thing she could think of.

"The doctor said I had a stroke because of my atrial fibrillation," the flight attendant fought the resistance of her exhausted body. "I knew I had it for years," he said. Rain from the cloud sauntering above the city drummed against the window. "I killed Dawnis."

Her clothes clung against her skin as she thought. The end of a man's life was playing before her eyes and she would give anything to stop the finale. The cold night at the Anchorage bar where they laughed together for the first time recollected in her mind, but his voice echoed in the emptiness between them. Like the final moments before a falling tree hits the ground, she felt powerless and inert.

"Then do something about it, Mac," the thought inserted itself into her head. "Don't end it like this." The words came as if someone whispered them to her. He remained unmoved but the lines in his forehead creased at the thought. "You owe it to her to make a difference, Mac." She could count the swollen vessels in his eyes.

*I killed someone. I do not deserve to live.*

"Mac, put the gun down," she felt a bead of sweat falling down her back. Her hands were still extended but her feet hadn't moved.

"Mac… please," the meager flame of hope that remained was battered by relentless subzero winds. "You made a mistake," she stood taller, "now take responsibility. This is not the type of man you are." The tension in his face eased almost imperceptibly but could be recognized by a friend.

*Finally, be the man who has the strength to stand up.*

His jaw clenched and his hand trembled. *Don't let this be how it ends.* His mind waged a battle of uncertainty and the noise was deafening. The years of an empty life pressed into him and the lies urged him to squeeze the trigger. He thought of all he'd sacrificed that was now lost. The pistol's discharge would bring relief, but her words permeated. *This is not the type of man you are.* He wondered what type of man he was and what part of his story would live on.

"Don't be a coward, Mac," Shari pleaded.

It was finally time to be brave. His ears buzzed and his adrenalin crest. So much of his life had been in the way of ease, with quick solutions and temporary contentment, but it left him lonely and hollow. Now, he could be the person he'd always wanted to be but failed. He knew what needed to happen and discovered the reason to source strength to do it.

The gun fell into his lap.

# Chapter 31

June 2016 | Federal Aviation Administration Investigation
Seattle, WA

Captain Robert "Mac" Frank opened the heavy wooden door and walked through the center. He felt the sideways stares from the suited occupants around the table and the compressive air of anticipation. *The one they have been waiting for.* The shuffle through briefcases and quiet chatter dissipated as he closed the door behind him. It took every ounce of his focus to step towards the battle when his gut urged him to do otherwise. The balding lawyer signaled him to take a seat at the center of the table. The months of waiting had finally come to an end.

"Good morning, Captain Frank," said a younger man in a three-piece suit. He had a slight smirk and hair that was greased back so each strand pointed directly at the wall behind him. "We're going to get started in just a second." Mac nodded and tried to look calm. He wanted to run but was in the belly of the beast. *I know what people are thinking.* They didn't know the whole story, but they wanted a direction to point their finger. *People love a good airplane story.* The world would be listening closely, and the eagerness only grew stronger. Today, he had one objective though it would be one few expected.

The room where so much would change was small and inconsequential. The ceilings were tall, with bright fluorescent lights and oak panels enclosing the walls. A long conference table made of dark maple ran along the center of the room with worn leather chairs along the outside walls. Shari found a seat within eye shot of the pilot and a single voice recorder sat in the middle of the table. A suited man reached over to flip it on.

Mac's uniform smelt of last night's defeat. *I'm a coward.* He needed to make it right.

The chief pilot and lawyer filed next to him and they exchanged formalities. *They work for the airline, not me.* He wanted to feel comforted that his senior was beside him, but his allegiance was clear. *I hardly heard a peep from him since the incident.*

"Hi Mac," the Chief Pilot said putting a hand on his shoulder. "How are you feeling?"

"I feel like shit, Steve," said Mac. He looked at Shari studying the floor. *We have her to thank.*

"Hang in there, Mac. We're going to get you back in the air soon," he said. Mac nodded but knew he was about to change everything.

The bald man took a sip of burnt coffee out of a Styrofoam cup and coughed. "The recess is now concluded, and we will now hear questions for Captain Robert Frank." The investigator looked up and gauged the pilot sitting across from him, knowing the battle would bring blood. Mac suppressed the urge to flee. *This is where it ends.* He exhaled deeply and leaned forward. He was here for one reason, but the conclusion was already clear.

"Now Mr. Frank," he studied his notes through the glasses perched on his nose. "We have heard statements from First Officer Julie Sampers and several aviation safety experts. We have also heard statements from an FAA physician and a neurologist about your case," the paper fell on the table. "We would now like to hear your perspective of what occurred on Jet Stream Air flight one forty-four," he pulled the glasses off his nose. "Please know everything said will be in the official record and used in the investigation."

Mac's pupils were full and dilated. He leaned forward into the microphone, "I understand." His foot tapped under the table and his uniform creased with each movement. *I can make this right.* He tried to sit tall but felt small no matter how much he extended.

"Captain Frank, were you the acting captain of Jet Stream Air flight one forty-four on February second, 2016?"

Mac nodded.

"This hearing is recorded, and we need you to speak all of your answers," the investigator pushed the bridge of his glasses up again. The eyes around the room were curious and unwavering.

"Yes, that is correct," Mac eyed Shari again in the corner. He fought for his own life for so long but today it wouldn't be about him.

"Mr. Frank were you the sole pilot aboard the flight deck on flight one forty-four at twenty forty-eight local time?"

Mac affirmed.

"Cockpit flight recordings show the autopilot was disengaged and inputs the left yoke put the airplane into a thirty-degree left bank and a twenty-five-degree dive," he read as he spoke. "This action resulted in an over twenty-thousand-foot descent at a dangerous speed," he looked up and his eyes studied Mac. "Can you please explain what happened at this time?"

Mac shifted in his seat and looked around the room. *The years of lies.* The millions he put at risk over the years suddenly felt real and urgent. He thought of all the times he evaded and wished he would've pulled the trigger.

*Today is when I make a difference.*

"I would…" his voice trailed, and he leaned into the microphone. He felt detached from the situation surrounding him, but his mind was loud and chaotic. It was unlike anything he'd done in his life. "I would like to make a statement," his hands were cold and his foot sustained a tap.

The questioner frowned and waited for him to go on. Every muscle in the room was stagnant and the air congealed in staunch anticipation. "Please go ahead, Mr. Frank," said the examiner.

"I lied." He expected a reaction, but instead a dozen pressing eyes waited for more. It was like his body was being controlled from somewhere else, but he didn't fight it. "I am completely responsible for the death and injuries of those aboard flight one forty-four."

Freed from a trance, the room shifted into anxious chatter. Some sifted through new stacks of paper while others typed vigorously into phones. Dennis's words played in his mind in loop, *"…you know what you need to do."*

"I'm sorry, Mr. Frank?"

"I had a stroke while flying," he shifted again in his seat but remained locked on the investigator. "I had a stroke while I was flying that caused me to think the airplane was in a sudden spin," he said. The length of his spine grew with each passing word.

"Captain Frank, certainly the medical aspect is…" he was interrupted.

"The physician said this stroke was because of atrial fibrillation, which they discovered on my heart monitor when I came into the emergency room." He paused and looked around the room. The chief pilot sat holding his breath and the chatter quieted.

"February second, 2016 was not the first time I was in atrial fibrillation. In fact, it has come and gone for *years,*" he looked down at his hands. "I knew I had the condition but never reported it." He leaned forward into the microphone again to hit the point home. "I knew my career would end if I saw a doctor." The whispering grew louder, gazes turned into confusion, and another photo was taken. *Do it for Dawnis.* Mac's eyes met Shari's and she remained stoic and enduring.

"The day before the flight, I woke up in atrial fibrillation with weakness in my arm. This improved over several hours and I flew the next day," the investigator stirred. "This was likely a TIA." He spelled out each letter and the volume grew.

"Everyone please be quiet!" the questioner tried to regain control. "Order in this room!"

"I didn't take responsibility for my actions for many years, I put thousands if not millions of people at risk," he was resolute, and his words were stronger. "I'm here to change that." *Today, I am the man I was supposed to be.* He thought about Dennis and the last night with his wife.

"Mr. Frank," said the questioner as rogue conversations began to dissolve. "Are you admitting to negligence while operating a commercial airliner?" A piece of the investigators greased back hair now pointed towards the ceiling. *Yes.* His notes remained on the table for the rest of the session.

"I understand what I am doing," he spoke with more purpose than he had in years. "I need to take responsibility for what I've done." He sat back in his chair poised, "This should never happen again." *This industry has blood on its hands and needs to grow.*

Mac looked around the room while suited officials pretended to page through notes to avoid his gaze. *Today, I am a captain again.* His eyes locked with Shari's, who sat stiff but eloquent. He owed her his life. *Now she will save other lives.*

"Pilots are afraid to seek medical care because they will lose their license and their livelihood if they have a medical problem," the words came to him has he rehearsed overnight. "I was too afraid to see my doctor about the heart palpitations I experienced because I knew I would have been grounded for months to years, if not indefinitely." He looked at the voice recorder on the table. "If I could have sought medical care without retribution, perhaps I could've been treated and kept flying." The commotion continued and the gavel hit again. "Dawnis would still be here today."

*I decide how it will end.* Each phrase heralded the next with new clarity. "The health care system pilots are faced with *must* change. The system put in place to keep people safe does the opposite." His heart beat steady and firm. "Though I made a mistake that I will pay for the rest of my life, I hope this unnecessary death will help our profession learn."

"Mr. Frank," said the questioner, trying to stumble back to his feet. "This admittance of guilt will likely lead to criminal charges."

"So be it," he made that decision only hours before, but it started percolating long before, "but this should never happen again." While he relished his final moments in the uniform of his profession, the room fell to silence and his dissonance faded.

"The investigation has no further questions at this time, Mr. Frank."

The pilot wondered if this was the yield of his life's work and sat with a new clarity. *"You know what needs to be done..."* A wave of peace enveloped him like he had never experienced before.

*Julie.*

Her face appeared within the crowd and he leaned forward in his chair. He would've expected her to leave for his testimony, but she remained, and her eyes were red and engorged. Mac wanted to shake her hand. Their narratives were so intimately intertwined, but he sensed their story was only beginning. *We need you to make a difference in the world.* It was now clear what set his student apart and he spoke directly to her:

"I understand I will not be the leader of this campaign as I face further investigation and perhaps charges," their eyes were locked, and her chin raised. "Someone must be the leader to change this problem that faces our profession and the millions of people that entrust us to fly."

It now made sense to him and he smiled.

# Postscript

## September 2023 | Scottsdale, Arizona

Red sedimentary stone vaulted into the horizon as oranges and yellows painted across the valley in the setting sun of the American southwest. Vast expanses of desert were punctuated by the rolling fields of cactus arms and the towering fortress of Superstition Mountain in the east. The city lights were just beginning to glow in Oldtown Scottsdale as tourists ambled the streets among stores selling shirts and keepsakes. At a restaurant along a center street in town, Julie sat at an outdoor table in the desert warmth and brought a glass of wine to her lips. The velvet Chardonnay flavors of lemon and melon swirled in her mouth while the acidity brought out the oaky dryness of Burgundy, France. She was early and looked out across the historic storefronts and admired a mother holding the hand of her child no older than seven. They walked down the sidewalk, the mother smiling down at the child holding an ice cream cone melting over her hand. The mother laughed and Julie smiled. Times like these begged her to appreciate the simple joys that life brought.

Today loomed in her mind since she heard the news. She'd flown into Phoenix dozens of times without ever stepping out of her hotel room, but the circumstances brought her to explore the city. She took a few days off work and wanted to have a little fun despite everything.

The exhaustion from the near vertical, 1,280-foot ascent of Camelback Mountain that afternoon mollified her but the views from the peak were exquisite and renewing. She was enchanted by the stunning 140-acres of cacti in the Phoenix Desert Botanical Garden but walked the enclosure preoccupied with tonight's meeting. Travel remained a favorite part of being a pilot, but today it was hard to focus.

"Julie?" the woman approached from behind and pushed a strand of hair behind her ear. Julie set her glass of wine down and came to her feet without a word. She smiled and admired her familiar face for a moment. She pulled a roller suitcase behind her and a purse was draped over her shoulder.

"I'm so glad we could do this," Julie was surprised to feel her eyes begin to well.

"I am too, Julie," she smiled and opened her arms. They embraced among the diners eating burgers and telling stories of their travels. She took a seat at the opposite side of the table, mirroring Julie's swollen eyes. The whirlwind after the incident had changed their lives and their worlds had diverged over the past few years.

"Looks like you just flew in," said Julie trying to catch a tear before it caught in her eyeliner.

"Yea," she slid her purse under the table. "I could only take two days off from my clinic." She looked older but her eyes were still soft, and her skin pulled slightly below her jaw.

"It's hard to believe," Julie spun the wine glass between her fingers and studied across the table. The woman shook her head slowly and exhaled.

"I didn't think it was going to end this way," she crossed her legs. "I wanted to see her again, but I never had the chance."

"She would've just been glad you could come to the funeral, Megan," Julie leaned forward and smiled. A waiter passed by and put another menu on the table and shuffled away. Julie wished there would've been more time with her but was glad she made one final phone call a few days before Shari passed.

"At least she was able to enjoy a good year of retirement in the warmth of Arizona," the doctor said. Her black sweater pulled around her trim figure and Julie nodded. "Leukemia can beat even the strongest among us." The moment waded in silence while Julie took a sip of wine and Megan admired the mountain. Death itself didn't scare Julie but the thought of missing out on the world was unsettling. There was so much left to see and do that a death so young challenged her to consider what was important.

"So, I hear you've had some exciting news," Megan turned back to the pilot with a lighter tone, though her eyes were still red.

Julie nodded and tried to smile. Her mind was elsewhere, and she sought to refocus it. "I just finished my final round of interviews last week," she adjusted in the chair. "I accepted the job."

Megan leaned forward, "Congratulations, Julie!" her smile was sincere amidst the lingering grief.

Julie blushed but didn't conceal her excitement. "I'll move up to Grand Forks in this summer and will begin teaching this fall." It was still hard to believe. She always assumed her career would be in the cockpit, but the thought of teaching stirred within her the past few years. Between her performance reviews with the company and the moderate publicity after the incident, she was a competitive candidate and accepted a position as an assistant professor of aerospace at her alma mater.

"It's a well-deserved promotion, Julie," the doctor was animated. "You're going to make a big difference to the future of aviation." A waiter set two more glasses of white wine on the table.

Julie looked down again and stirred. She hated bragging about herself but there was a reason she wanted to meet with Megan the night before Shari's funeral. "I understand you completed the training to become a flight doctor, is that correct?" asked Julie.

"I just finished about six months ago, "Megan smiled and took a sip. "I actually see pilots one day a week in my clinic. It's nice that there was some good that came out of this whole mess."

"Well, that is part of the reason I wanted to see you, Megan," Julie continued to look at the table. "I was actually approached by a publishing company about writing a book." Julie's eyes rose and she closely studied the doctor across the table. The message came while she was flying just over two weeks earlier and had sat in her voicemail box since. First there was shock and wonder, but it later began to make sense. A difference could finally be made after everything that had happened.

Megan's eyes were wide, and she sat forward again, "Julie, that is wonderful!" Some diners looked over but went back to their meals and Julie blushed again. "I'm so happy to see some good came out of this for both of us."

"Well, this is the reason I wanted to talk to you," Julie held her breath. "I think we should write this book together." Megan's expression changed, not expecting the words. "I've been putting a lot of thought to it and I think we can really make a difference."

Megan was dazed with thoughts flowing through her mind. "I just," she was at a loss, "I hadn't considered that."

"I think a book we wrote together could take hold and maybe get at the issue Mac said all those years ago." Megan's new training as a flight surgeon and her experience in the air would build credibility that would maybe call people's attention. "The problem isn't a new one but maybe we could be a part of the solution."

Dr. Megan Delaney looked back out over the mountains and put another strand of hair behind her ear. The sun had set behind the horizon and the moon was just coming over the eastern sky. Tourists sat with their families and friends, laughing and conversing, among the energy of the bustling city. They would go back to their hotels tonight and eventually onto airplanes that would take them home safely to their families and lives.

The doctor turned back towards the pilot and smiled. "I would be honored, Julie."

Made in the USA
Monee, IL
12 December 2019